DEATH IN SHANGRI-LA

DEATH IN SHANGRI-LA

A DOTAN NAOR THRILLER

YIGAL ZUR

Translated from Hebrew by Sara Kitai

OCEANVIEW PUBLISHING

SARASOTA, FLORIDA

ISBN 978-1-60809-299-4

Translation from Hebrew by Sara Kitai

This translation published in the United States of America by
Oceanview Publishing, Sarasota, Florida

www.oceanviewpub.com

10 9 8 7 6 5 4 3 2 1

PRINTED IN THE UNITED STATES OF AMERICA

Acknowledgments

To Murray Weiss, my agent, for your wise counsel and commitment. To Gregory Bekerman, for your help in Russian-Israeli slang. To Felix Khachaturian for your vision. To Sara & Ammnon Grushka for putting up with me and my stories for so many years. To all the team at Oceanview: Pat & Bob Gussin, Lee Randall, Autumn Beckett, and Emily Baar—thank you for welcoming me with open arms. To my beloved sons, Kay & Nitai, for the light. And to my wonderful wife, Karin, for unlimited love.

DEATH IN SHANGRI-LA

PROLOGUE

A year earlier

"You're delusional," Willy said. "You have no idea what you're talking about. Spiritual my ass."

I didn't respond. I was calculating how many emotions a person can cram into one sentence.

"My world is ugly, but at least it's real," he went on, hard-nosed as ever. "The spiritual world is a load of crap."

We were sitting in his office in one of the many towers that had sprung up around the Diamond Exchange in Ramat Gan. They're all built in the sterile style that passes for luxury in the New Age Israeli economy and hide more than they reveal. The office blocks are home to import-export companies, insurance agencies, law firms, and of course, the headquarters of arms dealers like Willy. They're all secretly linked together in an infinite web of vested interests, affiliations, commitments, and animosity. A lot of animosity.

The twenty-fifth floor looked out on hundreds of identical glass windows that reflected the red-gold glow of sunset. In just a few minutes it would be replaced by the harsh glare of neon lights illuminating the work of the countless minions who toiled to fatten the bank accounts of the privileged few.

"You're so predictable," I said.

"Really? Don't count on it."

Willy seemed preoccupied. His feet were up on the large, beautifully carved Indonesian desk he had hauled back from one of his many trips overseas. He was the picture of a businessman after hours, not giving a shit because he didn't have to, not answering the phone after his secretary left for the day—"They can go to hell for all I care."

On the desk between us was a bottle of aged Talisker from the Isle of Skye, with its hard-rough taste evocative of the ocean. Two heavy glasses held generous shots. It was just the type of whiskey I'd expect Willy to drink. On the wall behind him were framed mementoes: Willy and the gang; Willy in a jeep in the Himalayas; Willy on a yacht holding an enormous swordfish and smiling at the camera; Willy on safari with an African guide standing next to an elephant; Willy in an Australian pith helmet with a huge cigar in his mouth, a camera around his neck, and a grin on his face, jauntily striking a pose à la Hemingway or Clint Eastwood. He knew he was living the good life and the adrenaline was flowing.

Over to the side were several smaller pictures of Israeli guns and weapons systems. Each had a signature in the corner, but they were too far away for me to read. A single, even smaller, photograph stood on the desk: Willy with a Yankees cap on his head, crouching down to hug two little kids, a girl and a boy, in front of Cinderella's castle at Disneyland. It was the near-perfect picture of the ideal family. Only his ex-wife was missing. I assumed the picture had been taken on a bonding trip after the breakup.

Willy caught me looking at the picture. "That was the happiest day of my life," he said. "You know how much I love my son, don't you?"

I gave him an answer I knew would provoke him. "I know you think you love him. But you're a lousy dad."

My words drew the anticipated response. He threw me a scathing look, but quickly damped the fire in his eyes.

"Explain."

Willy is a cut-the-bullshit kind of guy. Every now and then someone tries to blindside him, especially one of the wannabes who pop up from time to time, mostly retired generals who now have to put an "ex" before their rank and imagine doors all over the world will automatically open for them because of who they used to be. They think they can use their connections to get the drop on him. And then all of a sudden, they take a sucker punch and they haven't the faintest idea where it came from. It's only after they've already suffered the blow, particularly to their super-inflated ego, that they discover it came from Willy. He showed them who's in charge.

I remember him telling me once, "If there's one thing I learned growing up on the streets of downtown Haifa, it's that life is a constant fight for survival."

There's only one way to talk to Willy. You have to give it to him straight, like pouring lye down a clogged toilet even when you know all the shit is going to rise to the surface. "You'd do anything for your son, except the one thing he really needs right now," I said, aiming for the heart. "Accept him for what he is, without judging him."

He gave me that sidelong look of his. "I think your mind's gone to mush," he said. "You've been sitting in the lotus position too long."

I laughed at his dig, but Willy didn't let up. "I gotta say I liked the previous version of Dotan Naor better, the hard-assed Security Agency guy."

What could I say? Give him a full rundown of what I've been doing since I was kicked out of the Agency a few years ago? Ever since I opened the detective agency with Shai, I've spent my time looking for one lost Israeli or another, learning martial arts, and sitting at the feet of spiritual guides in the East. He wouldn't understand.

I realized we hadn't spoken since I'd struck out in this new direction, but, of course, he knew what I'd been up to. So, I threw him a line I was sorry about later, because some things are better left unsaid. "I still have to rough someone up now and then; it comes with the job, but as a way of life it seems meaningless to me these days."

He gave me a steely look. "So now you're judging me?"

"No. You asked if I believe you love your son, and I gave you my answer. You don't like it, no worries. I'll shut up."

"Go ahead, kick me in the balls. I can take it."

I could hear the bile rising in his throat, like the burning sensation you get from eating toasted white bread.

"You want me to go on?"

"You wanna squeeze them, too? Be my guest."

"It wasn't so long ago that you were the smug dad of a bright kid with an active mind, a prodigy on the way to making a name for himself."

"Exactly right. And what's wrong with that?"

"What's wrong? He changed, and you refuse to accept it. You think it's just a phase. Even worse, you think he's turning his back on his true destiny. He was supposed to become one of the leading attorneys in the country. You already imagined how proud you'll be when he's the youngest person ever to make partner in a prestigious law firm. To make a long story short, you thought your son would stroke your paternal ego. You never stopped to ask yourself if he was happy."

"Happy? Happy is a hefty bank account. When you can afford everything you've ever wanted in this shitty life. And you can't deny it, life is full of shit."

I was about to give him a serious answer, but I decided to keep my mouth shut. I knew if I didn't choose my words carefully I'd lose him, and I could see how upset he was about his son. That was the essence of the message he was sending.

Willy refilled his glass, raised it to his nose, and sniffed the whiskey with obvious pleasure. "You're very good at fucking with a guy's head," he said, taking a sip and licking his lips indulgently, a sure sign he'd cooled off. "Want a cigar? I just got back from the Dominican Republic. I brought home some of the finest."

I didn't ask what he'd been doing there, in that hidden paradise yet to be discovered by Israeli tourists. Willy could always surprise me. I knew he had a number of footholds in Southeast Asia. There was even one country, whose name it's better not to mention, where he was the unofficial king. If the admiral of the fleet had a disagreement with the commander of the army, they called on him to mediate. But Willy was too restless to stay put in any place for very long. He was always on the lookout for new clients. The greatest potential was in unstable Third World nations where the dictator at the top of the pyramid was under threat, or better still, deranged. It was best if there were hostilities with some neighboring country. Quiet borders didn't yield profits. The border the Dominican Republic shared with its impoverished neighbor, Haiti, wasn't quiet. That was enough for Willy to go sniffing around, and not just for cigars.

"Later," I said. "It's too early for me."

He laughed. "Let's have dinner. There's a new Italian place downstairs. Not bad, and the waitresses are a thing of beauty. The wine, too."

Willy took another sip of whiskey and looked at his glass appreciatively before going on. "It's easy for you to talk," he said. "You come and go as you please. No one to answer to. No lasting relationships. I'd like to see what you'd say if you paid through the nose so your twenty-one-year-old daughter could study dancing for two years at the most expensive school in Amsterdam, and then she brings her Portuguese girlfriend home and announces, 'Dad, I'm a lesbian and we're moving in together.' Of course, she wants you to pay for that, too. What would you say then?"

"It happens."

"It happens?" He looked like he was about to explode. "And she's just the first course. My darling boy Itiel. The perfect kid. I was so proud when he finished first in his class at Tel Aviv University Law School, and then one of the biggest law firms in the city invited him to do his internship there. You don't get an offer like that every day. That's why it was so hard when the kid comes and tells me he doesn't want to be a lawyer anymore, that— how did he put it?—that the material world has lost its appeal for him, and he's decided to go live in northern India and become a Buddhist. He's going on retreat to an ashram, he says. God knows what that means. You tell me, is that what I busted my ass for all these years? Didn't I fulfill my moral obligations to my family? Didn't I give them everything so they wouldn't have to eat shit like I did? I paved the way for them. Not just any way, a red carpet they walked down with a silver spoon in their mouth. And what do I get in return?"

Willy made an obscene gesture that involved his elbow. "You know what? I'm willing to bet whatever you want that it's all bullshit. Itiel's spirituality is bullshit, just like his sister being a lesbian all of a sudden. It's trendy, they're experimenting, all part of the crazy mixed-up thinking that comes from the fucked-up, so-called liberal society we're living in today."

I kept silent. Anything I said would just add fuel to the fire. His tone had turned sarcastic. "Nowadays, if you're not gay, you're not sensitive enough, if you're not spiritual, you're material. It's all crap. Believe me, if I had him here now, I'd give him such a shaking his mother would turn over in her grave."

"You think that would help?"

"You better believe it."

"I don't think it would."

"Wanna bet?" he asked, and his face instantly broke into a huge smile. It was the smile of an innocent babe, of unconditional delight.

Willy is a betting man. He'll bet on anything any time. If he loses, and that happens sometimes, he always holds up his end of the bargain. He once flew a friend from London to New York and back again, by Concorde, after he bet him dinner in a famous restaurant and lost. His payoffs are legendary. Always on a grand scale.

"You pick the stakes."

"I still don't know what we're talking about."

Willy didn't answer. He refilled the glasses again. By now the bottle was half-empty. The sun had set long ago.

"You're right. I'll start at the beginning." He took a long swallow before going on. "Itiel's in a place called—just a minute, let me check. I marked it on Google Earth."

He reached for his reading glasses and perched them on the end of his nose. The small gesture suddenly revealed him to me in the clear light of age, a man over fifty suffering a certain mental fatigue. But that still didn't explain his bitterness. Maybe Willy was finally starting to understand that true happiness doesn't come from power or money. Probably not. He didn't get it yet. A man like him doesn't get it until life punches him in the face.

"Found it," he said, pointing to the computer screen. "It's a state in northern India, Sikkim. He's at some retreat outside a large monastery called Rumtek with twenty others, Tibetans and Westerners. He says he spends most of his time reading sacred texts and meditating, and he's also doing community work and something ecological. What, you can't do community work here? With the money Itiel would be making, he could start a dozen charitable organizations. And wouldn't I give him a leg up? You bet I would."

Willy fell silent. He adjusted his glasses with an impatient gesture. I realized it was a new thing, those glasses, the kind of thing that hit his huge ego right where it hurt. Then he got to the point.

"It's his last e-mail that's really got me worried. He says that at the end of the year he's going to an even more remote retreat to meditate for three years, three months, and three days. He'll be cut off from all contact with the outside world."

He paused, puffing silently on his cigar and taking a sip of whiskey.

"Any questions so far?"

"No," I said evenly, as if it were a routine matter, something I talked about on a daily basis. "It's a traditional Tibetan form of meditation. They usually do it in the dark."

He gave me a long, penetrating look. The added information was like gasoline dripping onto a flame that had already been burning for some time. "I can't let that happen, and I won't," he said finally. "I have to do something before I lose him for good."

I didn't respond. I could see he was weighing an idea, probably one he'd been turning over and over in his mind before he'd made his decision.

"Here's where our bet comes in," he said.

"I'm listening."

"I'll bet you that within a year from today Itiel will be here in this office with a wife and baby, and he'll say, 'Dad, you were right about everything.' What're you willing to bet?"

I hesitated for a minute, and not because I was afraid of losing the bet. I was afraid of things I had intimate knowledge of and Willy didn't have a clue about. I knew what happened when you started messing with a person's karma, even if it was someone close to you. You nudge them a little in a certain direction, but you never know where they'll end up and what the collateral damage will be. It's like standing on top of a cliff and kicking a small stone that starts rolling downhill and suddenly there's a massive rockslide.

A tense silence hung in the air between us. We both knew what came next. When Willy was in a "sporting" mood, fueled by half a bottle of fine whiskey and enveloped in a cloud of cigar smoke, there was no way I was going to get out of taking that bet. And it was obvious he planned to win. Willy viewed life as a war zone. "Winning is the only thing that matters," he liked to say. That was also the reason that the only book on the shelf behind him, aside from the Ministry of Defense's *Guide to Military Exports*, was a Hebrew translation of Sun Tzu's *The Art of War*.

This time he was going to lose. Big time. But I didn't know that then.

If I were as wise as Sun Tzu, I would've opened his book and read it out loud to Willy: "If you don't know the enemy and you don't know yourself, you will succumb in every battle." But how many of us are as wise as the ancient Chinese general? There probably isn't anyone on his level today even in China.

So we bet a bottle of single malt.

"I'm making a note on my calendar," he said, turning the screen around so I could see. "Today is April 20th. Exactly one year from today, same time, same place, you're putting a bottle of Talisker on my desk and Itiel is standing here with his wife and kid and a big grin on his face."

"Agreed."

Willy emptied his glass and puffed on his cigar without speaking. "Tell me, Dotan," he said finally, "would you have agreed if I'd just asked you to do it as a favor to me?"

It took me a minute to grasp his meaning. "Try to convince your son to change his mind?"

"Uh-huh," he grunted, sending an aromatic smoke ring into the air.

"I'm glad to have the chance to get to know him better. He always seemed like a good kid. And as your friend, I'm happy to talk to him for you. But I'm only doing it to put your mind at ease, so you can stop worrying that he's off his rocker."

"That's all?" he asked, examining me closely.

I kept silent, trying to figure out what he was getting at. And then it dawned on me. This wasn't just a casual conversation; it had been mapped out very carefully in advance. The bet was the culmination of typical Willy strategy. Every detail of what I had thought was simply two old friends catching up had been programmed precisely. It was the work of a shrewd arms dealer who thought solely in terms of confrontation and war, who planned three steps ahead to make sure he was always on the winning side. I wondered if he'd ever been beaten when it came to business.

"Yes," I said, "that's all."

"But it's what you do—you rescue Israelis in distress, bring kids back home."

"Yes and no."

"What's that supposed to mean?"

"I try to save lives," I said, "not always by conventional means, but I do what I can."

"Isn't that what I'm asking you to do?" he persisted.

"No, not at all. You're asking me to convince Itiel that the path he's chosen is the wrong one. That's not the sort of thing that can be accomplished by using reason, or even force."

I didn't add that there was only one way to do it, with love. I'd tried to tell him before. He didn't get it, or maybe he didn't want to hear it. In retrospect, I was sorry I hadn't kept at him, that I hadn't said it then, when there was still time. "Listen," I should have told him, "the only thing your son needs from you is love. Everything else will work itself out." Maybe he would have listened and maybe something would have sunk in and the whole thing would have played out differently. Maybe.

But I didn't say it. Willy nearly leapt out of his chair. "You're wrong," he said angrily. "Someone has to show him who's the boss. Put some sense in his head."

I took a deep breath. The last thing I needed was a raging Willy.

He thrust his hand out for the bottle in an effort to calm himself. It was empty. "Let's do the Italian place some other time," he said.

"No problem."

I left him sitting in his chair with his feet up on his expensive desk, lost in thought within a cloud of smoke. I had no idea it was the last time I'd ever see Willy alive.

There were a lot of things I didn't know.

Would I have taken the bet if I'd known that as a result Israelis would be murdered, innocent people would die, the popular Israeli image of India would be shattered, India and Pakistan would be on the verge of a violent conflict that threatened to spiral into a nuclear war, and the valleys of the Himalayas—the Shangri-La of earthly paradise, the isolated land of eternal happiness—would be set ablaze by the fires of terrorism?

The answer is obvious.

But what I know now I didn't know then. How could I?

CHAPTER 1

It took me a while to realize the phone was ringing. My flight from Mumbai had landed at Ben-Gurion Airport a little behind schedule at three fifteen in the morning. It was close to four by the time I got home.

I picked up the phone and answered in a hoarse, decidedly unsociable tone, "What?"

"Dotan?"

My partner, Shai. The last voice I wanted to hear at the start of my day. It meant only one thing—trouble. And at this hour of the morning—big trouble.

"Yeah?"

"Have you heard? Willy was murdered in India."

I sat up abruptly, totally awake. "What? When?"

"The night before yesterday, apparently. They found his body in some fleabag hotel in Delhi."

"I'm listening." My mind started running a marathon. What the hell was Willy doing in a no-star hotel in Delhi? It wasn't his style.

"It looks like an execution. The body was decapitated."

"Go on."

"That's all I know," he said, hanging up.

Stunned, I looked at the clock. 6:47. There went my sleep, or what passed for sleep.

I was in the shower when my cell phone rang. As I climbed out, it rang again. The screen read "withheld." I answered anyway.

"Good morning, Dotan Naor. You alone, or have you got some sexy young thing in your bed? You know you can be charged with molesting a minor, don't you?"

"Jealous prick."

It was Barnea from the ICIU, the International Crime Investigation Unit. The guy had the uncanny knack of landing on me at the worst moments.

"I'm on my way," he said. "Put the kettle on. And while you're at it, throw a few eggs in a pan with a lot of oil. My partner's a big hungry guy and he's partial to fried foods."

"Don't push your luck," I said, disconnecting.

Ten minutes later there was a knock on the door. I opened it and found the two men standing there.

Barnea is a bruiser. Almost my height at six foot one, forty-five pounds heavier than me, and as strong as an ox. In the Agency, we used to call him Mincemeat because of the way a suspect's face looked after it came in contact with his fist. He mellowed a little after he went over to the police force and gave them the benefit not only of his brawn, but also his massive brain and extensive experience.

He allowed himself the hint of a smile when he walked in, an unfiltered Camel between his lips as usual. "This is Shuki," he said, introducing the sergeant who followed him in.

The guy was a butterball, a shapeless mass of blubber. The second he came in, his restless greedy little eyes made a beeline for the kitchen.

"I'm gonna take a look around," he said.

"Make yourself at home." The sarcasm dripping from my voice went right over the head of the creep, who was focused only on the door to the kitchen.

Barnea let out a sigh. "Where were you this time?"

"Mumbai. I got back this morning."

"You really got it made. I'd sell a kidney right now to be on a plane anywhere far away from here. What were you doing there?"

"I was trying to extract a kid who got himself picked up at the airport with five kilos of grass."

Barnea whistled. "And?"

"I greased every palm I knew or had to or wanted to. I threw cash in every direction, but it didn't do any good. Nada. Zero. The Indians want to take him to court and they won't budge. They want a show trial. They're sick of all the Israeli potheads who've settled in with their chillum pipes and aren't going anywhere, except north and south with a supply of weed in their backpacks. I tried explaining he was the son of a 'very important general,' but zilch."

"What did you expect? They're Gentiles."

Sergeant Shuki appeared at the kitchen door. His upper lip was studded with crumbs from an old box of crackers I'd opened before I left.

"Don't you kids get milk and cookies at the station in the morning?"

The pig cleared his throat and spat the remains of a cracker onto the floor, which admittedly wasn't particularly clean to begin with. I could see he was looking for an excuse to have a go at me. Barnea saw it, too, and shifted gears.

"What's your connection to Willy Mizrachi?"

"Old friends," I said, feigning innocence. "Why?"

It was evident to Barnea that I was toying with him, and he started losing the little patience he had. "Why? Because you're the only son of a bitch whose name is on his calendar for today."

I didn't respond. I was thinking. Then I remembered the date.

"I got in at three in the morning," I said, "El Al direct from Mumbai. Check the passenger list."

"Don't tell me what to do," he fired back, lighting another cigarette.

I swatted at the smoke he blew in my face.

"Your Indian friends found him the night before last, slaughtered like a pig, and that's putting it mildly. What do you know about it?"

"Whose work does it look like?" I asked, trying to figure out why the ICIU was concerned with Willy's murder.

"Butchers. What do I know? The Indians are investigating. Meanwhile, they don't have any leads. They think he was carrying a large amount of cash."

"That doesn't make sense. He knows what he's doing. He's gotten mixed up in more than one sticky situation in his life."

"Let's get back to your meeting with him. What was it about?"

"We get together every now and then to finish off a bottle of whiskey."

"And see whose is bigger," Barnea cut in. "Cut the crap, Dotan. Give me something. Were you involved in one of his arms deals in Asia?"

"Why would I be?"

He looked at me skeptically. "Is that a yes or a no?"

Shuki had a different idea. "Just gimme a minute alone with him, Barnea, and he'll start singing the national anthem," he offered.

Barnea laughed. Laughter is a blessing, and it's good for the health, too. Of course, he almost choked at the end, but that was probably due to all the cigarettes.

"Take it easy, big guy," he said. "All he has to do is go 'ahhh' and you'd go flying."

I didn't say anything, but I stretched my back and flexed my shoulder muscles just in case the crazy hippo gave me a reason for a morning workout.

"He's got a black belt in things you've never even heard of," Barnea added before turning back to me. "Remind me, where was it you went head to head with Putin?"

"Vladimir Putin?" the sergeant asked incredulously. "The president of Russia?"

"Shaolin Monastery, central China."

Martial arts enthusiasts and fans of the *Kung Fu* movies know Shaolin. It's the home of the fighting monks, the ones who devised combative strategies using their bare hands, sticks, and swords. "Soft as cotton, light as a swallow, hard as steel," it says on the temple gate. I had a funny shot of the Russian president after our fight, which wasn't so funny. He won. Putin is no pushover. But we went into the contest drawing on different sources of strength. He wanted to win because he's hungry for power, but I was on a quest for something else. It began when I left the Agency and it isn't over yet. That's why I lost.

Shuki looked me over from head to toe. "Bullshit," he said. "No way."

"It's true." Barnea laughed. "I saw the picture."

Some things shouldn't be flaunted, I thought. *Not even as a joke.* In a flash of ego, I once showed Barnea the photos from my grueling kung fu training at Shaolin. That was a mistake.

"When was the last time you got together?" he asked.

"Who? Me and Putin?"

"Quit fucking with me, Dotan. You and Willy."

"Exactly one year ago. That's when we set a date to meet up again this afternoon, before the holiday."

"Some kind of ritual?"

"It just turned out that way."

I thought of our bet and how important it was to him, and not just because he wanted to win. But I had no intention of sharing the details with Barnea.

"I travel a lot. So does Willy. We try to get together once a year, usually just before the Seder. If we can connect some other time, that's fine, too."

"Where did you meet last time?"

"In his office."

"What kind of man was he?"

That was a tough question. How could I define Willy? What makes an arms dealer the man he is?

"Tough, cynical, calculating, ruthless."

That seemed to say a lot about him, but it was really very little. I was about to go on, but I was interrupted by the sound of phones and beepers going off. Both cops' devices all came to life at the same time.

"What's going on? Are we under attack?" Barnea asked.

He answered his phone while reading the message on his beeper. I saw a grimace of pain followed by fury, which was replaced in turn by a pensive look. Shuki started sweating. Barnea disconnected and lit another cigarette. For a change, he puffed on it in silence.

My phone rang. I ignored it.

"Don't bother. I can tell you what it's about," Barnea said. "Terror attacks on a number of Israeli targets in India. From what we're hearing, it looks like a coordinated action. Strikes on Chabad House in Manali and guesthouses in Rishikesh, and what seems to be the abduction of an Israeli couple in Kashmir. Everyone's in shock. The Indian prime minister is on the hotline to ours. We're at war, and this time it's not on our own turf."

My phone rang again. I didn't pick up.

Barnea started for the door. Butterball trailed after him.

"Don't go anywhere for a while," he said. "We haven't finished this séance. I may have more questions for you."

The sergeant threw me a look that said "I'll be back."

After they left, I kept thinking about the word Barnea had used. Séance. Communicating with spirits no longer of this world. You should never try to commune with the dead, I thought. But what choice did I have?

My phone rang a third time.

That didn't bode well.

CHAPTER 2

Northern India, Himalayas
Chabad House, Manali, 2 a.m.

THE PICTURESQUE TOWN lay blanketed in a nocturnal mist that rolled down from the Rohtang Pass over the tops of the cedars covering the mountain slopes. The apple trees in the valleys, heavy with fruit, were licked by dew. Under makeshift tarps, crates of apples were stacked up waiting for the trucks that would take them to the Delhi markets in the morning. In the Manali Bazaar, a few auto rickshaw drivers wrapped in blankets sat around a small dung fire smoking bidis, the poor man's cigarette. Several lights someone had forgotten to turn off were still glowing at the entrances to the Shiva and Rama guesthouses in Old Manali. Save for the gentle sounds of cows and buffalos chewing their cuds as they moved in the dark among the old buildings, the town was quiet.

They came down the mountain in two columns, dressed in dark clothes and armed with automatic weapons. The multiple pockets of their vests were filled with cartridges and hand grenades. Each column carried an RPG launcher, six rockets, and explosives. The three-man team in the vanguard advanced through the thick forest of the Hadimba Temple. As they passed the intricately carved wooden structure, the leader spat in the direction of the doorway and mouthed a verse from the Koran: "Fight those who do not believe in Allah and who do not adopt the religion of truth from those who were given the Scripture." Moving silently, they crossed the narrow concrete path and continued on past the secluded houses below the temple. Opposite them was the long white building whose third floor was home to Chabad House. They halted for a moment at a bend in the road and checked to make sure the coast was clear.

A few yards away, the sadhu, the holy recluse, readjusted his position. The old man sat cross-legged by a fire that had gone out long ago. The chillum pipe between his thighs had also gone out. They didn't see him. But having spent so many years sitting there awake through the night, he saw them, and he saw their target. The sadhu closed his eyes and called to Shiva, the god of destruction, death, and time, to come and be present on the battlefield.

A yellow light above Chabad House blinked twice. The three terrorists who had come from the direction of the temple signaled back in red. If anyone happened to notice, they would assume it was the blinking light on the side of an auto rickshaw. The yellow light belonged to the other team of four who were taking cover in the forest above Old Manali.

Two members of the first team stayed behind at the bend in the road just before Chabad House, prepared to stop any rash attempt at interference by the Indian police. The third man strode quickly toward Old Manali, taking up a position not far from the Moon Café. He dropped to the ground by the side of the road, becoming one with a mound of dirt, ready to shoot anybody who stepped out of one of the cheap hostels nearby. The working premise of the operation, planned long ago in Peshawar, Pakistan, was that the first to appear would be Israelis, who accounted for most of the tourists in Manali at this time of year and had a reputation for being curious and reckless. The more of them they got, the better.

From the Shiva Guesthouse came the music of "Bitter Sweet Symphony" by the English rock group The Verve. Although the sound faded off into the night air, it was still possible to make out the words.

The members of Team One held their positions in silence, waiting patiently for the music to stop.

RISHIKESH, 2 A.M.

The green truck with a canvas tarp made its way down the mountain toward Rishikesh. It stopped at Lakshman Jhula, one of the two suspension bridges over the Ganges. Two men in dark camouflage crossed to the other side carrying a heavy load of weapons and gear, their running feet causing the bridge to sway gently. Quickly, they positioned themselves for their mission: to block off the bridge.

The truck continued toward the second bridge, Ram Jhula. Two more terrorists leapt down, one landing on a sleeping beggar. "Leprous dog," he spat in Urdu, the language of the Muslims, giving him a kick before moving on. The beggar hunched up tighter under his burlap sack and turned over. The terrorists passed several pilgrims returning from an early immersion in the river. One was Surya Kumar, a retired police officer. After leaving the force, he had decided to follow the custom of devoting himself to a spiritual life of yoga and meditation in Rishikesh, the city of the rishis, the ancient seers. Even at the age of seventy, he was extraordinarily fit and light on his feet. As the figures passed, he caught sight of their weapons and the RPG launcher. He grabbed hold of the edge of the cloth around his loins and began running as fast as he could. Shaking a drowsy auto rickshaw driver, he shouted urgently, "Chelo, chelo," go, go. Five minutes later he walked into the police station, startling the desk sergeant, who rose to his feet, saluted the old brigadier, and went to wake the duty officer. "Sir, Kumar Babuji is here," he said, using the honorific for the former high-ranking officer. "He says there's a terror attack."

The six men on the third team came by car from downriver. One jumped out along the road to block any attempt at escape. The other five continued on toward two guesthouses, Israel House and Benny's Retreat, both popular with Israeli kids due to their proximity to the ashram of the noted yoga teacher Ivan Sekeli, known universally as "the Hungarian." Benny, a former Israeli hi-tech entrepreneur, put a cool two million dollars in his pocket when an American company bought his start-up. The profitable exit gave him a chance to realize his secret fantasy—to be free to dedicate himself to yoga and meditation.

The five terrorists advanced toward their targets, chosen a month earlier. They passed the entrance to the Vishnu temple where the Brahmin sat before a burning oil lamp reading from the Sanskrit Puranas and clapping two small cymbals. As he raised his hand to bless the fire, he saw the figures slipping past the temple gate. He felt a cold draft of air that threatened to extinguish the flame. Creeping quickly and carefully to the gate, he watched as the strangers moved stealthily, sticking close to the buildings. He could tell one was a woman from her stride and the long ponytail. A dog lying on the sidewalk started growling menacingly. The woman kicked at it with a whispered "motherfucker." The dog whimpered and got up to look for a safer spot.

Three of the terrorists headed up the stairs to Israel House, a narrow building with twelve rooms spread out on three floors. The other two went a few yards farther to the small structure that housed the five rooms of Benny's Retreat.

MANALI, 2:15 A.M.

The deployment phase was complete. The four terrorists at Chabad House moved quickly up the broad stairs. As expected, the door to the long corridor was open. Two turned into the first bedroom where Rabbi Yehuda was sleeping with his wife, Jocheved, and their two young children, Leah Miriam, aged three, and Joseph Gedalia, only a year old. The other two continued on to the dining hall, where three mattresses had been placed on the floor for the Chabad emissaries who had arrived specially to help prepare the Seder. They were anticipating at least a hundred Israeli backpackers for the holiday meal.

They opened fire as soon as they entered. The sleeping men had no chance. One sighed as if in a dream, another crawled a yard along the wall, managing to mouth, "Hear O Israel, the Lord our God . . ." before a bullet shattered his skull. The third slithered into the corner, where the heavy curtain that served as a partition between the men's and women's sections during Friday night services was piled on the floor near the desk. He curled up and covered himself. As soon as the terrorists went to check out the kitchen, he reached up to the desk, praying that no one had touched the computer since he'd sent his last e-mail earlier that night. His prayer was answered. His Gmail account was still open, showing the address of his close friend Shimon Assiag, a Chabad emissary in Bangkok. Quickly he typed: "Under attack. Terrorists. May God protect us." He pressed "send." As he crouched down again, he knocked into an empty vodka bottle left over from the welcome party held in their honor. The bottle rolled across the floor, attracting the attention of one of the terrorists, who fired off a round in his direction. Twenty-year-old Shmuel Elhanan, who had adopted a religious way of life just a short time before, knew he would never raise another glass, never again dance on the holidays, and never get the chance to leave his mark. Darkness descended on him. The bullets ravaged the computer, but the message had already been sent.

Yehuda and Jocheved Witzner awoke with a start. Two flashlights were directed at them. They recognized the dark shapes of gun barrels. "Be strong, darling," the young rabbi whispered to his wife. One terrorist stuck a gun to his head while the other bound his hands with cable ties and left him lying on the bed. Jocheved was tied up in a sitting position. "Have pity," she said in an American accent. "We have two little children."

Without a word, the man walked toward the other bed. He shined his flashlight on Leah Miriam, revealing her golden curls. The little girl blinked her eyes at the blinding light. Joseph Gedalia was sleeping peacefully beside her, his breathing regular and his side locks, damp from the night air, stuck to his cheek. The terrorist grabbed the baby boy. That was his last breath.

"God have mercy," Jocheved screamed.

Facedown on the bed, Rabbi Yehuda heard the bones cracking, his wife shrieking, and he knew. He prayed they would die quickly, without suffering, but that was not to be.

His daughter burst out crying. The terrorist by her bed put a pillow over her face and pressed it down with his foot. He held it there for a whole minute. The little girl stopped crying. He removed the pillow. Leah Miriam gasped for air, her lungs rising and falling like a bellows.

Jocheved fainted, toppling over sideways onto the mattress, her head landing on Yehuda's back. He knew they would not get out of this alive. He remembered Rabbi Gavriel Holtzberg and his wife, Rivka, may they rest in peace, who had been killed in Mumbai not long before. They would soon be joining those saintly souls. They had been destined to die as martyrs. But why? Weren't they here on a holy mission?

RISHIKESH, 2:15 A.M.

The terrorists lay in wait, holding their positions. At precisely 2:15 they began kicking down the thin wooden doors and firing in all directions. The deafening noise caused panic among the backpackers, who had been asleep in their rooms on cots or mattresses on the floor. The orders were to kill as many as possible with the first volley, and then herd the rest into Benny's Retreat.

Blood soaked into the rubber mattresses, flowed along the floor toward the backpacks, sneakers, and socks that had been tossed aside before the youngsters went to bed, and spattered on the walls.

They moved methodically from room to room, switching magazines as they went.

Benny was alone in his cottage adjacent to the guesthouse. It took him no more than a second to grasp what was going on. Climbing out through the large window, he ran for the nearby woods where the Maharishi Mahesh Yogi had once sat with George Harrison and other followers. It was known throughout the world as the Forest of Divine Peace, a place of meditation and prayers for peace, both personal and global.

Awoken by the sound of shooting, Yoram in Room 3 quickly shook Dorit awake. "Terrorists," he whispered. He carried the thin mattress to the door and propped it up in an attempt to shield them from the first shots. "Jump," he ordered, shoving her toward the window. As she landed on the ground, the bullets cut through the flimsy wooden door and stained rubber mattress like a knife through butter.

Yuval had gone to sleep on the roof of Israel House to save a few rupees. He heard the shooting and knew it wouldn't be long before they found him there. Scurrying across the roof, he hid in the narrow space between the large water tank and the crumbling gutter made of white bricks. In Room 12, which cost only a hundred rupees a night, Yarin and Yoav also heard the shots. They ran barefoot out the slatted door, heading for Lakshman Jhula. A figure rose up at the edge of the bridge. Yarin was shouting a warning—"terrorists"—when the first round struck him. Yoav saw the flash of light and could tell from the sound that the shots had been fired from an AK-47. He started to turn and run back in the direction they had come from when another figure rose and shot him in the back. The two terrorists gave each other a thumbs-up. "Itbach il-Israil, death to the Jews," they exulted.

Lake Dal, Srinagar, Kashmir, 2:30 a.m.

The rowboat slipped quietly through the water toward Ali's floating home. Ali had been warned not to spend the night in the houseboat with his young wife, Fatima. He'd had to apologize to Yael and Oren, the cheerful young Israeli couple who'd come to Kashmir on their honeymoon after seeing the fabulous pictures of the houseboats on Lake Dal on the Internet. "A magical land at the foot of the Himalayas, the real Shangri-La," they read on every tourist site.

Although realities in the region have changed, the locals still say that Lake Dal in Kashmir Valley is a true paradise spread out below the green slopes of the snowcapped mountains. The secret of its magic lies in the harmony between the wonders of nature and the works of man, between water and earth.

Their families weren't thrilled when they chose India, but Yael and Oren assured them with utter confidence that everything would be fine. "You don't expect us to go to New York again, do you?" they asked. Their parents had no choice but to accept their decision. Still, Yael's mom never missed an opportunity to call and tell her about any new caution issued by the anti-terror unit, which recommended "strongly" that Israelis refrain from visiting Kashmir.

They landed in Delhi and spent two days wandering around Paharganj because Yael wanted to see where all the backpackers went. Oren bought her a cute little bag with colorful scenes embroidered around the edges. It was perfect for her contact lenses and cleaner.

They'd arrived in the Kashmir capital of Srinagar two days ago. Unlike the other boat owners, Ali didn't accost every potential client. He stood all by himself in a corner of the large square where the buses from Delhi stopped, and waited for the customers to come to him. Flustered by the commotion around them when they got off the bus, Yael and Oren went in search of a quiet spot, and lighted on Ali's broad smile.

Yesterday he'd taken them out on Lake Dal in a small boat to see the man-made floating islands. In the evening, they dined on the aromatic lamb pilaf Fatima cooked in the stern of the houseboat. At midnight, before they went to bed, Ali apologized and said that Fatima wasn't feeling well, she might be starting labor, and they were going to sleep in her parents' house on shore.

"Good luck," Oren said. "We'll see you tomorrow."

After Ali and Fatima had rowed away, the newlyweds cuddled together on the carpet in the bow of the houseboat and sat gazing out at the lake. "You're as beautiful as the moon on Lake Dal," Oren whispered in his wife's ear. She smiled up at him. He pulled her closer and they made sweet tender love in the light of the moon, which cast changing shadows as the clouds moved across it.

Oren awoke at around two fifteen and felt the houseboat rocking. A breeze blowing over the enchanted lake, he thought, going back to sleep. He awoke again at five and went out on deck. They were being tugged by a smaller boat on which a young woman was standing. She was pointing a gun at him. A man with a rifle across his back was at the wheel.

"Sit down and I won't have to hurt you," the woman said.

"Who are you?"

She fired a single shot that whizzed past Oren's ear.

"I told you to sit down. I'm not going to say it again."

Oren heard a noise behind him. Yael had pushed the covers aside and come out on the flat deck.

"Sit down, sweetheart," he said quietly. "I think we're being hijacked."

CHAPTER 3

TEL AVIV

AFTER THE COPS left, I turned on the TV. Every station was broadcasting bulletins about the terror attacks in northern India. Channel 2 had already dubbed the events "Terror in Shangri-La," and the name would stick. The crawl on Channel 10 read "Himalayas under attack. Israelis targeted by terrorists in northern India."

The newsreader was having trouble pronouncing names that had long become part of the Israeli backpackers' vocabulary: Manali, Rishikesh. It was obvious that after completing his military service at the army radio station, he hadn't opted for the usual rite of passage in India, but had chosen to accept the tempting offer of a job as an anchor for a commercial TV station instead. Like many of his genre, he didn't understand that what you learn from personal experience is very different from what you can glean from news agencies, no matter how good they are.

"Based on what we know so far," he reported in a tone verging on hysteria, "terror attacks were launched this morning in India and are still going on as we speak. At least two sites frequented by Israelis appear to have been targeted. One is almost certainly Chabad House in Manali. There are also reports of a second attack in the region of the guesthouses in Rishikesh. It is not yet known whether there are any casualties. We go now to the Foreign Ministry for its response."

The ministry's press officer came on screen, looking tense in his suit and tie. "We have been receiving reports from the scene in Manali and Rishikesh," he stated, "but they have not yet been corroborated by any official sources. We are in contact with the local authorities, including the army and the police."

Shit. As usual, they haven't the slightest idea what's going on. They never learn. You'd think the attack in Mumbai never happened.

"Can you confirm that the targets are Chabad House in Manali and two or three guesthouses in Rishikesh?" the anchor asked.

"For the time being, I cannot confirm anything. We are in direct contact with the Indian Foreign Ministry and the Israeli embassy in New Delhi, and are awaiting their reports."

"Do you know if any Israelis have been hurt in the attacks?"

The question set off alarms in thousands of Israeli homes. Even before the press officer replied, hundreds of mothers, fathers, brothers, sisters, and friends were on the phone, eager for a sign of life from their own personal backpacker, one of the ten thousand Israeli kids currently in India.

The press officer wiped away a bead of sweat that had formed on his brow. The viewers' eyes were peeled to the screen, anxiously taking in his every gesture. "We do not yet have that information," he admitted.

By now it was obvious that the press officer didn't have a clue. The anchor went on the attack. "Is it possible, sir, that additional incidents are taking place that you know nothing about?"

The press officer answered—but it wasn't the anchor he was answering. It was his phone, which had started ringing. "Elisha here," he mumbled uncomfortably, adjusting the crocheted yarmulke on his head. He listened for a moment, his face going white, and then turned back to the camera. "That's all. The ministry will apprise the public of any further developments as soon as the information becomes available."

In a dramatic voice, the anchor read out the phone number of the hotline hastily set up by the Foreign Ministry, repeating it twice as it crawled across the bottom of the screen. Within five minutes, hundreds of calls had come in and the hotline crashed.

"If any of you receive information from any source—e-mail, telephone, text message, Facebook, Twitter—please share it with us. We have opened a special line. Here is the number to call." A new caption appeared on the screen. The anchor listened to something in his earpiece and then announced, "We can now show you the first report to come in from the scene, a message received just a few minutes ago from Manali." The text of the message filled the screen:

ISRAELI GIRL'S BLOG
Israelit-manali@gmail.com

Thursday, Passover eve. There's a rumor going around Old Manali that terrorists are attacking Chabad House. It started with Yaron David, who's staying at the Sharma Guesthouse with friends, including Anna and Osnat Belikov. He went downstairs and then came back and said someone shot at him. There are bodies on the road to the bazaar. The road is blocked off. More later as soon as I hear anything.

Here is the link to a picture uploaded by Zigzag at 7:10 this morning.

The text was replaced by the picture of a pale asphalt road with dark trees in the background and small houses closer by. A body lay facedown at the edge of the road. It looked to me as if someone had realized what was going on, tried to run, and was shot in the back.

Cut.

My phone rang again.

"You finally decided to pick up," I heard Tammy say. "Good God, Dotan. It's not easy to get hold of you. Did you hear what's going on?"

"Yes."

"Hey, Dotan, are you with me?" she said, trying to get more of a response out of me. "We want you in the studio later this morning to commentate on the events. Any chance you'll do it?"

"Um," I hesitated. "I don't know. I just got back this morning."

"From where?"

She was as sharp as a whip, that girl. Nothing got past her.

"Mumbai."

"So, you slept through the flight. That is, unless you were fondling one of the baby air hostesses in the toilet."

"Just fondling?" I said, playing along.

I knew the same image was going through both our heads. One of our so-called quickies that didn't end until Tammy was summoned back to work at Channel 10. The irregular hours of a news producer have their advantages.

"Come on, it's a piece of cake for you. I know you. You can go for days without sleep."

She was right. But I was on to her game plan. Unlike other people in my profession, I didn't mind public exposure, and she knew it.

"I'll send a cab. We need someone who's familiar with the area, someone who feels comfortable in our virtual studio. I don't have to spell it out. You know what I need from you. And don't let me see you on Channel 2."

It was hard to refuse her. Like most men, I turned to jelly around her. I never asked her what she did when she wasn't with me. It was none of my business. She only appeared on air when she had to replace an anchorwoman who called in sick at the last minute, but whenever it happened, an electric current ran straight from the TV to every male viewer. They sat glued to the screen, staring at her amazing face, brilliant blue eyes, natural blond hair, and seductive cleavage. There was no doubt in my mind that they envied the lucky bastard who was fucking her. I knew one of them. I never understood what she saw in an old wreck like me who had recently moved into an age bracket whose first digit was 4.

In addition to the sublime sex, we had a mutually beneficial relationship, a fair exchange of give and take. She fed me information and I gave her good stories and was a regular guest on the morning show. Every now and then, you might catch my face on the screen in the evening as well. She knew she could count on me for something interesting, real facts on the ground from places most people would like to visit but never get any closer to than the National Geographic channel.

"I have to see what my day looks like," I said. "What do you know about what's happening over there?"

"It's chaos. Not surprisingly, the Indians were caught with their pants down again. They're barely functioning."

That didn't sound good.

After the attacks in Mumbai in 2008, I was interviewed by a number of Mossad and Security Agency departments, despite objections to my presence. It wasn't hard to guess what my detractors had to say: "He's a nutcase"; "How can you bring in someone who was booted out?"; "He's a bad joke these days. He thinks he's some kind of lethal combination of Bruce Lee and Mahatma Gandhi." But there were still some people around who knew better, who would have countered that no one knows the region or understands the Asian mentality better.

I offered them my opinion, that Mumbai was just the opening shot. But I've got to admit that even I wasn't expecting the next volley to come so soon.

At the time, I talked it over with other people, too. In the course of my work I've made quite a few friends, and no small number of enemies, in all sorts of odd places around the world. Brigadier Tanwar came to mind. He was forced out of the Indian police because he tried to shake things up after the fiasco in Mumbai. The chief of police didn't like him interfering. Weak people hate anyone stronger than them. Tanwar was politely shown the door. That's the way a system loses good, reliable individuals and institutionalizes incompetence, indecision, and cowardice. Not that it was any different in Israel. I'm a case in point. I realized I ought to call Colonel Krishna, but Tammy broke my train of thought.

"We're barely getting any information," she said. "We're trying to reach Israelis in the region. The networks have just started sending their crews in. CNN, Sky, and the BBC have already cut into their broadcasts with breaking news, but they don't have anything solid to report either."

My cell phone rang. I didn't even bother to look. I figured I knew who was calling. There's nothing new under the sun.

"Hey, Dotan," Tammy asked. "Do you happen to know any Israelis who live around Manali or Rishikesh?"

I laughed.

"What's so funny?"

"The ones I know would never agree to be interviewed on air."

I thought of Ran, known as "El Pashtun" along the winding roads of the Himalayas, from India through Kashmir to Pakistan, and from there to the opium fields of Afghanistan. His ecological house stood on the terraced hillside above the road between Manali

and Nagar, unquestionably one of the most beautiful roads in the
world. In the heart of the fertile valley that grows narrower as the
mountains close in on it, among the streams flowing to the Beas
River, he'd built the most stunning retreat I'd ever seen. I could
never figure out how a man with such potential, a guy who grew up
on a kibbutz and served in an elite army unit, had become one of
the toughest and most highly regarded drug lords on the Pakistan-
Kashmir-Manali-Nepal opium road. I hadn't imagined that events
would bring us together again.

As soon as I got off the phone with Tammy, Chen called. She was
a news producer on Channel 2.

"You're too late, baby," I said.

"Don't tell me Tammy got to you first?" There was more than a
trace of envy in her tone. "Never mind. I'll find someone else. There
are plenty of so-called experts waiting by the phone. You owe me
one."

I hung up, realizing there was one person I really owed. Willy. I
wondered how I'd gotten mixed up in this mess and what I'd learn
from it. I knew that every step in life is a lesson on the journey to
the final lesson of all.

CHAPTER 4

TEL AVIV

I'D JUST PUT the kettle on when I heard a knock at the door. This
was getting out of hand. I plodded to the door and looked through
the peephole. Whoever got the idea of a peephole, I have to give
him credit. It's saved me from a bullet or two over the years.

The man on the other side of the door pulled out his ID and
shoved it up to the hole. It didn't make much of an impression on
me. For all I could tell, it was an exterminator's license. He had
waiting eyes. They get them at the end of the course, together with
the dark glasses.

I opened the door. There were two of them in regulation garb.
He was in dark blue trousers, white shirt, dark jacket. The fold on
the left-hand side of the jacket hid a standard-issue service gun. She
was in a short blue skirt with the same white shirt under her jacket,
albeit a bit more form-fitting. I assumed she kept her gun in the bag
slung over her shoulder.

"If this keeps up, people are going to have to take a number to see
me," I grumbled. "What's going on?"

"We want to talk to you," the man said.

"I haven't even had my coffee yet and I'm already running an
information bureau. Why don't you go wait in a café while I have
some breakfast and take a dump. Whaddya say, can you let a man
start his day like a human being? I just got back and I haven't had a
chance to breathe."

"This isn't the time to breathe," the woman said. "Your girlfriend at Channel 10, did she call yet?"

They strode in and took a quick look around my shabby characterless apartment. I sized them up. He was cast in the model of the typical agent. Utterly synthetic. Dark. Handsome. The type who went straight from an elite army unit into a field job with the Agency or the Mossad.

But she was something else entirely. They sat down on the sofa, and I pulled up a chair and took a seat opposite the most amazing legs I'd seen in a very long time. She crossed them, giving me a clear view of the little triangle closing before my eyes, as if to say: "First you have to earn it, bud." Wherever I looked, it was sweet. A saucy face with little freckles on an upturned nose. Blond hair tied back in a ponytail. Slim, with a terrific figure. She couldn't have stood more than five foot five, but every inch was worth its weight in gold.

"Okay," she said, "have you finished taking inventory?"

Smiling, I asked, "You wait for the uniforms to leave before coming up here to pester me?"

He nodded. I wondered which of them was in charge. I hadn't figured it out yet. They were working like a well-oiled team.

"My name is Arnon Shai," the man said. "This is Maya Kfir."

"That's quite a name," I said to her.

She laughed. "Better than Leibder. That's lion in Yiddish. I changed it to Kfir when I was in the course."

I hadn't been referring to her last name, but to her first, and all the mystical meanings of Maya. I wondered what kind of experience I was in store for this time; was she a seductress or an opportunity? I found it all very appealing: her laugh, the dimple at the side of her mouth, the gleam in her blue eyes.

"How can I help you?" I asked.

There was a moment of silence before Maya took the lead. "Willy Mizrachi," she said.

"What about him?"

They exchanged glances, trying to decide whether I was really an idiot or just putting on an act.

"Barnea from the ICIU was here, so you know the story," Arnon said.

I nodded. I decided I might as well be straight with them.

"Barnea must've asked you about your connection to Willy. That's his business," Maya said. "What we're interested in is the wreckage he left behind."

"If you're asking me if I know anything about it, the answer is no."

I saw the skeptical look they exchanged. They were already getting on my nerves. Too little sleep? More visitors than I generally have in a month? Whatever the reason, the result was that Dotan Naor was beginning to feel cranky. And that doesn't happen often.

"You seem like nice kids, but I suggest we get this over with fast before I kick you outta here. I'll give you five minutes, no more. And I've got a very short fuse at the moment, so don't try me."

Arnon scrutinized me. Like all twentysomethings, he was sure he was smarter than me. On top of that, the idea that a guy in his forties might be able to take him on seemed preposterous. I let out a sigh. Maya, on the other hand, got the picture. "Don't even think about it, Arnon. He could clobber you with one hand tied behind his back." Turning to me, she said, "Stop flexing your muscles. We read your file and what we need is your brain, not your biceps."

I liked that. She was just what it took to make me melt even before Tel Aviv was hit by the heat and humidity of summer. I'd already learned there was something special about the hard-nosed beauties this country grew. And it really got to men like me, men who are stuck perpetually in middle-age.

"What do you want?" I asked matter-of-factly, a tone I could only manage by not looking at her.

"We want you to work for us," she said.

"No way, kids. That goes way beyond the usual bullshit."

"You still in the resentful stage because they kicked you to the curb?" she asked, not smiling this time. I could see the fear of failure in her eyes, the existential angst of every agent.

"No. I'm just not on your side anymore. Haven't been for a long time."

"And if I told you we think you're the only one who can clean up Willy Mizrachi's mess?"

I did the math. One, I was definitely intrigued. Two, I knew I couldn't just walk away.

"Go on."

"As soon as it gets out that the Israeli arms dealer Willy Mizrachi was murdered in Delhi, a lot of shit is going to hit the fan all over the world. And it won't be long before it all points back to us. To be precise, to our military industries. It's no secret what kind of aggressive tactics they use and how many officials they bribe in countries we're interested in selling weapons to. To say nothing of the fact that they also trade with places that might be considered sensitive or problematic in terms of foreign relations."

"You've just wasted a lot of words without giving me any facts."

"Willy Mizrachi brokered large deals for government-linked organizations like the Defense Ministry, Israel Aerospace Industries, Rafael Advanced Defense Systems. He had his own markets. And he also had a license to sell weapons and a valid permit from the inspector of military exports. But when the competition got tougher and the commissions dried up, he went to war. And the wars of the Jews are always the worst. He started acting as a go-between for deals between third and fourth parties. Things like T-55 tanks that were bought in Russia, retrofitted in Israel, and sold to the Ivory Coast, or weapons from Romania or Bulgaria that were sold through Switzerland to Guatemala, Myanmar, and God knows where else."

I whistled silently to myself. Now I understood where the fancy jeep and the expensive cigars came from, and I also understood the reason for Willy's frequent visits to places that might be natural destinations for me, but not for the average tourist.

"So what?" I said. "At least fifteen countries export weapons, including superpowers like the US, Russia, and China. Not to mention lots of smaller unsavory nations. They're all in competition with each other. What's the problem?"

After a short pause, Maya explained. "One, a lot of money has changed hands in the past few years, sometimes under the table, and that's always a problem. Two, Willy apparently had some kind of personal interest in one of his deals, and we suspect he sold weapons through an intermediary to someone we're not very partial to. Three, we don't have any leads to his murderers. And four, we can't investigate."

"I followed you up to number three," I said, "but you lost me at four. Why not?"

Maya seemed to be fond of counting. "One," she said, "Israel wants to keep its hands clean. People are starting to say the Israeli government turns a blind eye to arms dealers operating in the gray area, maybe even offers them support. Two, the Foreign Ministry would never acknowledge what he was doing because we don't even have full diplomatic relations with some of the countries he was involved with. Three, we don't know the region as well as you do. Four, we're not authorized to operate there."

"I still don't understand what you want from me."

She pulled out my Agency personnel file. I had to laugh. We live in the digital age and the Agency still hadn't computerized its files. All the documents were in a yellowing cardboard folder held together with a rubber band that had started disintegrating when I was still in the army. "You can laugh," she said, "but we read it all, every word."

"And what conclusions did you reach?"

As soon as she started to say "one," I cut her off. "I hate laundry lists."

"You seemed to like it before," Maya said, recrossing her legs and looking me straight in the eye.

I nearly fell off my chair. I shut my eyes for a second, thinking of what it would be like to see her lying beside me on a long white beach. Koh Samui? Too many tourists. Southern Mexico? No, the minute she untied her bikini top, a cop would descend on us with his hand out for a bribe that would feed his family for the rest of the month. I considered Cayo Limon at the northern tip of the Samana Peninsula in the Dominican Republic. The classiest beach you'll ever find, spread out around a glorious symmetric bay. The perfect expanse of white sand between the gentle waves of the sea and the palm trees murmuring in the breeze. Maya, me, and a bottle of honey-colored extra viejo rum.

"Hey, you still with me?" she asked.

"I wish," I said, not able to resist the temptation, although I knew it was the last thing you're supposed to say to a woman.

"What's the story, Maya?" Arnon intervened when he saw she was creating what's called in the profession a "connection" with me. "How come all the old fogeys come on to you?"

I undid a button on my shirt. I saw Arnon's eyes widen. At least I'd gotten a reaction from him. Sighing, I lightly scratched my most recent chest tattoo, a Himalayan panther. Maya, however, chose to remain professional.

"Can we get back to business?" she asked.

She was very pretty when she was angry.

"One, you knew Willy Mizrachi. Two, you were involved in a deal of his in Thailand."

"Hold on a minute," I interrupted. "That was a onetime thing. I let him take advantage of a contact I had. We stayed friends, but I asked him never to get me mixed up in that kind of thing again."

"Can I ask why?"

"You want the short version?"

She nodded.

I offered a terse explanation, my eyes fixed on her. I wasn't sure she'd get it, but I gave it a go, not knowing where it would lead.

"Blood money," I said. "That's not me."

She gazed at me with eyes I could dive into and never reach bottom.

"I'm not sure I understand."

"I'm not sure I could make it any clearer even if I wanted to."

I didn't feel like explaining that I was into saving lives, even if I sometimes had to break the law to do it, as long as it didn't involve anything that might cause lives to be lost. That's why I stuck to more straightforward cases, like looking for kids who disappeared or trying to arrange quietly for an Israeli's release from a foreign prison. Three hundred dollars a day plus expenses. It seemed reasonable to me, and I didn't need any more. I slept well at night, relatively speaking, of course. Sometimes I had to keep my eyes open to make sure a Thai punk didn't stick a knife in my back or a Kazakhstani thug didn't try to rough me up.

Maya didn't push it, deciding to get back to the business at hand. "We want you to work for us on the Willy Mizrachi case."

"Why?"

"Nobody knows the region like you. You can move around easily. And we know about your humanitarian bent. Anyone who ever worked with you abroad says you never leave scorched earth behind. That's not a typical Israeli trait."

She leafed through the file, and I noticed how thick it was. That surprised me. Someone had taken the trouble to keep it up-to-date, but I knew what the last entry would be. Three months in a Buddhist monastery in the Isaan district in northeast Thailand. There wouldn't be anything after that.

"The answer is no," I said.

I saw the hint of disappointment in Maya's eyes, but she'd been trained to control her emotions. *Not bad*, I thought. A heart of steel. I could work with that. She showed the potential of a good student.

"Why not?" she asked.

I debated whether to answer and decided to give it a try. Maybe something would sink in. "The seventh Dalai Lama phrased it this way: 'If there is a way to free ourselves from suffering we must use every moment to find it. Only a fool wants to go on suffering. Isn't it sad to knowingly imbibe poison?'"

After a moment's silence, she asked, "Is that your final answer?"

"Yes."

"They're not going to like it."

I laughed. Despite what was going on in India, and despite what happened to Willy, I couldn't help myself. It was a cathartic laugh, because I realized I was finally free. They couldn't make me feel like I owed them something anymore. It was over. At least, that's what I thought at the time.

"If you change your mind, give me a call," she said, taking out a business card and placing it on the bureau.

"Any time?" I couldn't resist the urge to flirt a little more.

"Any time," she said with a smile, "day or night."

I knew I was making an ass of myself. I was still the same lame-brain as ever around women. They were the only ones who brought that out in me.

CHAPTER 5

It was a lot to process for one morning. There was no way I was going to get any more shut-eye. I glanced back at the TV and zapped through the channels. They were still scrounging for information, looking for the most reliable commentator, trying to make contact with Israelis on the ground. On Channel 1, a university professor who specialized in terrorism was lecturing on the spread of Islamic terror. On Channel 2, an Israeli named Boaz was on the phone from Rishikesh. "I'm in my room in the guesthouse," he reported breathlessly. "It's right opposite the Lakshman Jhula bridge. We can hear gunshots across the river. There're Indian forces down below. I can't tell if they're army or police, but from here they look like a bunch of clowns. And the rifles they're carrying look like broomsticks."

Loud gunfire could be heard in the background. Anyone with military training would recognize the sound. It came from an AK-47, the terrorists' weapon of choice.

Boaz became even more frantic. "The Indians are being fired on from the bridge. They're all taking cover, except for one big Sikh officer. He just ran to a jeep and he's screaming into the radio."

The call was cut off abruptly. The buzz of the empty phone line echoed in the studio. That was my cue. I got my yoga mat and left the apartment. I stopped at the juice stand and began the session with a glass of bitter wheatgrass juice.

"What's up?" Kobi asked from behind the piles of mango, papaya, pomegranates, and carrots. "Did you hear what's going on?"

I nodded.

"It's awful. The kids go there to get high for a couple of months and look what happens."

I mumbled something unintelligible to indicate that I shared his sentiments.

"What've you been up to? I haven't seen you around for a while. Picking up a new skill in the East?"

"Something like that."

His eyes lit up. Guys like Kobi rush into some trendy new business venture hoping to get rich quick, and then the years go by, and they're stuck with the business, but the dreams are gone. He handed me another glass of wheatgrass juice, on the house, just so I'd give him a little more to fantasize about.

"What?" he asked eagerly. "Spill."

"I took a few lessons in urumi in Kerala in southern India."

"Hey, take it easy. Too many words. What's urumi? Never heard of it."

"You're not the only one. Most people haven't. It's a long sword with a flexible steel blade that curls up on itself. It's lethal."

"You're killing me. Where do you dig up these things? You're making it up."

I laughed.

He turned away from me to squeeze a large glass of carrot juice for a pretty young thing who, judging by her tights and the bag she was carrying, was on her way to the gym.

"Tell me more," Kobi said when he had served her.

"It'll have to wait, bro."

Terror attacks in India, an Israeli murdered in Delhi, and in Tel Aviv life went on as usual.

I continued down the boulevard looking for a nice olive tree to spread my mat under. It was a bit exhibitionistic, I know, but in this city, nobody gives a fuck what you do. Anything goes. I took off my shirt and slipped out of my flip-flops. After an hour of stretching, I started feeling normal and could put behind me the ten and a half hours in the air followed by six hours of bad news, unwanted guests, and too little sleep. Over a cup of coffee in a boulevard café, I began running scenarios in my mind. I thought of Willy. What the hell was he doing in a sleazy hotel in Delhi? I suddenly realized what was bothering me. It wouldn't be fair for me to win the bet just because Willy was dead. It was a dumb way to think, but it's what started the wheels turning.

CHAPTER 6

I DECIDED TO call Cochi. She'd know. Well, it was her job to report daily on who was doing what, where, and with whom. These days her column filled a whole page in the paper. I guess they had to fill it with something. She was a bottom feeder, but she was hot.

"Hi, handsome," she answered. "I'm so glad you called. Any chance we can get together for a drink later, or are you still with Michal?"

"Michal?" I didn't like admitting how quickly I lost track of them. I didn't even remember their names. All they left behind was a vague memory: an image, a sensation, the feel of a feminine touch.

"I get it," Cochi said. "You want to come and cry on Mommy's shoulder?"

"Cut the bullshit, Cochi. Tell me, where can I find Sylvia?"

"Sylvia Bazonkas?"

Cochi can be uber-malicious, but I had to laugh. "That's what she's called these days? Last I heard it was Sylvia Drill Bits."

"I guess you haven't seen the work she had done."

"I'm not really in the loop."

"Does it have to do with Willy?"

I didn't answer. How the fuck had she found out already?

"I can hear your cogwheels turning, sweetie. It's my job to know things. You know you can't keep a secret in this country for more than five minutes. Write down her number. After you see her, tell me what you think of her new look and whether it will do her any good."

She read out Sylvia's cell phone number, then added, "A big boy like you shouldn't be wanking off at night in front of a porn flick. Pick up the phone. I'm always ready to take care of you."

I blew her a kiss over the phone and hung up. Then I called Sylvia. "Sylvia, darling," I said.

"Dotan, my love. Where are you?" She was so excited she could hardly speak. "You're not going to believe this but I've been thinking about you all morning. I went through all my papers looking for your number. Nada. It's like you disappeared into thin air."

"When can I come over?"

She burst into tears. "Now. Come now. I'm so miserable."

The address she gave me was in the Akirov Towers on Pinkas Street. *Not bad, Willy*, I thought, *keeping your mistress in a super luxury building.*

My bike was still chained to the same pole where I'd left it. I'd tried to get Arieh the Romanian to let me put it up for sale in front of his junk shop at the flea market, but he said the eyesore would drive his "customers" away. He was referring to the junkies he bought stolen bikes from for fifty shekels.

I pedaled as fast as I could to the towers and marched over to the Peeping Tom behind the bank of computer screens in the lobby. I knew his type, the kind who flex their muscles for the residents in the hope of humping one of the ladies in a top-floor apartment. The guard didn't like what he saw. A sharwal and a cotton Indian shirt with two heavily tattooed arms sticking out. But he was no moron. He saw me take in the security system in a single glance and hit a button in front of him.

"You can send out an all-clear," I said. "I'm here to see Sylvia."

"Sylvia what? I need a full name."

"I only know her as Sylvia Bazonkas."

At least I got a smile out of him. "Ex-Agency?" he asked.

I gave him the name of my division. That broke the ice. With a big grin, he told me to leave an ID with him and handed me a visitor badge.

"Fifth floor," he said. "I'll let her know you're on your way up."

I nodded and headed for the elevators. I didn't like the cold, angular building. I preferred traditional Tel Aviv architecture, crumbling four-story houses that still displayed a glimmer of their former glory.

Sylvia opened the door. I almost fell over, and it takes a lot to get a reaction like that out of me. They were huge, especially for a petite babe like her, five foot one at best. Her lips had also been transformed into a silicon soufflé and her hair was now platinum blond.

She showed me to a chair in the middle of the space she called the living room. Everything was cold and white, the antithesis of Sylvia herself, who was, without question, the crowning jewel of the apartment. She went into the kitchen, put a capsule in the espresso machine, and made me a strong shot of ristretto. For herself she poured a glass of no-cal flavored mineral water.

We sat opposite each other, drinking in silence. Through the wide window I had an amazing view of the Tel Aviv inhabited by the little people, the working folk.

She waited for me to finish my coffee before asking, "What's happening over there?" Her tone was no longer that of Sylvia the coquette, the extrovert, the spoiled child. I was one of the few people she'd ever let see her serious side.

"I haven't the foggiest idea," I said. "I came here to find out what you know."

Sylvia took a sip of water and looked me straight in the eye. "Very little, to say the least," she said. "People think men pour their hearts out to their mistresses. Maybe they do. But not Willy. He was a secrecy freak."

"When was the last time you spoke to him?"

"Three weeks ago, something like that. Willy wasn't the type to call every day. He phoned, said he was going to northern India to a place called Sikkim. I could tell he was troubled. I could hear it in his voice. And you know Willy. He kept his feelings to himself. But he was worried about something. I'm sure of it."

"Did he tell you about his son?"

"Yes."

She walked to the window and stared out at the city below. Then she turned back to me. "Willy was here a couple of weeks before," she said. "I could see he was upset. We talked about his son, and he said, 'I have to bring him home, now more than ever.'"

"Did he say why?"

"When I asked him, he looked at me with that piercing glare of his, you know what I mean, and said, 'I screwed up.'"

"That's all?"

She nodded. "I'm not being much help."

Yes, you are, I thought. If Willy said he screwed up, he was in deep shit. What kind of shit? I had no idea.

Sylvia moved away from the window and came to stand next to me. Passing her hands over her double Ds, she asked, "What do you think?"

I almost choked. "Impressive," I said.

"You think so? It was Willy's fantasy. He had a lot of stupid ideas about women and how they're supposed to look."

I knew Willy was a bastard, but I didn't know he had a kinky side. This was getting interesting. But how do you ask a lady about her dead lover's sexual preferences?

Sylvia wasn't a dumb blond. She understood.

"Ask me whatever you want," she said. "You know what, don't bother. I'll tell you. Willy fucked all the time, wherever he was. He'd hump anything that moved."

I didn't like what I was hearing. I've known a lot of men who were brought down by their dick. As soon as they let it run wild, it took over, and they were done for. In the business culture of Southeast Asia, sex is a perk you get from your host for closing a deal. And Israelis love free gifts. Most of them don't know there's no such thing, that it's going to cost them in the end.

"Did Willy leave any papers here?" I asked.

She was standing with her back to the window, a small but imposing silhouette. She hesitated for a moment before saying, "I have a key to his office."

She went into the kitchen and came back with a key ring. "There's a safe behind one of the pictures. The code is 1426#." She handed me the keys. "You're going to find out who killed him, aren't you?" she asked.

"I'd like to think so."

On my way to the door, I turned around. "Will you be all right?"

"Don't worry about me," she said with a smile that didn't hide the tears. "The next Willy is already waiting his turn."

CHAPTER 7

I WENT BACK to my spot on the boulevard and picked up my exercise routine where I'd left off, although I didn't have much hope of completing it. My cell phone rang less than a minute after I began the first breathing exercise. When I saw who it was, I knew she'd keep calling until I picked up.

"Well," Tammy asked, "can I send a cab? It'll take all day for you to get here on your rusty old bike. The guys here are fed up with all the so-called experts, all the professors who've never even been over there. Come on, let the viewers see your pretty tattoos. You got any new ones?"

"Yes."

"Incredible. Where? Tell me where."

"It's not really a tattoo. Send a cab to the boulevard. The cabbie will find me."

"Don't keep me in suspense, Dotan. Tell me what it is and where you put it. Please. Now, before I have to hang up."

"A little pearl on my dick," I whispered.

"That's sick, man. You're killing me," she moaned. "You're a dead man if I find out some chick got to play with it before me. Ciao, baby. I've gotta run."

The phone fell silent. I stood up on the mat, closed my eyes, and breathed deeply from the abdomen. Then I started a set of exercises I learned from Mahatra, the scar-faced laughing yogi who lives in a tiny hut in Rishikesh on the banks of the Ganges. The idea is to combine laughter with breathing exercises. It's an ancient technique every yogi knows but not all of them use. It has nothing to do with jokes or funny situations, but you do need a sense of humor. I breathed and laughed, opening my mouth wide and letting out a big laugh. The passersby stared at me quizzically. An old lady walking her dog crossed anxiously to the other side of the boulevard.

I laughed again, cleared my mind of all thoughts and images. A total vacuum. Laughter and an empty mind. Laughter and an empty mind. A wave of positive energy flowed through my body. Then I was ready to start the series of more demanding exercises. It's no easy ride on the banks of the Ganges. I stood for fifteen minutes on one leg, the other bent and resting on the thigh of the supporting leg, my hands clasped in front of my chest. The minutes ticked by as if time didn't exist, like everything else in the non-physical world. Then I switched legs. Another fifteen minutes. The only thing in my head was the image I'd carved on my memory: the sun rising across the river over Ma Ganga, Mother Ganges, with the three of us, Mahatra's students, standing as we did every morning on the thin strip of sand that appeared at low tide.

I heard honking. I opened my eyes. The cabbie stuck his head out the window. "You the one for Channel 10?" he asked.

I nodded.

"Let's go," he said. One of the drivers behind him was already leaning on his horn.

I rolled up the mat, stuck it under my arm, and picked up the orange shoulder bag that's gone with me everywhere since my first monastic retreat. I leaned my bike against a tree, commanding it to be the ugliest one in the neighborhood, and climbed into the cab.

On the way, I called Shai. I'd dissolved our ailing partnership after the search for Sigal Bardon in Bangkok, but I still worked with him as a freelancer.

"You have anything urgent going on?" I asked.

"No. Just a boy who fried his brain, probably with that hallucinatory plant. What's it called?"

"Datura inoxia."

"He was last seen in Manali. But the family hasn't signed anything yet. They're still hoping the insurance will pay part of the cost of the search."

"I get where they're coming from. I may be going to India. I'm not sure yet."

"Are they on your back because of Willy?"

Sometimes Shai can be almost human. Not often.

"Yeah. I'll let you know."

I gazed out the window, thinking about the Israelis in India who were going through the most shitty experience of their lives. The cabbie seemed to be reading my mind. Some of them have that power. "It's lousy, what's going on in India," he said. "But it's all in God's hands."

I ignored him, sinking deep in thought until he pulled up in front of the Channel 10 building. The security guard at the entrance nodded at me in recognition, apologizing for the new regulations that required me to leave an ID with him. He gave me a badge that allowed me access to the studios. I took the elevator to the newsroom on the sixteenth floor. Assistants glanced at me as they ran down the corridor. There were new ones all the time, each of them dreaming of the day they'd be sitting behind the anchor desk. One stopped and asked, "Are you Dotan?"

She led me to makeup. As usual, the makeup artist gave me a huge grin. "I haven't seen you around in a while," she said. "Where've you been hiding?"

"Here and there."

"You're really something."

Tammy burst in and hugged me from behind. "I'm hooking you up to the studio," she said. "You won't believe what's going on."

"Give me the latest."

"From what we've heard so far, there were two attacks, one in Manali and the other on two guesthouses in Rishikesh."

"Which side of the river? There are guesthouses on both sides."

"No idea."

"Can you pull up a map from Google Earth?"

"We'll try. But let me finish. There are also indications that Israelis may have been abducted in Kashmir Valley." She glanced at the notes in her hand. "Srinagar? Did I pronounce that right? A place by the name of Lake Dal."

"You're kidding. That doesn't sound good."

"You planning to go on air in that rag?" Grimacing, she pointed to my wrinkled Indian shirt. "Mirit, who's on wardrobe this morning?"

"They didn't think they'd need anyone."

"Let's go through the closet and see if we can find something that fits."

They tried, but everything was either too tight or hung on me like a sack. A parade of girls passed by the wardrobe room trying to get a peek at my gallery of tattoos. Tammy waved them away and closed the door. "You have to stop seducing minors," she said.

They put me on air. I attempted to give a realistic picture, describing the problematic location of Chabad House at the very foot of the road that ascends to Old Manali and the fact that it occupied a floor in an industrial building rather than being in a separate compound or an isolated spot. I explained the somewhat complicated geography of Rishikesh on both sides of the Ganges and the position of the two suspension bridges. I went into detail about the road from the south that came from the direction of Haridwar and how it could easily be blocked off. I spoke about the geopolitics of Kashmir and expressed the concern that if Israelis were abducted there it would be a simple matter to sneak them over the border to the Pakistani side of Kashmir.

Toward the end, I was asked if the attacks could have been prevented. I gave a cautious answer. "This wasn't a spontaneous act," I said. "It's a terror attack that was planned down to the last detail a long time in advance. I would guess it took at least a year to gather the intel, choose the targets, train the terrorists. Could it have been prevented? No. Could the risk have been reduced? Maybe."

The anchor, who was no idiot but no genius either, asked his next question: "How do you assess the response of the Indian military and the local police force? The events aren't even over yet, and we're already hearing quite a bit of criticism, mainly from the independent Indian press, in particular about how slow they were to respond."

"The security forces in India are very large entities," I said. "After the attacks in Mumbai, they conducted serious investigations and set up special operations platoons in each battalion called Ghatak Units. And police anti-terrorism squads are stationed throughout the country. But India is very big. If I'm not mistaken, the Ghatak unit closest to Manali and Rishikesh is in the city of Chandigarh, which is a nine- or ten-hour drive away. It takes time to deploy specially trained forces. There are a lot of them in Kashmir, but the situation there is so sensitive that they might have hesitated to call them out to avoid inciting the Muslim population."

I left the studio. Tammy was waiting for me. "You did great," she said.

"I can't stay."

"Don't be like that."

I kissed her lightly on the forehead.

"Will you be back for the evening news?" she asked with a smile, showing off her natural assets, which were bounteous.

"I'll see. I've got a lot to do."

"Okay. Give me a hug before you go. I love your hugs."

I put my arms around her. Why not? But my mind was on Sylvia's tears. Her tears had convinced me I had to go to India.

I knew it was a mistake, that I should sit still and not do anything. But that wasn't an option. No way. I owed it to Willy. Maybe to myself, too. How did Guru Mahatra put it: "You complete one cycle. It isn't over. The second cycle begins." He meant the cycles of life and the pain that accompanies them. I meant that as soon as you shovel away one pile of shit, you've got another one to clean up.

CHAPTER 8

THE SECURITY GUARD escorted me up to Willy's office and punched in the alarm code. I opened the door with the key Sylvia had given me.

"How long will you be?"

"An hour, maybe more."

"No problem. Press this when you're ready to leave," he said, pushing a button on the secretary's console. The security desk at the entrance to the building showed on the computer screen. "I'll see you and come up and turn the alarm back on."

The office looked exactly the same as the last time I'd been there, a year before, except that the brown leather chair was empty. I pictured Willy in it, leaning back, his feet up on the large wooden desk, a thick cigar in his mouth. Willy and the good life. I forced the image out of my mind. I'd come to look for clues, not to reminisce.

I checked the drawers. Just the usual suspects. Office supplies in the top drawer, including a Mont Blanc pen in its box. Undoubtedly the real thing. Willy wouldn't buy a ten-dollar knockoff. Another drawer held a few cigar lighters and cutters, the basic accoutrements for a cigar smoker.

I turned to the computer. Family pictures alternated on the screen at regular intervals. Itiel's college graduation, his daughter's final dance recital somewhere in Europe. Willy seemed to like defining moments, at least the ones that fit his definitions. I didn't even need a password to get into the computer. Sometimes the most cautious people in the world are convinced their front door gives them all the protection they need and don't bother to secure what's behind it. They're apparently unaware that even the fanciest lock demands no more than a few extra seconds of concentration from an experienced burglar.

I went into Outlook. There were a lot of unread messages. I wondered if Willy had checked his mail in India or if he'd had it routed to a different address. The list was impressive. I saw messages from Romania, Holland, Ukraine, Liberia, India, Angola, Guatemala, Panama, and the Cayman Islands. I opened one from a law firm in Amsterdam and another from someone called Abdul Aziz Wani in Delhi. It contained just two words: "Delivery completed." I wondered what it meant, although I could make an educated guess. I decided not to waste time reading the reams of correspondence, and printed out the mail from the last month along with Willy's list of contacts, planning to go through it all later.

The safe was behind the photo of Willy in the Himalayas. It was a dinky affair, a metal box with a simple keypad set into the wall. The absence of stricter precautionary measures surprised me. It wasn't like Willy, I thought. I guess at a certain point, he started to feel invincible.

I punched in the code I'd gotten from Sylvia. Inside was a long leather folder stuffed with bills: dollars, euros, Swiss francs. Beneath it was a large pile of documents. I pulled them out and flipped through them. I knew each one might provide a lead, but it would take me a long time to wade through it all.

I hit pay dirt when I saw the document at the bottom of the pile. It bore the logo of an Indian company by the name of Nandi

Corporation Arms Dealers. The heading referenced the sale of five hundred TAR-21 assault rifles. I let out a long whistle. Way to go, Willy. I knew a lot of weapons dealers don't like to mess with small arms. Too little profit and too big a headache. You can get an AK-47 these days at bargain-basement prices, no more than a hundred dollars a pop. And nothing can compete with it for price or performance. It's the ultimate weapon for crimes against humanity, ethnic wars, and any other type of killing spree. Give any nutter who thinks he's the new messiah an AK-47 and wait for the blood to start flowing.

Willy was nobody's fool. I did the calculations. Five hundred guns at a thousand dollars each equaled five hundred thousand dollars. And that's not including the optics, magazines, and ammo, which the TAR-21 spit out at a rate of nine hundred rounds a minute. His cut would be at least 15 percent. Not bad. Stapled to the sheet was another page with the same company logo. I scanned it quickly, trying to get the main gist. It was the cargo manifest for a ship that had sailed from Cyprus to the Black Sea port of Constantza in Romania, where it took on forty-six tons of weapons of various sorts. In addition to TAR-21s and associated ammunition, the long list included Dragunov sniper rifles, AK-47s, and Sagger missiles. The ammunition was given in tons, not rounds, and the different types of mines were catalogued in precise detail. The unnamed ship, flying a Cypriot flag, was headed for Bhavnagar, India.

I also found the record of a bank transfer of twelve million dollars to an account in a Turkish Cypriot bank in the name of a Ukrainian company, Euro-Wex. Another document detailed transfers of funds into the same company's account in a branch of the Chase Manhattan Bank in New York.

I was starting to sweat. It wasn't going to be easy to follow the convoluted trail of weapons and money transfers. That was Willy through and through.

Under the papers I found a book of business cards. It held ten cards arranged on pages of three, with a single card on the last page. I manipulated the numbers. I'd always liked to play with the meaning of numbers. What seems meaningless to other people can be very significant to me.

Nine plus one makes ten. In Indian astrology, nine is the number of heavenly bodies that influence a person's fate. There were also the first nine days of the Hindu month Ashvin, when the triumph of good over evil is celebrated. On the tenth day, the prince god Rama slays Ravana, the demon king, and the goddess Durga slays the demon Mahishasura in the guise of a buffalo. And ten is the number of avatars of Vishnu, the different forms he takes when he descends to save the world.

Ten business cards. I concentrated on the one filed on its own. "Abdul Aziz Wani, agent, Manchester and New Delhi." No surprise that the name of the company was Nandi Corporation Arms Dealers. The card contained an address in New Delhi, telephone numbers in England and India, and an e-mail address. If I played the tables, I could say that the tenth card I drew was my lucky one. My gut told me that what I had in my hand was a lead that could very well prove invaluable.

The buzzing of the cell phone in my pocket interrupted my thoughts. I placed the contents of the safe next to my bag before answering.

It was Maya Kfir. "The Foreign Ministry didn't like what you said on TV," she said without any preamble.

"I'm not surprised. They're good people, but they don't understand that there's no substitute for the insight you can gain on the ground. They get pouty when it turns out someone knows more than they do."

"They called you a mad dog that bites the hand that feeds him."

I didn't reply. It wasn't a very flattering description.

"So what've you decided?"

The phone vibrated to indicate another call coming in. Sylvia's name showed on the screen.

"I've got to take this," I said. "We'll talk later."

Sylvia sounded agitated. "FedEx just brought me a package. It's from Willy. There's an envelope addressed to you inside."

"Open it," I instructed.

"It's money. A bundle of hundred-dollar bills with a rubber band around them. Hang on, there's something else."

I heard the rustle of paper.

"It's a letter. It's too long to read out to you over the phone. Are you near a fax machine?"

I looked around and found the office fax. The number was written on a label over the dialer. I dictated it to her and she started writing it down. Then the penny dropped.

"That's Willy's office."

"You got it in one," I said.

Sylvia didn't respond. I heard the machine come to life and pages began to spill out. Each sheet was covered in closely spaced handwriting, but I could see it was legible.

"Did you get it?"

"Yes, babe. Thanks."

"The money will be waiting for you here. Ciao."

CHAPTER 9

I SAT DOWN in Willy's chair, put my feet up on the desk, and started reading.

Dotan,

I won't say you're like a brother to me, because you're not. I wouldn't even call you a close friend. Frankly, I don't have any close friends. But I've managed to tolerate you pretty well. There's something I feel I have to share with you, and that's pretty unusual for me. You know I've never been good at baring my soul. I bet you're thinking: "Wow, Willy is a changed man." Don't kid yourself. I'm the same son of a bitch I've always been, and you better believe it. A whiner? Not me. Not where I come from.

I'm sitting at the window in a room on the second floor of a seedy hotel. It's on a street called GB Road. To say this isn't the cleanest hotel in the world would be an understatement. I've seen lots better, but very few as filthy as this one. Never mind. Outside I can see Indian whores and all sorts of exotic things you could probably give a name to, mister India expert. I'm keeping my eyes on the FedEx office across the street, waiting for it to open so I can make sure the hotel clerk delivers the envelope I gave him. It's addressed to you and Sylvia. I promised him five hundred rupees, and that's a lot of money for a rodent like him.

There's a bakery across the street that sells every kind of Indian confection you can think of. You once told me the name of that sticky ball. Gulab jamun, right? I'm glad I can still remember something. Anyway, besides the cakes and the swarms of flies, there are two nasty looking characters in the shop. Going by the silly hat on his head, I'm pretty sure one of them is Kashmiri. See, I learned something. I'm also pretty sure he's got a gun in his pocket. The guy sitting next to him is probably Tibetan. I'm guessing by his broad face. I've got nothing against Tibetans. On the contrary, I've done a lot for them. Maybe he's from Nepal. There's something hard about the Nepalese I've run into. The bad ones can go to the darkest extremes. The one across the street scares me. When he came in he was carrying a sword or machete or something in a long wooden sheath. How come the Indians still let people walk around with weapons that belong in a museum?

I won't go into the Tibetan thing now. Maybe sometime, if we ever get the chance. You know I'm no do-gooder. I only made an exception because I thought it would improve my chances of winning our bet. I hope you haven't forgotten it. I haven't, but I'm afraid it may cost me my life. I swear, even if it does, I don't regret a minute of this whole crazy year I've spent doing everything I could for the sake of the bet. Scratch that. I've been doing it for my own sake.

That may sound wacky to you. You can laugh or not, but I'd like for you, more than anyone else, to believe it. The journey I made to try and convince Itiel to change his mind turned into something entirely different. I started out as an asshole. Then I met the most amazing Tibetan woman here, Tenzing. She's an integral part of our bet, but I'm guessing you'll find that out for yourself. That is, if you still give a rat's ass about me. That was the start of the strange path I followed, strange at least for me. I just remembered something else you once taught me. I don't know if it means anything, but I'll quote it anyway and you'll know what I'm talking about: "Om mani padme hum," the jewel in the lotus. For whatever that's worth.

So, as they say, so long, my friend. That sounds much better than "bye, dude," doesn't it? The next time you're in some dive drinking single malt, remember who taught you how to drink. Pour out a double, breathe in the aroma, examine the color. Here's to you, bro.

Someone's knocking on the door. I hope it's the waiter. I ordered a glass of kali chai with a lot of sugar. If it's not the waiter, there'll be a lot of blood instead.

I sat in Willy's office staring at the letter for a long time. Then I leaned back and closed my eyes to help me concentrate. Eventually, I folded the sheets, set them on the desk next to the pile of documents from the safe, and went into the kitchenette. I found a bottle of aged Talisker and two glasses and brought them back to the desk. This time I didn't sit down behind it, but on the opposite side where I'd sat the last time I'd seen Willy. I poured out two glasses and placed one in front of me and the other in front of his chair. I examined the glowing amber liquid and breathed in the heady aroma.

"Here's to you, Willy," I said, raising my glass and sipping the whiskey.

I took a cigar from the drawer, cut off the tip, lit it, and set it in an ashtray next to the untouched glass. Gazing out the closed window, I saw a small cloud crossing the sky and thought of the year that had elapsed since I'd last been here. I realized that Willy had made the bet with me because it was the only way for him to take some kind of action, and he wasn't ready to give up yet. But it was also a trap, and no trap is deadlier than one you deliberately set for yourself. I knew I was about to do the same thing.

The ash fell from the cigar as it burned itself out. Willy would have been upset by the waste of a good Dominican. I got up, washed the glasses in the sink, and left them to dry on a towel. Then I took out Maya Kfir's card and dialed her number.

"I'll do it."

There was a short pause before she answered, "Good."

"There're conditions."

"Give me twenty minutes. I'll meet you at the Masaryk Café. That's your favorite watering hole, right? Okay with you?"

"I need an hour," I said. "I have to take care of something first."

"Fine," she said, disconnecting.

I stuffed the papers into my shoulder bag. Acting on a gut feeling, I picked up the photograph from Willy's desk and stuck it in the bag. Then I shut the safe and left. The office door closed behind me. I knew I'd never be back here again.

CHAPTER 10

I WENT BACK to Sylvia's to get the money Willy had sent me, and within an hour, I was sitting at my regular corner table in the Masaryk Café with my back to the wall enjoying a large cappuccino. Nora, the longtime waitress, asked, "How's it going? You have anything to do with what's happening in India?"

I smiled. A smile comes easy when there's such a vision in front of you. Slim, an ample perfectly proportioned bosom, flowing red hair. Wherever you looked, figure or face, she was a sight for sore eyes, even though she wasn't a kid anymore. Besides, you could tell she wasn't weighted down by the burden of a permanent man in her life.

"Yup," I said just as Maya plopped down in the chair across from me.

She threw Nora the kind of glance that only women can conjure, and the waitress walked away sullenly. I took advantage of the few seconds until Maya brought her eyes back down to me to examine the goods. Deep down inside I breathed a silent sigh.

"It's official," she said. "We got authorization for you to go to India."

I gave her a piercing glare. "What's the catch?"

She laughed. I liked the look of her teeth. They seemed to have a laugh of their own.

"I'm coming with you."

The expression that came over my face wasn't a smile. Leaning forward, I stared into my cup. I wasn't trying to read the future. There was nothing to see there except for stray coffee grounds floating in a cloudy liquid. It matched my mood perfectly.

"No way," I announced.

"Why not? Think about it for a minute before you give me one of your laundry lists. It would probably start: one, chauvinism; two, chauvinism."

I laughed. The girl was an experienced tease.

"One, I work alone. Two, I'm not a tour guide. Three, it's the Indians who are chauvinists, not me. Instead of pumping them for information, I'll have to spend my time removing their hands from your sexy ass, and that's just the best-case scenario. And four . . ."

"What?"

"You make me nervous."

"You won't know I'm there," she said with a smile. She could tell I'd surrendered even before any shots were fired.

And that was the problem. I wanted to feel her. I looked at her blue eyes, moved on to the freckles skipping along her slightly upturned nose, and I wanted to grab at them one by one. If I could, I'd tell the little guy under the table to calm down. Years of meditation and martial arts and I couldn't even control my own dick. I knew I'd have to find a way to create a distance between us in order to get the job done. Otherwise, everything would fall apart. Including me.

To my surprise, she got there ahead of me. "It doesn't mean we'll be joined at the hip. It means we share information and agree on a plan of action," she explained.

"I can live with that. But you've got to understand it doesn't mean I'm bound by any decisions your guys back home make."

She paused before saying, "That's the way we want it."

When she left, I knew I'd fallen into their basket like a ball in an NBA game. But it was just netting.

It took me no more than a minute to pack. A toothbrush and my yoga mat. I hardly needed anything else. The antithesis of the typical Israeli with an old-style drawstring kit bag or a fancy backpack with all the useless bells and whistles. To Maya's credit, she also moved quickly. She called from downstairs, where she was waiting in an inconspicuous company car. Someone had spoken with the Indian embassy and they opened it just for us. We filled in the forms and, without any questions asked, we were issued visas that were valid for one year, allowing the bearer to enter the country three times during that period.

Maya was on the phone for most of the ride to the airport. I also took a call. It was from Tammy. When I told her I was on my way to India, she nearly fell off her producer's chair.

"I get the exclusive, sweetie," she said in a tone halfway between an order and an entreaty. "You don't talk to anyone from the Israeli media except me. Do you want me to describe how I'll repay you when you get back?"

I stole a glance at Maya and decided not to respond to Tammy's foreplay. "Chances are by the time I get there, it'll all be over," I said, keeping my voice businesslike.

Tammy instantly pulled out her serious claws. Women are such pragmatic creatures. "The way things look now, that doesn't seem likely. Nobody really knows what's going on. According to the Indian Broadcasting Network—they were the first to report from Mumbai—Indian forces are exchanging fire with the terrorists in three or four locations in Rishikesh. They've been broadcasting pictures of at least two people trying to jump from the roof of one of the guesthouses. There are also reports of heavy fighting in Manali."

"I'm not sure I'll be heading for the battle zones."

"The Dotan I know isn't going to miss the action. Be careful, and if you find out anything, just remember to text me a few words, where and what."

Tammy disconnected. Maya concluded her call as well. We looked at each other and laughed.

"Who goes first?" she asked.

I gave her a brief summary of my conversation with Tammy. It more or less fit what she'd been told. The last thing she said before we both fell asleep on the plane was, "India has really cast its spell on you, hasn't it?"

I nodded and yawned, realizing I hadn't gotten any serious sleep since I'd landed. Maybe it was time I did.

"India is a land of *and*, not *or*," I mumbled, half asleep.

I remember catching a glimpse of the question in those blue eyes of hers, but I'm not sure whether I answered it.

CHAPTER 11

DELHI

BEFORE WE LANDED in Delhi, they peeled the blankets off us and placed what they call breakfast in front of us. I discovered I had a headache from here to Timbuktu. The next discovery I made was that another head was growing from my shoulder, the head of a woman I knew very little about. By the way, that's not unusual in India. Quite a few of the forty thousand or so gods have two heads or more, and they can differ not only in gender, but in personality, too. They're evidence that duality is at the foundation of existence. The head that had settled itself in the pit of my shoulder didn't look all that bad. It didn't feel all that bad either. I didn't like that. We hadn't even arrived yet and she had already insinuated herself into my flesh. I shook her gently. Maya opened her eyes and said "Morning" with a big smile. What can I say? One look at that smile and my discomfort and the shitty taste left in my mouth by two Scotch and sodas were gone. I was back on the positive side of the planet.

At immigration, a bleary-eyed officer handed her passport to another officer behind him who stamped it. Typical Indian efficiency. When he got to my passport, he was stumped. He leafed through it in search of a valid visa. "You left Mumbai three days ago," he said, raising eyes that were red from lack of sleep, not unlike mine.

"That's right, sir," I said, using an Indian-like intonation to show I was an old India hand. It didn't make the slightest impression.

"What is the purpose of your visit this time, sir?" he asked deliberately, stressing the "sir."

"Business," I said, aping his tone and accent.

He turned the passport this way and that, drawing the process out to demonstrate what he thought of Israeli documents. They opened the wrong way around and were therefore irregular and automatically suspect. Then he asked me to wait. He got up from his post and showed the passport to the shift commander. "Sir, please go to that desk over there," he instructed when he returned, pointing to the man in charge.

"Go ahead," I said to Maya, whose passport had already been stamped. "I'll meet you at the carousel."

I went where I was told. The immigration officer took my passport and said, "There's a phone call for you, sir."

I picked up the phone. "Dotan," I said and heard the voice of Colonel Krishna from the Central Bureau of Investigation, the Indian security agency. "How are you, my friend?" he said.

I could picture him as if he were right there in front of me. He would be standing by the window in his office, looking out at the green boulevard of New Delhi that ran as straight as an arrow, every crease in his uniform ironed perfectly. The man always demanded the maximum, from himself and from life.

The first time I met him, which was quite a few years ago when I was first starting out in the search and rescue business, it had to do with the murder of an Israeli backpacker. He was standing by the window then, too. When I came up beside him, he pointed to the homeless who lived on the street below and asked, "Can you identify any of those people? Can you tell what ethnic group they belong to?" I couldn't. "The woman wrapped in white is a Jainist nun, possibly from one of the Mount Abu temples. The man in the white turban with a red earring is a Rajput from Rajasthan. The one with the three lines on his forehead and shaven temples is a Shiva priest. The woman in the burka is a Muslim, but you probably know that."

We stood there for some time. "The street you are looking at is a single breathing organism with many heads, arms, and legs," he explained. "It is not a random collection. There is order and logic to it, with well-defined divisions and subdivisions. Every corner will lead you to more strata and substrata of caste, occupation, and any number of other categories. Learn to look, my friend, or you will never understand India."

It was at that window, after the Israeli kid's body had been flown back home, that our friendship was sealed. It would probably be more accurate to call it a mentor-disciple relationship. It took years of visits to India before I understood that his method of teaching was to let me watch him in action, to witness his embodiment of what appeared to be impossible contradictions. He was a senior police officer who still sought, and found, the divine in every human being, in all the refuse he encountered. Gradually, very, very gradually, I acquired the patience that led me to an understanding of what Colonel Krishna had meant when we first stood by the window together. I came to realize that India is much more than just a picturesque mosaic of people, landscapes, animals, colors, odors, and sounds. That what we see with our eyes is much more complex than the Western patterns we were taught to see, think in, and perceive. "If you look carefully, if you learn to look," Colonel Krishna told me then, "you will see that time and space are different for us than they are for you. In order to solve the case of a missing person in India, you have to learn how to look at us. Otherwise, you will not see and you will not understand."

In a country as hard to navigate as India, I found the colonel to be an extraordinary ally. It is a place where almost everything is in the hands of bureaucrats, but he could get things done as if the words "no," "maybe," and the Indians' favorite phrase, "you have to fill out a form," didn't exist. Everything required mountains of paperwork and countless stamps and signatures. They did whatever they could to stall, pigeonhole, and avoid making decisions.

"How are you?" the colonel repeated, his voice bringing me back to my surroundings at passport control.

"Fine," I said. I wondered how the old fox knew I'd arrived in Delhi and why he was in such a hurry to get hold of me even before I left the airport.

He was never one to waste time on idle words. He went on as if there'd barely been a pause in our last conversation. "I had every intention of meeting you in person at the airport, but since you are not alone, it is better this way."

"I'm listening."

"My friend, you and the lovely lady need to turn around and go back where you came from."

I didn't reply. I was busy going over in my head all the information I had about the attacks and trying to figure out what he was driving at. He was waiting for an answer.

"Can't do it," I said.

"I was not expecting you to say anything else. I will not stop you. Do what you have to do."

Krishna always reminded me of the people who have no qualms about informing you that you have dandruff on your collar. Nobody likes to be told, but that doesn't make the dandruff go away. He knew how to scratch at the open sores, the thoughts that had nagged me during the flight and even before I got on the plane. What was my real reason for coming to India? Did I owe it to Willy? Was it the bet? Or was I trying to pay off some other debt?

"Just remember what I taught you," he said. "Things are not always what they seem."

I listened in silence. There are things that are said in silence, especially between people who have known each other for a long time.

"The temptress is called Maya?" he asked.

"That's right," I said, wondering how he knew. But I wasn't surprised by the keen intuition displayed by the pain in the ass.

"That is an enigmatic and rather dangerous name for a Mossad agent." He chuckled. "Who knows what it may lead to here in India." Returning to the real reason for his call, he said, "Be careful. Israelis are being targeted."

I gave him a noncommittal "okay," knowing that, without saying it in so many words, he was telling me that, whatever happened, I could count on him.

"Take care, my friend, and may Vishnu be with you."

Vishnu, the protector, descended to earth nine times, each time in a different form, to save the world and preserve the divine order. There was one more time to go. I was hoping it would be now.

CHAPTER 12

MAYA WAS WAITING by the carousel. We collected our bags and headed for customs.

"Don't we need to exchange money?" she asked.

I stopped at the bank. "Do it here, not at the exchange office. Their fees are exorbitant."

When you enter India, you find yourself on the offensive and the defensive at the same time. You have to do battle with yourself, with rationalism. I knew very well that a difference of ten rupees in the exchange rate was insignificant, but I had an inane desire to shield Maya, to protect her, to keep the smile on her face. It had been stuck there since we woke up on the plane, but it was already starting to fade. I wasn't surprised. The Delhi airport is large and spacious with an added bonus—the stink of urine and Lysol that announces loud and clear: "Welcome to India." Maya was showing signs of the shock experienced by everyone who lands in India for the first time. There's no simple cure. It's natural to feel repulsed and flustered. I let her take it like a big girl. It was just the beginning. We went out into the arrival hall. The smell of the garlands of flowers with which the hordes of waiting relatives strangled their loved ones added to the stench.

"This is India?" Maya asked, choking.

"Just an appetizer. Before the main course."

I wondered if I sounded as hard-core as I intended. I couldn't go easy on her. Classic Zen, or like Colonel Krishna liked to say, "In order to learn, you first have to know how to breathe. With the air you inhale comes the odor, and it's not always pleasant."

We left the building and headed for the line of taxis that stretched as far as the eye could see. They inched forward in a cloud of carbon dioxide that would pose a serious challenge for any gas mask. The driver who pulled up next to us was covered in as much soot as his cab. It was even stuck to the tufts of hair that protruded from his ears. Maya watched in concern as he unsuccessfully pumped the gas pedal. A couple of drivers volunteered to give him a push. The engine coughed a few times before catching. The cabbie took out a comb, passed it quickly through his hair, and asked irritably, "Where to?"

The cabbies in Delhi are always irritable. They have a million reasons to be. They're mad at the owner of the taxi who demands a high percentage and doesn't fix the broken springs in the driver's seat, at the incessant traffic jams, at the rising price of gas, at the roads that are flooded in summer and strewn with potholes in winter.

"Paharganj," I said.

"The backpackers' quarter?" Maya asked, puzzled. "That's where you're taking me?"

The cabbie added his two cents. "I know a very good hotel, sir, and very cheap. The hotels in Paharganj are no good, not clean."

I saw the first sign of doubt in Maya's eyes. It was aimed at me, of course.

"I know a place there. It's in a convenient location," I told her with as much conviction as I could muster. GB Road ran past Paharganj. I wondered again what the hell Willy was doing in one of its sleazy hotels.

"Take us to the Hari Rama Hotel."

"That is a shitty hotel, sir. It is not at all suitable for a lady."

He threw Maya a hopeful glance, eager for the small commission he'd receive if we agreed to let him take us to the hotel he recommended. I was sure it was just as shitty. Thankfully, the lady decided to trust me. We pulled out of the suffocating lot into the unrelieved smog of Delhi.

Maya was in shock. "How do they breathe?"

"Every person in Delhi is a medical miracle. They're mutations that have adapted to living on air low in oxygen and high in sulfur dioxide and nitrogen. Yoga breathing exercises train them to require less oxygen, and they get their other survival skills from poverty and hunger."

Living proof of my theory arrived in the form of a wide-eyed boy in threadbare khaki trousers and a t-shirt a few sizes too big. You could tell just by looking at him that he slept on the street, or in a cardboard box under a bridge at best. He stood at the exit to the parking lot selling English-language newspapers. The unblinking eyes of the small, tattered figure reflected all the sorrow and suffering of human existence. But that was only if you knew how to look. Some people didn't see anything.

I instructed the driver to stop. The boy ran to the open window. "I have the *Times of India*, sir. An excellent article about terror on the front page. I have the *Hindustan Times*, the whole cricket league and Bollywood gossip. Very good, sir." He gave me a wink and the most mischievous smile I'd ever seen. I winked back and took them both. The boy turned to Maya and tried to tempt her with a selection of magazines with seductive pictures of celebrities on the covers, but she just smiled back at him.

"Such an adorable kid," she said as we moved forward. "And so sad."

The girl was beginning to get it, I thought. Not bad.

Maya kept her head turned to the window, taking in the scenes. The dense traffic, the roads and bridges constantly under construction, the hordes of people crammed into buses, taxis, and rickshaws, riding motorbikes, or walking aimlessly in the street. I paged through the papers. Huge headlines spoke of the events in Manali and Rishikesh. The *Times of India* reported that IBN had received an e-mail that night reading: "In the name of Allah, we, Himalaya Mujahideen, have struck again. Death to the infidels."

I'd never heard of Himalaya Mujahideen. In recent years, Islamic terrorist organizations had been springing up like mushrooms in India and Pakistan. They changed their name every few months in order to pay tribute to some hero, cover their tracks, or simply raise morale. I thought of the incongruous conjunction between the Himalayas and terror, a situation that aroused intense anger and pain in the Hindu population. For them, the snowcapped mountain range was the land of the gods. The most majestic of all mountains, imposing and eternal, the Himalayas were dotted with shrines to Shiva, Tibetan monasteries, and Sikh temples. The driver cleared his throat loudly, interrupting my thoughts. The Indians are famous for their throat-clearing activities, especially in the early hours of the morning. "You are Israeli," he declared. "India and Israel should bomb all the Muslim countries and get rid of the problem once and for all."

Yeah, sure, I thought. *That's a great solution.* I knew there were lots of people in India, and in Israel, who'd agree with him. I decided to keep my mouth shut, turning my attention to the subhead of the article, which contained more information. It reported two explosions. The first was an empty truck in the Manali bazaar across from the bus depot. The truck driver and three civilians were killed and there was heavy property damage covering a wide area. Another empty truck was blown up near a train crossing between Rishikesh and Haridwar. It claimed the lives of the driver and four policemen whose jeep was parked alongside the truck. The explosion blocked the road, halting traffic in the direction of Rishikesh. There wasn't the slightest doubt in my mind. They were using the same tactics that had been employed in the Mumbai attacks. I wondered what more we'd learn in the coming days.

The cab slowed. Another boy selling papers hurried over. I saw at a glance that they were all in Hindi. I also saw the tiny girl beside him carrying a basket of overripe bananas. I rolled down the window and handed him a ten-rupee note. With gaping eyes, he stretched out his arms, offering me the papers. I chose one at random. The boy remained standing there, watching us drive away.

Spreading out the paper, I found a grainy black-and-white photograph. I was able to make out the figures of two terrorists standing by a suspension bridge in Rishikesh. Their weapons were pointed at an unseen target. Something in the picture nagged at me. Suddenly, I realized what it was and jumped up, banging my head painfully on the roof of the cab. I pulled a magnifying glass from my bag and examined the photograph closely. One of the rifles was easy to identify, mainly because of the curved magazine. An AK-47 with a wooden grip, made in China. But what had caught my attention was the other weapon. I checked every detail again and again until I was certain.

It was a TAR-21, a modern Israeli-made Tavor assault rifle. There was no mistaking its distinctive design with the magazine behind the pistol grip and trigger and the special cheek rest. I didn't say anything, just took a deep breath. An Israeli rifle in the hands of Muslim terrorists in India. Fuck.

Maya saw how agitated I was. I handed her the paper and the magnifying glass. She examined it, put it down, and said, "Why are you so upset about it?"

"You don't think it means that someone has crossed the line?"

"Do you really think we can control every ex-army officer, every retired Defense Ministry weapons expert or politician who found a way to make a killing? To say nothing of all the brokers who are only interested in their ten or twenty percent."

"So you're saying they can sell anything to anybody?"

"More or less."

"Then you're on their side," I said, pointing to the picture.

"Stop being so naïve. If we don't sell to them, they'll get what they want from the French or the Americans or the Chinese. Money is the name of the game."

I'm far from naïve. But this brutal reality was hard to swallow. I'd seen too many atrocities in too many parts of the world.

"There's no monitoring system in place?" I asked. "They can sell whatever they want—small arms, machine guns, missiles, armored cars, electronic fences, retrofitted planes, helicopters, night vision equipment, land mines, radar systems, anti-aircraft guns, training programs?"

Maya remained silent.

"So there's no reason for me to get worked up about Muslim jihadists in India with an Israeli assault rifle that can fire nine hundred rounds a minute?"

"I'm not saying we like it. That's why I'm here."

We continued the ride in silence. I spent the time trying to figure out why I cared so much.

"It makes my blood boil," I said.

Maya kept her eyes glued to the window. After a while she turned to me. "You're right. We're trying to plug the hole. Everyone has something they regret, no?" Her words were accompanied by the incredible smile that made her blue eyes sparkle and the freckles dance on her nose. One look at her and my anger was replaced by something entirely different.

"Even you?"

"Even me," she said, her expression becoming serious.

"What do you regret?"

"I was married to a hi-tech baron for three months."

It was the first piece of personal information she'd revealed since we met. But I wasn't ready to dive into our private lives yet. I decided to back away as quickly as possible.

"I want to make sure we're on the same page," I said. "What exactly did you come here to find out?"

She caught on. Seeing I preferred safe waters, she went along with me, adopting a businesslike tone as if we'd never started drifting toward the rapids of our private worlds.

"We only want to know one thing," she said. "Whether the terrorists' weapons came from the consignment of Tavors sold officially to the Indian special forces. If they did, it's India's problem. If they came from anywhere else, we'll have more than egg on our face. We'll be in deep shit."

"That's why you're so interested in Willy?"

She nodded.

This time the image of Willy that popped into my head wasn't tinted by friendship. I knew he was a greedy bastard. But was he totally without conscience? Maybe. But I still felt I owed him. I just didn't know why. Because I gave him my word? Because of a meaningless bet? I was having trouble deciphering my own motives. Suddenly India seemed like an endless maze. I wondered what twisted, distasteful path I'd have to take to find the answer. I sighed, apparently audibly, because Maya threw me a glance and asked, "What are you thinking?" Her tone had lost its businesslike edge and grown softer, so I shared my thoughts with her. "I'm worried that Willy's death is the start of a journey that will be covered in blood."

Her expression changed, as if she'd begun to look at me differently. I'd ceased to be merely Dotan Naor, field agent.

CHAPTER 13

THE ITEM APPEARED in a small box on page 5 of the *Times of India*, the page reserved for catastrophes, alongside reports of a bridge collapse and a train wreck. "The Hunt Continues," read the headline. "Chief Inspector J. B. Singh of the Lal Qila precinct in Delhi told our correspondent that the police are still conducting an intensive search for the people responsible for the death of Israeli businessman Willy Mizrachi. Information they have received points to GB Road. Mr. Mizrachi's body was found in a hotel on nearby Farash Khana which is owned by Mr. Muhammed Sajid. As previously reported, Mr. Mizrachi was brutally murdered and his head was severed. A leader of the Muslim community in Lal Qila stated that the community was shocked by the accusation that the district had become a death trap for foreigners. He issued a moving appeal not to allow the incident to heighten tension between Hindus and Muslims."

The picture showed the Sikh police officer leaning on his long baton and twirling an imposing mustache as he examined a chalk mark around a large dark stain on the ground. Blood, a lot of blood. A huge pool of it like you find in a slaughterhouse. Oh, Willy, what did you get yourself into?

I was making a list in my mind of the people I'd have to talk to when the taxi bounced and I got another bang on my head from the roof. Maya laughed, covering her mouth. The cab bounced again and we heard the sound of rubber rhythmically hitting the asphalt.

The driver slowed and stuck his head out the window. "The front tire is flat," he announced.

The Indians are adept at changing tires, as long as there's a spare in the trunk. Otherwise, it can take a very long time—"five minutes" that can turn into hours. The cabbie got out, undid the rope that held the trunk closed, and took out something that appeared to be a spare with a rubber patch. Then he pulled out an enormous rusty jack designed for a truck and an iron rod. There's nothing that can't be recycled. Too restless to wait in the cab, Maya started to get out. "I'm going to look around," she informed me.

I looked out the window. We were near one of the small traffic circles that stud the roads in New Delhi. Despite its rather shoddy reputation, Delhi is a very green city. It's just hard to see it because of the dust. The place we were in looked okay, so I didn't try to hold Maya back.

I leaned back to take a nap, but I didn't have much luck. Thoughts were racing through my head. Giving up, I pulled out the book of business cards I'd taken from Willy's safe. Nine plus one. I focused on the last one: "Abdul Aziz Wani, agent, Manchester and New Delhi."

I must have dozed off because I was awakened by the sound of banging. I sat up straight and looked at my watch. Forty minutes had gone by. There was no sign of Maya. That wasn't good. I got out and saw the cabbie a short way off, hammering on the rim. A little farther away, several people were sitting in a circle under a tree. I headed rapidly in their direction.

In the center of the circle was a young Sikh with smoldering eyes. Like most Sikhs, he wore a steel kara bangle on his right arm. His right hand was clutching Maya's. She looked up at me with a sparkle in her eye and a smile on her face. "He says I have an extraordinary hand."

"We're leaving. Now."

Maya's face registered surprise at the urgency in my voice.

The Sikh raised his dark eyes to me. "You do not like to look into the future," he said.

"No," I answered. "There's nothing there. The future doesn't exist until I get there."

"I can see it in the furrow in your brow."

"Stop it," I said.

His eyes flashed. Not with hatred, but because of my attempt to dismiss him. "You are afraid? What are you afraid of? Everything is already there. Everything has already happened as it was meant to happen."

I tossed him a hundred-rupee note. He reached out for it with his thin hand, not taking his eyes off me. "A lot of blood has been spilled around you," he said. "A lot of skulls are hanging from your neck. Every place you have touched has seen only killing and devastation. You are different today, but you have not yet completed your journey."

I turned and walked away without looking back. He was spot on in his description of the dark times in my life when I frequented the deepest sewers of human existence. In order to pull myself out, I traveled throughout India in a frenzy. I learned there is nothing unclean in a world that is all Brahman—holiness. I managed to cleanse myself of the filth that had caused me to leave my profession and my country. I discovered the calling that had made me what I am today—a secular pilgrim. Searching for missing persons, solving disappearances, giving life a chance—they were all stations on the personal Via Dolorosa leading to my salvation.

Maya caught up with me. She kept silent until we'd moved far enough away and then asked with a curious expression, "You don't believe in that kind of thing, do you?"

"Actually, I do. The mind creates reality. Everyone has the potential to cause death and devastation. Thinking about it, raising it to the level of consciousness, is like a trigger."

"I see where you're coming from. You think your conversation with Willy triggered what happened to him."

The lady's no fool, I thought. We walked on in silence for a while. "Just so you know"—she laughed—"the things he told me were much nicer. But I don't understand why he got so excited when I said my name was Maya."

"In Hindi, Maya means illusion. It's the awareness that everything, every human being, every physical object, is an illusion. It represents a state in which we leave familiar reality and enter a different space. Like you left everything familiar behind and entered India without knowing what you were getting into and what you'd find."

My own entry into India this time was also different. I'd brought someone else along with me, something I'd never done before. I'd brought Maya, who appeared in many different shapes and forms. She could be soft and benevolent, but she could also be dark, impulsive, and vengeful. No man could resist her. I wondered which of her many faces was here with me.

The cabbie was passing a comb through his hair. "We can go now. New tire—very good."

*   *   *

The Hari Rama Hotel is no Hilton, and nothing like the Shangri-La. The owner, K. K. Gupta, was sitting in his usual spot behind the reception desk. He squealed in delight when he saw me. "So nice to see you. How have you been?" he beamed. "Boy, chai," he shouted in the direction of the kitchen. "And be quick about it for a change."

At first sight, Gupta was very intimidating. The closest a human being can come to Jabba the Hutt. It always seemed to me that he had a very good chance of being installed as a new god in the Indian pantheon, a figure with a totally bald, pointy head on a neckless body. He spent most of the day sitting cross-legged on a peeling leather chair. The only exercise he got was confined to the jaw region: yelling at his staff, stuffing sweets into his mouth, and chewing paan, an addictive mixture of betel nuts, lime paste, and spices.

When he saw Maya follow me in, his face broke out in a huge grin. It was as if the moon goddess herself had entered his fleabag hotel, bathing it in her light. "Madam," he said, attempting a bow and throwing me a brilliant smile. "I hope this is your intended bride," he declared presumptuously.

"K.K.," I said. "How many years have you known me and my solitary life?"

"Too many," he sighed theatrically. "It is time you settled down in India and gave us the benefit of your wonderful sperm. It would rejuvenate our tired ancient blood. Perhaps this divine lady can help you?" Again, he gave her the biggest, warmest grin in his repertoire.

"How long are you two going to keep this up?" Maya asked.

"Just till the tea arrives," I said reassuringly.

Gupta extricated the rolls of fat from his habitual chair and gestured me over for a private word.

"You can talk in front of her. Maya is an ally."

"Maya?"

Poor guy. After he'd finally managed to pull himself upright, he nearly collapsed back down when he heard her name. Gazing at her in awe, he said, "Madam, you bear one of the most wonderful names in our epic mythology. Maya is the epitome of the understanding that all is illusion."

Maya completely forgot that we were in a seventh-rate hotel in Paharganj. At least in that sense, Gupta was a champion. He even insisted on carrying her backpack upstairs by himself, although the effort gave rise to a lot of perspiring and grunting. Between sweaty moans and groans, he continued to rave about her name. Maya grinned from ear to ear, as if someone from above was unrolling a red carpet at her feet.

"An hour," I said. "Get yourself organized, take a rest, and then we head out for the Israeli embassy."

She nodded. "I'll set it up."

Just before she went into her room, I noticed the dreamy look in her eyes, which were still red from lack of sleep. That's India, I thought. It can open its arms and embrace you with a bottomless love that leads to peace, nirvana, but it is just as likely to be a place of violence and blood. A land of *and*, not *or*.

I walked into my room and burst out laughing. I could picture Maya's reaction when she took in her surroundings and the sight she was confronted with instantly wiped the grin off her face.

CHAPTER 14

KASHMIR VALLEY

THE SKY WAS growing lighter. Oren could see they were heading north, leaving behind the harbor where the houseboat had been moored, drawing farther away from Srinagar, from any chance of calling out for help.

Ahead of them was a broad valley stretching to the snowcapped mountains arrayed in a near-perfect crescent in the distance. The first rays of sunlight from the east were glittering on the white snow as the dawn rose over the Himalayas.

They started moving toward the shore. Oren spotted two dark-colored jeeps waiting nearby under cover of the lush vegetation. As they came closer, he saw two kneeling figures reciting the morning prayers. A third man was standing beside them, his arms crossed on his chest and his eyes peeled on the boat. He was a tall man with a white turban and a heavy beard. Oren's heart skipped a beat. The sight reminded him of pictures he had seen in the papers: a Taliban or Al-Qaeda soldier standing over his victim, who was on his knees below him, quivering, his hands tied behind his back. Within seconds, the terrorist's curved sword would come down and sever his head.

The man in the turban locked eyes with him. What Oren saw in those eyes was unmitigated hatred and contempt. He knew they were going to die. He put his arms around Yael, who was sitting hunched over, sobbing softly. The tugboat made a sharp turn and docked at the edge of the lake. The terrorist jumped off, pointed her gun at them, and ordered, "Move. Go get in the jeep on the left."

Just before they stepped off the houseboat, Yael must have remembered her contact lenses. Without thinking, she drew aside the heavy curtain that separated the cabin from the deck. The terrorist followed her every move. Slowly, Yael reached in and got the little embroidered bag.

As they climbed into the jeep, the tugboat released its moorings and chugged away, dragging the empty houseboat behind it. Oren assumed they would cut it loose somewhere in the middle of the lake, making it impossible to tell where he and Yael had been put ashore. The men finished their prayers, rolled up their prayer rugs, and settled themselves in the driver's seats of the two jeeps. The man in the turban got into the jeep with them, taking the seat beside the driver. The terrorist sat down opposite them in the back, laying her weapon across her lap. It was a TAR-21.

Oren recognized the rifle. He could even see the serial number embossed on an indentation in the barrel: 34800169. *Just our lousy luck*, he thought. They're going to kill us with an Israeli gun. "Where are you taking us?" he asked. "We're just Israeli tourists. Our country has nothing to do with the conflict in Kashmir."

"Really?" the terrorist jeered. "So what's this?" She pointed to the rifle.

She was quick. Oren didn't see it coming. Raising the gun, she struck him hard on the left cheek with the flat barrel. Yael started sobbing again. The terrorist gave her a derisive look. "I thought Israeli women were tough," she said.

Oren sat up straight, rubbing his painful cheek. The driver leaned on the gas pedal and the engine roared. They were heading north, driving through a dramatic landscape of mountains and more mountains. No one spoke. He wondered how long they had to live.

MANALI, THE FOLLOWING DAY

The two terrorists waiting at the bend in the road began their advance toward Chabad House. One ran forward in a crouch holding his AK-47 in front of him, while the other followed behind firing his TAR-21 at the Indian forces taking cover on the high road leading to the Manali bazaar. A police jeep was burning in the middle of the road. Three bodies lay beside it. A special forces unit that had landed at nearby Kullu Airport late in the morning was quietly making its way through the cedar forest, preparing to take up position at the edge of the woods. The forest, a national park that links the bazaar with Old Manali, was deserted. Whether out of respect for the awe-inspiring trees or because of the fences, the park had not become a refuge for the homeless or a public toilet. It was bordered on one side by a narrow paved road dotted with Manali's venerable hotels and on the other by the Beas River. Under the command of Major Daruk, the unit advanced without attracting attention, deploying among the trees directly across the river from Chabad House. The specialist marksman positioned himself on a small mound and slowly raised his TAR-21 to his right shoulder. He cocked the gun, and slipped a bullet into the chamber.

Peering through the sight, he saw the first terrorist stop and turn slightly toward him to provide cover for his comrade coming up behind him. The marksman aimed for the chest. He took a deep breath, released it slowly, and counted in Hindi, "ek, do, teen." When he got to three, he gently squeezed the trigger. One shot. That was all he needed.

The second terrorist started crawling toward the entrance to Chabad House. The marksman cocked his rifle again and slipped another bullet into the chamber, but the terrorist rose and began running before he had time to take aim. Caught by surprise, the marksman froze. Suddenly, he heard shots and saw the terrorist fall. The shots had come from the direction of the river, where five men with M-16s were hiding in the forest.

Major Daruk raised his binoculars and scanned the area, but saw nothing. No movement, no figures. He gestured for the signal officer, who approached in a crouch. "Base, any other forces above Old Manali?" he asked over the radio.

"Negative." It was the voice of Brigadier Rajkumar, commander of the special forces anti-terrorist squad headquartered in Chandigarh.

Major Daruk hesitated a moment before speaking again, well aware of the import of what he was about to do. "Are you certain, sir?" he finally asked.

The brigadier's angry response came instantly. "Affirmative."

"Sir, there is another force across the river from us. No question. They took out one of the terrorists three minutes ago."

There was a short pause before the brigadier's voice thundered back, "Bloody hell. Who the fuck are they?"

"No idea, sir. What do you advise we do?"

"Put your intel on it. I'll check with the higher-ups."

The radio fell silent.

Captain Vijay, the intel officer, crawled over to his commander. "Rumor has it there are Israeli drug runners across the river."

The major gazed at the captain in the dark. He knew that when Vijay said "rumor" he meant he'd already checked with reliable sources and learned enough to raise the information to the level of near fact.

"There's not much we can do about it now. It's almost dawn. We'll wait for daylight," Major Daruk ordered, passing two fingers through his beard.

* * *

Dawn broke. Five men lay close together on the ground, their eyes glued to Chabad House. Clad in dark camouflage, they blended into the landscape of hillocks and stone fences. One member of the group, an unusually large fellow, rose into a crouch and made his way to the man in the middle, falling to the ground beside him.

"What now, Ran?" he whispered.

Ran remained silent. He'd been trying to work out the answer to that question ever since they took out the terrorist. He enjoyed the mental exercise. His chosen way of life had accustomed him to making quick decisions and acting on them promptly. His reputation as the toughest drug lord in all of northern India derived in no small part from his ability to size up a situation in short order and respond swiftly, boldly, and shrewdly. He was a talented bastard who ruled over the region as if he owned it.

For some time, he'd been keeping tabs on the activities of the hostile Islamic factions who had spilled over into Kashmir from Pakistan and forged a path deep inside India, settling on the broad welcoming margins of the Islamic population. As long as they didn't threaten his routes, he didn't interfere. Still, he had predicted the terror attacks, believing it was just a matter of time. Israelis in India were a tempting stationary target, a spicy sauce into which every jihadist was eager to dip his pita.

"Gather everyone up, Victor," Ran instructed.

Victor had served in the "Chechnya" unit in the Israeli army. After seven years as a sniper in the Chechen war, he moved to Israel, joined the IDF, and continued to do what he did best. When he left the army, he looked for work in Israel's thriving security industry, but with nothing but "Rifleman Third Class" on his résumé, all he was offered was a job as a supermarket security guard. The very idea was sickening to him. That's when he got the call from India. It came from a man who had heard about him from someone who knew someone. He'd been working for Ran ever since.

The group gathered in silence. "We're moving out," Ran announced. "You'll take shifts manning an observation post on the roof of the Hari Rama guesthouse. The owner, Rajneesh, is one of ours. I'll find out if the Indian forces are preparing a rescue operation anytime soon. If not, we won't wait. We'll go in ourselves as soon as it gets dark. I hope the hostages are still alive by then. Are you with me?"

No one bothered to reply. There was no need.

As a matter of principle, Ran chose to keep his distance from incidents involving Israelis, which were not infrequent. When it came to drugs, he alone made the rules. Israelis just out of the army often came knocking on his door, but he always sent them packing. "Go see the sights. Stay out of this business, it's not for you," he'd say. The Indian prisons were full of young Israelis who didn't listen. But a terror attack on his own turf was something else entirely. That's where he drew the line.

Victor, Meir, Gadi, and Shimon, the newest member of the group, gathered up their gear, preparing to leave the forest. "May God protect them," Shimon muttered.

RISHIKESH, THE FOLLOWING DAY

Benny lay gasping for air in the bushes. He tried to steady his breathing, afraid he could be heard for miles around. He knew he had to get up and keep going, had to get as far away as possible and raise the alarm. He had to make it across the river to the houses and the police station on the other side. He had never been so scared before. His whole body was trembling. He wondered if there was any chance the kids back at his guesthouse would get out alive.

He was straining to pull himself up when a young girl pushed the bushes aside and banged into him. They fell to the ground, Benny flailing about with all his might to get out from under her.

"Stop it." The voice sounded frightened.

Benny lay still and looked at the girl lying on top of him.

"Are you staying at my guesthouse?"

"Who are you?"

"I'm Benny."

"Dorit. What do we do now?"

"We have to get help. Come on."

They started running.

"Slow down," she called behind him. "I can't go so fast in bare feet."

Benny slowed to a quick walk. Quivering in fear, they made their way silently along the sandy path beside the Ganges, heading for the lower bridge, Lakshman Jhula. A flash of light caught their eye. A reflection from the telescopic lens of a rifle? Instantly, they dropped to the ground.

"Terrorists?" Dorit whispered.

Covering her mouth with his hand, Benny nodded. Her fear was escalating into panic. He signaled to her and they began crawling backwards, increasing the distance between themselves and the two dark shadows he'd made out at the edge of the bridge.

"They've got sentries at both bridges," he whispered.

"What are we going to do?"

"The water isn't deep. I can swim across."

Dorit could see he was just as frightened as she was.

"What about me?"

"Move back from the river. Climb up to the houses and try to convince someone to take you to the bridge at Haridwar. If you run into the police or the military, tell them what's going on."

Benny took off. She watched him until he reached the sandy verge of the river, a dark shadow against the pale sand, and then heard a muffled splash. Dorit begged Ma Ganga not to claim another victim. There had already been enough victims tonight. Then she turned her back on the river and walked away into the darkness.

CHAPTER 15

PAHARGANJ, DELHI

THE SOUND OF singing accompanied by a harmonium wafted in through the open window from the Sikh temple next door, expressing endless devotion to the divine. At that moment, I knew I'd come home, to India, had made the unfeasible transition from the world of rationality and violence to the most profound serenity, the place where you can connect with any spiritual or religious act, like the music of the Sikh prayers filling my squalid hotel room.

I brought my hands to my chest, leaving a small, intimate space into which to direct the consciousness. Softly, I recited the daily Hindu prayer, "Lead me from untruth to truth, lead me from darkness to light, lead me from death to immortality." "Om shanti, shanti, shanti," I concluded, opening my eyes. I got out of bed and went to the window. Outside was an incredible urban labyrinth of concrete roofs gray from age and lichen, crumbling brick parapets, satellite dishes, black water tanks, laundry hanging out to dry, colorful fabrics stretched across bamboo poles. A family of monkeys was making its way surefootedly along the power lines that crisscrossed the scene. Diamond-shaped kites were caught on protruding iron bars. A flock of Persian pigeons was crossing the sky. Now and then one descended toward the rooftops, where it flew in dizzying circles until it rose to rejoin its companions. In the distance, the onion domes and lofty minarets of the Friday Mosque, the largest mosque in Delhi, towered elegantly yet severely over the decaying city.

My mind wandered to Manali, Rishikesh, and Kashmir, and then back to Delhi, the place where Willy was murdered. I had to get the details, to collect information, and then let my mind go to work and find the connection that would lead to an answer.

I closed the window and went to what was euphemistically called the bathroom. The water was cold and rust-colored. I decided to do without a shower. Taking off my shirt, I washed my face in the thin trickle of water that issued from the faucet in the sink. Sighing, I splattered as much water as I could on my head, neck, and armpits. Nothing had changed in Gupta's hotel. It was slowly falling apart, aging at the same rate as its owner. Feeling moderately refreshed, I put on a clean cotton Indian shirt, went out into the hall, and knocked on Maya's door.

"Dotan?"

"Yes."

"Come in. It's not locked. I'm in the shower."

The room was a mirror image of mine. The same bed with the same mattress that had seen better days, the same sheet struggling to cover it, the same light woolen blanket that used to be blue, the same noisy air conditioner, and the same slowly revolving ceiling fan. But there was one difference. Maya had gotten a lot done in just one hour. The rickety wooden table was gleaming, and the tubes and jars arranged in orderly rows on top looked as if they'd always been there. I picked up a brush. It smelled of Maya, the smell that had remained with me since the flight. Her clothes were already hanging or neatly folded on the shelves of what passed for a closet in the corner.

"I'll be out in a minute."

"Take your time."

Her laptop was open. I passed my finger over the touchpad and the screen lit up, revealing an e-mail that read, "Keep an eye on him. We think he knows more than he's saying." The sender was someone named Arnon. I was familiar enough with the address extension, gov.il, not to let the message upset me. It was predictable and pathetic.

Maya emerged from the bathroom wrapped in a towel with another on her head. The look on her face said it all. "Is that supposed to be a shower? I wait for fifteen minutes for the water to come out and all I get is a few paltry drops. And what's with the bucket and the pot?"

"It's part of the Indian way of taking a shower." I laughed. "The idea is to fill the bucket first, so if and when there's no more water, you don't get caught with shampoo in your hair."

"I don't want to hurt the feelings of your dear friend Gupta, but if it was up to me, we'd be out of here in a second. I'm more of a Hilton or Marriott girl. I could do with a clean towel."

She pulled the towel off her head and threw it aside with a look of disgust. I saw her glance at the computer. When she looked back at me, her eyes were as cold as a Himalayan stream.

I pretended not to notice.

"Should I come back in a few minutes?"

"No, just turn around so I can get dressed."

I did as I was told.

"I'm ready."

I looked her over. She'd gone for simplicity and comfort. Light cotton trousers and a matching blouse. *Good*, I thought. *The less attention she attracts, the better.*

We left the hotel and I flagged down a battered cab.

"Aurangzeb Road," I said.

"The Taj Hotel?"

"Do we look like the tourists at the Taj?" I laughed.

The driver had an impressive mustache that turned up at the ends and had been smeared generously with oil or wax or some other gunk that made it stay like that. He raised his eyes, twirled his mustache, and said conspiratorially, "A lot of people choose to look like tourists these days. People are not always what they seem. Sometimes they get into the cab looking one way, and when they get out they look completely different."

We reached our destination, and I gave him a twenty-rupee tip.

"All Israelis are so stingy?" He raised his hand, bringing two fingers together so that just a thin strip of light was visible between them.

I gestured "yes" with my head the way the Indians do, moving it sharply from right to left.

The cabbie laughed. "I will see you in the next life," he said.

Because of the terror attacks, the Israeli embassy was on emergency footing. We went through the necessary security procedures and were waved in. The security officer, Hanoch, was expecting us. To be more accurate, he was expecting Maya. He completely ignored me.

"You've come at a bad time," he told her.

I knew I should restrain myself, but I couldn't hold back. I'd tried to work with him on investigations several times before, but the son of a bitch always shut me out.

"We barely have our foot in the door, and you're already looking for a way to get rid of us," I said.

"Is this loser with you?" he asked Maya.

My muscles tensed. Under other circumstances I would have shown him who he was calling a loser.

Maya passed her eyes between me and Hanoch. "I see there's no need for introductions."

Hanoch erupted, like a pressure cooker when someone twists the nozzle.

"You try just once more to go behind my back and smuggle some Israeli out of India, and I'll personally make sure they never let you back in the country."

He was steaming, and he had good reason. As a result of the incident he was referring to, the weight of the whole chain of command came down on him, from top to bottom, and he was forced to eat shit. It began with an official complaint from the Indian Ministry of External Affairs to the Foreign Ministry in Jerusalem. In a blatant attempt to cover their asses, the Foreign Ministry sent an official reprimand to the ambassador on the order of, "What's the matter with you? How did you let this happen on your watch?" Fuming, the ambassador in turn called his security officer and gave him the mother of all chewing-outs. Hanoch, with no one farther down the line to take his wrath out on, was left to stew in his own juice. That is, until I showed up in his office.

"Guys, let's cool it," Maya said to calm things down.

Taking a deep breath, Hanoch said, "I'll give you a quick update. Save your questions for the end."

We both nodded, although he continued to ignore me, speaking only to Maya. I could live with that, except for the part where he leaned toward her bosom when he asked, "Okay?" Maya recoiled, and my heart smiled.

"Like you know, we've got two incidents simultaneously, one in Manali and one in Rishikesh. And there's a messed-up story about an Israeli couple being abducted in Kashmir. I'll start with Manali. A group of terrorists attacked Chabad House, and we think they're holding the rabbi and his wife and two kids hostage. The problem is we don't know who else is inside or if there are any casualties. There's an Indian task force on-site, along with the cops. According to the latest report, two terrorists were killed. We're waiting to hear if they're going to try to negotiate with the terrorists or take them by force. Chabad Online is reporting that they received an e-mail from one of their people in Bangkok saying two friends of his are in Manali. He got a message from one of them that said they were under attack.

He's worried they might already be dead. Two other Westerners were killed in Old Manali. They haven't been identified yet so we don't know if they're Israeli. And at least three cops are dead."

At that moment both my cell phones signaled receipt of a text message. I looked at the Indian phone first and then at the Israeli. Hanoch stopped talking and waited.

It was the same message twice. "Are you in India?" I recognized the number. It was from Ran. Interesting. I wondered what he wanted.

"Sorry," I said, typing an answer on the Indian phone." Yes. I'll call in 10."

Plainly annoyed at the interruption, Hanoch picked up where he'd left off. He wanted us out of his office as quickly as possible. "The situation in Rishikesh is more complicated, because of the location. Indian commandos are exchanging fire with the terrorists at several sites. Four terrorists are dead, but our sources estimate the number remaining at eight to ten."

"Where exactly?" I asked.

"Mainly by the two bridges. I persuaded the ambassador to send me there as his official representative. With my experience, I could give the Indians a few tips. But they politely refused our help."

Hanoch continued to blow his own horn. I wondered if he was capable of talking about anything besides himself. It didn't look like it. Totally self-centered. People like him feel so uneasy in their own skin that they look for a place filled with others exactly like them where they can all sing paeans of praise to their egos. That's why the Agency couldn't understand how I just got up one day and left without looking back, no anger and no regrets. I barely even bothered to say good-bye before leaving for good.

"It's too bad," Hanoch went on wasting our time. "I could've made a difference."

"The casualties in Rishikesh, are any of them Westerners, Israelis?"

"Westerners, yes, but we don't know yet how many or where they're from. Aerial views show two bodies by one of the bridges. We're assuming quite a few casualties at the two guesthouses that were targeted. I don't have to tell you that all this is confidential, right?" Looking directly at me, he added, "I know you've got an in with all the good-looking babes at Channel 10. I never could understand what they see in you."

Sensing we were about to lock antlers again, Maya quickly cut in.

"What about Kashmir?" she asked.

"We don't have any reliable intel yet. A Muslim reported his houseboat missing. The police are trying to match names with the list of people who entered Srinagar through the security check post. The rumors we're hearing, which haven't been confirmed by any official source, say that an Israeli couple, a man and a woman, were abducted off the lake by Muslim separatists. If it's true, we've got a big problem."

We listened in silence. The situation in Kashmir Valley was much worse than just a "problem." If the Israelis had been taken hostage, their abductors might be planning to spirit them across the border to Pakistan. From there the road to the Taliban was wide open. Something was buzzing in my head, like an idea that wasn't yet fully formulated. I had the feeling I was just about to put my finger on something, but what was it?

"Now, let's get to the reason you're here," Hanoch said.

As soon as he said that, the penny dropped. Was there a connection? Could Willy's murder have been the prelude to a series of events aimed at lighting a torch that would set the Himalayas on fire?

"Have they determined Willy Mizrachi's time of death yet?" I asked.

Hanoch gave me a cynical look. "You know even better than me how things work in India, Dotan," he said. "The only answers I get are 'maybe Monday' or 'probably Thursday'."

"Did you go to the crime scene?"

"The crime scene? Of course not. I haven't moved from the situation room here for the past thirty-six hours. It's a good thing it's earlier in Israel than it is here."

"What do you know about Willy's contacts in India? His business contacts."

Hanoch exchanged glances with Maya.

"He's cleared for now," she said.

"I hope it's not for long. If I were you, I wouldn't trust him as far as I could throw him."

"Leave that to me," Maya snapped.

"Look," Hanoch said, "we haven't had a military liaison here for six months. They sent us a cultural liaison, but the Indians figured out right away that he was Mossad and escorted him to the airport. I'm not supposed to know about all the people from the military industries who stay in the most luxurious suites in the finest hotels and spend God knows how much on fancy dinners. All I know is that Willy worked through a local agent. He may not be in the same class as the one they called the 'Hare' who used to be the go-to guy for Israel's weapons industry, but he's connected."

"What's his name?" I asked, although I was sure I knew the answer.

Hanoch turned to a document on his desk and scanned the second page. "Abdul Aziz Wani. His company's called Nandi Corporation Arms Dealers."

Bingo. Hanoch was a moron who had the nerve to call himself a security officer. He could easily have picked up the phone and found out more about the man. To go by his name, he was a Muslim.

Where did he get his education? England? What university? Is that where he made his connections? What languages did he speak besides English, Hindi, and Urdu? Maybe Persian? Pashto? They would be very useful in certain parts of western India. Where did his family live? Delhi? Hyderabad? Kashmir? There were a hundred questions you can get answers to in five minutes. It was no big deal. All it took was a little fact-checking.

It was obvious I couldn't rely on Hanoch. The man was a caricature.

"There are still no leads to his killers or why they wanted him dead?" Maya asked.

Hanoch shook his head.

*　*　*

When we left the embassy, I informed Maya we were splitting up. "I'll meet you back at the hotel in a couple of hours," I said.

"I don't like it that you're going off on your own. What am I supposed to do in the meantime?"

"Get some rest. The next few days aren't going to be easy."

She got the picture and gave in. She could tell she wasn't going to get any more out of me. I waited until her cab drove away and then called Ran.

"You're twelve minutes late."

"Sorry. I was at the embassy."

"With that gorilla Hanoch?"

"Yup."

"Listen, I'm outside Old Manali. I know you're on good terms with Colonel Krishna from the CBI. Give him a message from me. If the task force doesn't mount an operation tonight, I'm going in. They waited too long in Mumbai. I have no intention of waiting.

The window is closing. My gut's telling me they already slaughtered some of the Chabadniks."

"Do the Indians know you're there?"

"They saw us take out one of the terrorists."

"You know the army isn't going to like it, Ran. Greasing a few palms won't help you this time."

"Are you judging me?" he asked coldly.

"No, and I never have. But you're about to cause a diplomatic incident between India and Israel."

"I don't give a fuck. There are Jewish kids inside. If they're still alive."

"How many men do you have?"

He hesitated before answering. "Five," he said.

"And you think that's enough?"

Ran laughed. "Just give Krishna my message," he said before disconnecting.

Secretly, I crossed my fingers for him. I should have asked him something else, but by the time I remembered, it was too late.

I called Krishna and conveyed the message.

"I want to speak to him," he said.

"I can't give you his number."

He didn't ask why. "So we leave it to karma," he said calmly.

I understood. Whatever happens is what was meant to happen.

CHAPTER 16

THE OFFICES OF Nandi Corporation Arms Dealers were in Gautam Nagar in the southern part of the city. The address on the business card was the type only locals can understand and foreigners shouldn't even try to figure out for themselves. Building CV, 97. I had no idea what it meant. The only hint was the added geographical note, "near the glorious Qutb Minar tower."

I got out of the cab feeling lost, not knowing where the driver had left me off. That wasn't unusual. I'd been through the same experience innumerable times. Whenever I hailed a cab in Delhi, I prayed for the best. With incredible agility, the driver would twist his way through the chaotic streets until finally stopping and announcing that we'd arrived. Not sure I should trust him, I'd scan the area cluelessly and then give in, pay the fare, and get out, only to discover there wasn't the slightest connection between the address I'd given him and the place where I now found myself. The next stage was also routine: flagging down another cab, showing him the address, a shake of the head that meant "yes" rather than "no," and the whole procedure began all over again.

This time I was standing in front of an amorphous maze of buildings with entrances and exits everywhere. It was a pure stroke of luck that I was in the right area; I could see the tower nearby. I circled the buildings three times, but it didn't help me get my bearings. I was beginning to despise Abdul Aziz Wani even before I met the man. I took two deep breaths to calm my nerves, and then, by some miracle, I found the right entrance.

I don't trust elevators in general, and especially not in Delhi. I took the stairs to the third floor and hit the buzzer. The door was opened by the babu. Every office has one. The servant looked to be in his sixties, with no more than a few straggly hairs left on his head. He showed me into a large hall with dozens of cubicles occupied by dark heads, most wearing glasses with Coke-bottle lenses. Some had thick hair and others were bald, some had a mustache and others were clean-shaven, some had a tika on their forehead and others had a yellow stripe in their hair. It was a microcosm of India's amazingly diverse class of clerical workers. They looked up for a second when I entered, and then went back to the huge stacks of paper on their desks.

I was confounded by the location and appearance of the office. I'd pictured something entirely different, Israeli-style, expecting to find the arms dealer in a fancy office tower or a heavily fortified warehouse. But this was India. It has its own way of doing things.

Without warning, a man in a dark blazer and Ray-Ban aviator glasses appeared in front of me. He was a big fellow. His dark slicked-back hair gleamed from a heavy-handed application of the oil Indian men are so fond of and he had a pleasant face despite his attempt to look tough. To make himself appear even tougher, he sported a thin mustache meant to convey ruthlessness.

"Can I help you?" he asked, although his tone said something very different. More like, "get lost."

"You look like that movie star, Shahrukh Khan," I said.

I didn't get a response.

"You've got his good looks," I added.

"Do you have an appointment, sir? If not, I am going to have to ask you to leave." This time his tone said, "I'll rip you apart, you motherfucker."

"I thought I was paying you a compliment. I was thinking of the movie where he plays that psychopath who'll do anything to get the girl. Let me show you the scary face he made, just in case you didn't see the film with your boyfriend."

I twisted my features into the most sinister face I could muster. It didn't matter much. No Bollywood actor can really look scary. My last comment hit the mark.

"Out. Now," he said, taking a menacing step closer.

"My name is Dotan Naor. I'd like to speak with Mr. Abdul Aziz Wani."

"That is not possible."

The intercom crackled. "Tarik, let him in."

Reluctantly, Tarik moved aside.

Abdul Aziz Wani sounded like the name of a big man, but when he stood up and walked toward me, I saw he was a short, slim, sprightly Kashmiri with scrawny limbs. Still, two things about him were big, or more precisely, stood out prominently. One was the disproportionately large nose on his face, which revealed his Semitic roots. It was more like a hump than a nose. I wondered if that horn on his face banged into the rug every time he prostrated himself in prayer. The other outstanding feature was his squared-off beard, much like the kind you see on ancient Hittite or Assyrian sculptures. It maintained its perfect symmetry even when he moved his head. Unlike the gray beards on stone sculptures, however, Abdul Aziz Wani's was bright red, signifying that he was a haji, a man who had made the pilgrimage to Mecca.

Without offering to shake my hand, he motioned for me to take a seat and clicked his tongue in the direction of the door. *I guess the guy doesn't like unbelievers*, I thought. A moment later, the babu came in and placed a silver tray with two small porcelain cups and a pot of black tea on a low table.

"Kashmiri tea," Abdul said, handing me a cup. "Tea for men. It is not cloyingly sweet like Darjeeling or vapid like Assam."

Going back behind his desk, he sat down in an imposing chair and sipped his tea, absently pulling at his beard and twisting one of the big gold gemstone rings that adorned each of his fingers. He didn't take his eyes off me the whole time. On the wall behind him was a large green rug embroidered with gold threads depicting the Grand Mosque in Mecca, with an inscription in stylized Arabic calligraphy. Even with my little Arabic, I could easily make it out: "Prepare, for the time is near." The other walls held an impressive collection of swords and daggers.

Abdul watched me taking in the objects displayed around the room. He rose, walked over to the wall on his right, and said, "Let me show you my favorite."

He took down a large curved sword and pulled the sharp blade from its sheath, which was studded with precious gems. "It is called Maooz i-Dariya. It belonged to my ancestor Timur Lang the Lame. You may know him as Tamerlane. He called himself the Sword of Islam."

He returned the sword carefully to its place on the wall, and I could swear I heard him whisper a prayer to the weapon that had decapitated who knows how many unbelievers, leaving behind towering constructions of skulls outside Delhi.

I started to say something, but Abdul held up a finger between me and his beard, bidding me not to speak. "I know why you are here," he said.

I remained silent. If he knew, let him do the talking.

"I do business with Israelis, but only because they are as corrupt as the Indians," he said, leaning forward. His red beard nearly found its way into my teacup. "You grease palms, you play dirty. You are the sons of Satan, but you are better at the game than anyone else.

And you love money. Oh, how you love money." He laughed, causing his beard to bounce up and down.

"Anyone who says you do not belong in the Middle East does not know what he is talking about. You fit in perfectly. You are the bad boys of the Middle East."

"You forgot to mention our expertise in weaponry."

"Allah kareem," he answered, clapping his hands. "No one can surpass you for instruments of destruction. Except those other unbelievers," he added, spitting onto the floor twice and stroking his beard before saying, with a laugh, "Those maniacs, the American devils."

"Willy?" I asked.

This time he laughed so hard he almost choked. "The granddaddy of unbelievers, no more of this world. The man had no god. Not yours, nor mine. He has no one to turn to now to ask for forgiveness for his sins. Willy only worshipped one thing—money. Oh yes, and his shaft. The one-eyed monster was his true master. He thought he had found eternal paradise here."

"In Delhi?" I asked in surprise.

"Just Delhi?" Abdul sneered. "You think we only eat thali at home? A man is free to find his pleasures wherever he can."

Willy patronizing prostitutes? I'm not naïve. You get propositioned in India all the time. But I always thought it was a recreation reserved for anthropologists, or for men who think they can find redemption in the sewer.

"You are shocked," Abdul said. "Perhaps you did not know the real Willy. There is an Urdu saying: 'What does a monkey know of the taste of ginger?' That hairy monkey knew. He liked to taste it all, anything that moved. There was nothing he would not try. Not really. 'You only die once,' he used to say. I have never seen another unbeliever like him. Whenever he got a whiff of a new experience, he would lose all sense of reason. Have you ever known a Westerner to visit the village of whores? You are familiar with that place, are you not, on the road between Jaipur and Agra, near Fatehpur Sikri?"

I took a deep breath. It was a pitiful little cluster of crumbling clay houses just off the highway. I pictured the heavily made-up women—young girls, mothers, grandmothers—beckoning for you to enter a tiny room and lie with them on a bed strung with twine or strips of canvas for a hundred rupees, while outside life went on as it did in any Indian village. The husbands worked the land, the children played with bicycle rims, cows and buffalos chewed stalks of dry straw and deposited dung and urine on the ground, goats scampered about, bleating. And the little girls watched and learned. Their time would come soon enough.

Abdul caught my incredulity and went on. "We were on the way from Jaipur to Agra. Willy was dozing in the car. I woke him and told him about the village. He became very animated, as if he had just drunk ten cups of fine Kashmiri tea. 'Forget the tourist sites,' he said. 'I've seen enough of them.' I told him, 'Willy, we are going to see the Taj Mahal, the jewel in the crown of Mongolian art. It has the most sublime symmetry of any building in the world'. Do you know what he said? He winked and said with a grin, 'My dear fellow, the Taj Mahal has millions of tourists, but the one I choose here will have only one Willy.' I pulled off the road. He came back about twenty minutes later. He was smiling. No, smiling is the wrong word. He was beaming. He had doled out a hundred dollars. The whole village was trailing behind him, kissing the ground he walked on. Only Gandhi, or maybe Mother Teresa, ever got such a show of love from the peasants. Even Tarik, the man you met when you came in, he has seen a lot in his time. Even he said, 'That unbeliever could compete with any Indian truck driver.' A compliment like that from Tarik does not come easy."

It was time to get to the point.

"Willy wrote me about GB Road," I said.

This time when Abdul laughed I wasn't surprised. He wiped his huge nose, and then reached in a drawer and took out a small leather pouch of snuff. He rolled it between his fingers, and stuck a wad in each nostril. Sneezing, he rang a little bell. The babu appeared with a tray of fruit and a bowl of water in which fragrant white jasmine flowers were floating.

Abdul took a juicy peach and smelled it with obvious pleasure. "Try one," he said. "They are from my orchards in Kashmir, the true Garden of Eden."

He bit into the peach, delighting in the flavor as the juice dripped down his chin and along his beard. Then he dipped his hands in the bowl of water and wiped them on a small towel draped over the old babu's arm. "Yes, I took him to GB Road, the red-light district," he said finally. "Where else would I take a client? Another restaurant? Not every client, of course. Most Israelis are too yellow-bellied. But Willy, yes, I took him to a brothel in Delhi."

I knew he was trying to draw me into his dainty concoction.

"Mr. Wani," I said, "the documents I found in Willy's office refer to the sale of TAR-21s. A very large transaction."

Abdul leaned toward me. "See here, infidel. You come here, drink my fine Kashmiri tea, eat the fruit of my orchard, and then you ask me about such things?"

"No worries," I said, starting to rise. "With your permission, I have to make a call. Colonel Krishna at the CBI. He'll be very interested to learn that I'm sitting in your office eating fruit from your Garden of Eden."

"Krishna is a Hindu dog with fleas."

"Maybe, but he's also a colonel in your Central Bureau of Investigation, and I'm sure he'll be glad to hear about an arms deal made under his nose without authorization from the Division of Acquisitions. And he'll be very interested in finding out how much money changed hands under the table and who benefited from it. I remember there was an exposé on the sale of Israeli arms to India in one of your papers that said: 'There seems to be a direct pipeline between Tel Aviv and Delhi.' It was quoted in all the Israeli media."

"Okay, Mr. Dotan. I will make a deal with you. Making deals is, after all, what I do for a living. I will tell you what I know and you will leave me in peace. But not here and not now. Do you want to see where I took him?"

I nodded.

"Then we shall go there."

"Like this?" I asked. My clothes were wrinkled and dirty. "Can we stop at my hotel for five minutes on the way? Just a short detour."

"Fine. All of Delhi is one long detour."

CHAPTER 17

ABDUL AZIZ WANI'S black Mercedes with dark windows was polished to such a high gleam you could have shaved in it. Tarik opened the door for Abdul, pointedly leaving me to fend for myself on the other side. But a boy sitting on the curb with a shoeshine kit got there ahead of me. He threw himself at the car door, opened it wide, and held out his hand for a tip. I gave him a handful of coins and got in.

"What you did, it is not good," Abdul said.

I didn't reply.

"These children are worse than rats. They are all thieving rascals."

Leaning forward, he opened a bar installed in the back of the driver's seat. "Scotch?" he asked.

I wasn't surprised. He wasn't the first Muslim I'd ever met who had a fondness for alcohol. He pulled out a small bottle of Antiquity, a blend of Indian and Scotch whiskies, and poured out two shots. We didn't clink glasses. There was nothing to toast. "Willy always said we Indians are masters at ruining good Scotch," he said, laughing.

I'd barely taken more than a sip when we arrived at Gupta's hotel.

"Five minutes," I announced, getting out.

I took the stairs two at a time. Maya heard me in the hall and opened her door. I gazed at her as she leaned against the doorjamb.

She was a sight for sore eyes. I told her who I was with and where he was taking me, and promised to be back around ten.

"Are you sure it's okay?" I could see the concern in her eyes.

"Absolutely."

"Is that how you're going?"

"No. Leave the door open."

I went into my room and changed. Two minutes later I came back out. Her sweet lips opened wide in surprise. I was dressed like an Indian par excellence from head to toe, in an off-white knee-length kurta over matching cotton pants and sandals made of plastic, not leather, God forbid. I had a Kashmiri scarf around my neck as a subtle gesture to Abdul. I knew he wouldn't miss the slightest detail of my attire. Maya didn't either. She looked me over from top to bottom, and I could see she liked what she saw.

"Don't you need a turban?" she asked.

"No." I laughed, heading for the stairs.

Downstairs I encountered the worried face of Gupta, seated in his usual spot opposite the front door. His eyes took in everything that went on outside his little dominion.

"My dear friend," he greeted me, "what business do you have with a Muslim arms dealer?"

Gupta had an unusual habit for an Indian—he asked direct questions. This time I didn't know if his query came from affection for me or lack of affection for Muslims.

"You know him?"

"Mister Wani? Of course I do," he said, spitting a moist red wad of paan through the door onto the sidewalk. "When you kill one man, you go to prison. When you kill dozens, you become a hero. And when you kill hundreds, you run for parliament. He was a candidate for Kashmir's Muslim party until a reporter published an exposé about his dirty business and he disappeared into the oblivion that is India. Sadly, Mr. Wani is the type of man who can re-emerge at any time."

Gupta spit out a second wad, missing me by inches as I walked out. I was always amazed by how he invariably hit his mark on the sidewalk. Years of practice, I guess. He had perfected the ultimate paan spit.

"I am taking you to the very same place I took Willy almost a year ago," Abdul said as I got back in the car beside him.

We reached GB Road. As Abdul's black Mercedes cruised down the street, the ladies on the balconies and in the windows tried to entice us with erotic innuendos. A skinny man emerged from a doorway and ran alongside the car. The moment we slowed down, he leapt at the handle and pulled the door open, bowing his head to Abdul and offering an endless litany of greetings accompanied by gestures of respect.

Abdul acted like he owned the place, blowing kisses to the ladies in the windows. As far as I could tell, all of them were fat and ugly with grotesquely painted faces. He stopped in front of a building with a legless beggar sitting in the doorway. The man held up a small can, wheedling "please, sir, please." Abdul walked in as if he didn't even see him. I stopped to drop a ten-rupee note in the can.

We climbed to the second floor, making our way up a typically repulsive Indian stairwell littered with torn paper, plastic bags, scraps of food, and goat droppings, the walls spattered with spit and crushed bugs. One of the fattest women I've ever set eyes on was waiting on the second-floor landing. I couldn't get the full picture because a large part of her was hidden behind a counter and another large part was covered by a humungous sari, but what I did see was enormous. It consisted of a fleshy pockmarked face and arms whose flab alone was bigger than both my arms put together. As soon as she caught sight of Abdul, she broke into a smile and the whole place came alive.

We were led into the lounge. I can't say it was attractive, but at least it was clean. A young barefoot boy in pants that were much too tight for him brought in a tray with chai smelling strongly of masala. He stood in front of Abdul, who took out a twenty-rupee note and waved it before his eyes while his other hand slid down and slowly stroked the boy's thigh. Bringing his hand back up again, Abdul pinched his cheek and handed him the bill, remarking, "These boys have the eyes of the virgins in Paradise."

I kept silent. To each his own. We sipped the tea. Abdul turned to me with a mischievous look in his eye. "Would you like to bite into a luscious apple served up by a beautiful girl?" he asked.

"Does it matter what I say? You'll do whatever you want."

"So I shall."

He clapped his hands, setting in motion a procession of the ladies of the house, if that's what you can call the creatures who appeared before us one by one. I thought I was going to puke. I assume he was purposely trying my patience. Each girl was uglier than the next. There were Nepalese girls with pitted faces, dried-up Kashmiris the worse for wear, and Indian women with rolls of fat sticking out between their halter and the skirt of their saris.

"Couldn't you have taken me to some Bollywood night club?" I groaned.

"No." He laughed. "I want you to see that there are treasures to be found even in the sewer. Willy understood that. In that way, he was more of a Buddhist than you are."

Abdul clapped his hands again. This time, only three girls presented themselves, each more beautiful than the one before. He watched the surprise come over my face. "Every one is a mumtaz i-mahal, a jewel of the palace."

He was right. The first was a slim Indian girl around fifteen with smoky eyes. The next was Kashmiri, barely more than a child, with braided hair and dark almond-shaped eyes she kept fixed on the floor. The third was a young Tibetan with a broad face who gazed at me with tranquil half-shut eyes that spoke of the majesty of the Himalayas. I couldn't stop staring.

Abdul took a noisy sip of tea, selected a gulab jamun from the plate in front of us, swallowed it whole, and licked the rosewater syrup from his fingers. "If you want her, she is yours," he said. "My treat."

The other two girls rose in silence and retreated behind a screen. The Tibetan girl sat down at my feet on one of the pillows scattered on the rug. As I continued to stare at her, our miserable surroundings vanished. All I saw was her face and the blush of youth that issued from her like water from a spring chanced upon by a thirsty traveler.

Abdul took a cham from the plate. The confection, made from condensed milk, was thickly coated with almonds, pistachios, and coconut. After wolfing it down, he rinsed his mouth. The Tibetan girl leaned forward and filled his cup.

"What are we doing here?" I asked.

"This is the safest place in town. No government official would dare to plant a bug here for fear he, too, might get caught on tape."

He took another sip of tea and replaced the cup. "I did good business with Willy, Mr. Dotan. I made a lot of money thanks to him, but he could also be stupid. Like the rest of us, he got emotional when it came to his son. When it is your own flesh and blood, your emotions can take over."

"Why are you telling me this?"

"Because it was in a place like this, in front of a girl like this one, that he devised his plan."

I stared at him in astonishment.

"You seem surprised," he said, "but Willy was very creative. He never did things in the conventional manner. That is not a bad trait for an arms dealer."

"What do you mean?" I sensed I was missing something.

"Willy had a good eye. The first time he saw Tashing, he knew right away."

"Just say what you mean."

"Your bet," he said.

"I still don't follow."

"When he saw Tashing, he knew she was just what he needed to get his son—Itiel, right?—to leave the monastery."

I leaned back and took a good look at the Tibetan girl on the floor. Stunned, I realized that Abdul had used her to give me an object lesson. So that was Willy's plan. How did it play out? More to the point, what went wrong?

"Willy bought her," Abdul explained. "It took a few days of haggling with the madam. It was a routine negotiation for Willy, but he treated it as if he had succeeded in selling four patrol boats to the Indian navy. And he got the same pleasure from it, maybe even more. When you deal in weapons and ammunition, you know just what you are getting. But that is not the case with human beings."

"What do you mean?"

"Tashing brought with her everything that made her who she was. And that was the trouble."

"Go on."

"I wish I knew more," he said. "All I can tell you is that everything Willy did from that moment on was related in some way to Tashing."

"Are you talking about arms deals?"

"Yes," Abdul answered firmly.

"A particular deal?"

"More than one."

"With who?"

"A Tibetan group that wants its young people to take up arms against the Chinese. They are opposed to the Dalai Lama's policy of compromise and reconciliation."

"Do you know their name?"

"FFFT, Fighters for Free Tibet. You can see their graffiti throughout Delhi."

"Who was Willy in touch with?"

"A man called Lobsang."

"There are hundreds of Lobsangs. Half the men in Tibet are called Lobsang."

"His full name is Lobsang Jigme. The group keeps a low profile. They do not wish to be found by Indian security forces. Permission for their presence in India can be revoked at any time."

"Can you arrange a meeting?"

"No. All I can give you is a phone number."

"Do you know who killed Willy?"

"No." Abdul paused before adding, "You will hear many things about me. Some are uncomplimentary to say the least. Many of them are true. But I can promise you one thing: Willy's blood is not on my hands."

I remained silent. The man sounded sincere and he'd given me quite a bit of information. But people like him are professional liars, and the higher they rise, the more money and power they acquire, the more they look you straight in the eye, the more lies they tell. Some of them even become psychopaths. I hadn't yet figured out how much of what Abdul Aziz Wani had told me was a fabrication. I knew I'd get to the truth eventually. He and Willy could have fallen out over a business transaction and then the bad blood between Muslims and Israelis could have taken over. But I thought they were both too shrewd to fall into such a simplistic trap. The slice of meat they cut for themselves was much too juicy to throw to the dogs.

Abdul's show-and-tell was over. The Tibetan girl vanished. The magic of a thousand and one nights faded, taking with it all its captivating charms. All that remained was the reality of an Indian brothel. The fat madam showed us out with a smile. The beggar in the doorway held out his can again when we passed. I threw him another rupee. Tarik opened the door for Abdul, and I got in by myself on the other side. We drove back in silence.

Night had fallen on Delhi. Most of the city lay in oppressive darkness, relieved only by the dim bulbs at the entrances to houses. Guards wrapped in blankets stood beside the iron gates of the wealthy who hid themselves behind walls. Small fires fed by leaves, torn newspapers, dung, and plastic sent thick smoke into the air on the street corners as hunched-up figures sat around them heating a pot of rice and dal and preparing for another cold night. Here and there a billboard advertised a new film with giant pictures of Bollywood movie stars.

"Have you heard what they say about us Muslims these days?" Abdul asked suddenly.

I looked over at him.

"The Congress party says we are fanatics, that we live in filth and reproduce like rabbits. They claim we have become too arrogant and should be locked up. 'Bloody Muslims,' that is how they refer to us."

We pulled up at the entrance to Gupta's shabby hotel. I got out without even saying good-bye. Abdul rolled down the window and called after me, "This is no longer the India you used to know. You would do well to remember that."

I knew what he meant. Moderate, gentle, nonviolent India with its inborn benevolence had gradually been eroded by waves of violence. I also caught the hint of threat in Abdul's words. The man exuded foulness. The driver put his foot on the gas, and the Mercedes disappeared into the darkness.

CHAPTER 18

WHEN I WALKED into the hotel, Gupta ran toward me as fast as his sizable body allowed. "About your lady friend, Maya," he said. I readied myself for what was to come. Gupta was a Brahmin. They're the yentas of India. It seems his wife was complaining that the woman upstairs, who was too skinny to begin with, was refusing to eat or drink anything she offered her.

"Only water? In my excellent hotel?" Gupta said, wiping the remnants of paan from his mouth. "My wife sent her up some curry, but she did not touch it."

"I'll take care of it."

Gupta sighed before shouting to the boy to bring him fresh paan from the shop, "and make sure it is sweet this time."

I took the two flights of stairs quickly and knocked on Maya's door. She was sitting cross-legged on the bed, her laptop in front of her and a bottle of mineral water at her side. "Ready for an update?" she asked.

I sat down on the fraying reed stool opposite the bed.

"I'll start with Manali. We're assuming casualties, but there's no official report yet. Our intel says there were seven terrorists and three have been killed. The Indian commandos are making plans to storm the building, but they still haven't decided whether or not they're going in tonight. The situation in Rishikesh is less clear. We've heard from several Israelis who made it out of the two guesthouses when the shooting started, but we still don't know how many are left inside. What we do know for sure is that there are casualties in Rishikesh. In Kashmir, the Israeli couple has vanished into thin air. It seems very likely they were abducted, and we're assuming they're being taken across the border to Pakistan."

"So you don't know much more than you did before," I said caustically.

She threw me a look, but I didn't feel like sharing my thoughts with her. Secret agencies are helpless in situations like this. It's unbelievable how incapable they are of finding out what's really going on. They rely on their counterparts abroad, who naturally hide the facts and offer up disinformation in an effort to cover their asses. Our people do the same thing. Concealment is the name of the game. You only get the real story from journalists in the field, the ones who go there, see for themselves, and report back.

I sat in silence. Maya closed her laptop. "Did you find out anything about Willy?" she asked.

I told her about my excursion and her face turned somber. "He's dangerous, Abdul. Do you think he's involved?"

"I'm sure he is, one way or another."

"With Willy's murder?"

"I have no doubt he knows more than he's saying. We have to follow the sale of the TAR-21s. That's the key."

"We were tracking some of Willy's deals."

I walked out, leaving the door open, and came back with the stack of papers I'd taken from Willy's office. Maya leafed through them. "Nothing we don't know," she said.

I raised an eyebrow.

"Don't look so surprised. We do our best to track every sale, although we don't always succeed. A lot of money is moved from one account to another, from one hand to another. The weapons trade is a black hole. It's very hard to trace the money."

"So we look for the Tibetan girl, Tashing," I said.

"And Willy's contact in the Fighters for Free Tibet, Lobsang Jigme."

"You realize that means we're going to get caught up in the web of Himalayan politics, right? We'll have to move very cautiously. It's like lying on a bed of nails. Touch one and you get jabbed, but if you spread your weight over all of them, they're like springs."

Instead of answering, Maya jumped off the bed. "I'm starving," she announced. "Did you eat?"

"No. I think Abdul lives on sweets. The amount of sugar he consumes is beyond incredible. I got the impression you don't trust Mrs. Gupta's cooking. Very wise. Come on, let's go find someplace to eat."

"Is that how you're going?" she asked, pointing to my Indian outfit.

I didn't need a mirror to know what she meant, but I took a glance anyway. I thought I looked pretty good, and more importantly, I was comfortable.

"Yup. We're in India."

We walked to the Main Bazaar on the central street in Paharganj. It was teeming with life, a sensory overload of colors, odors, and noise. Maya eagerly drank in the sights and sounds: "original" Samsonite luggage, embroidered bags from Nepal, plastic sandals—"only 50 rupees." Mountains of spices and henna, incense and fragrances. The smell of burnt oil and curry from the food stands, the stink of urine from the single urinal. Bells on rickshaws filled with beggars, hymns from the Sikh temple, love songs from the shops selling music tapes and disks. Most of all, there were mobs of people. Women in colorful saris, portly shop owners, quick-footed children carrying trays of steaming chai, men peddling sticky pink cotton candy.

It's a street of contrasts, a crowded thoroughfare in an open expanse, a place of intolerable noise, religious tolerance, and wild-eyed fanaticism, of compassion and barbarity, of freedom for every lifestyle. Here Israeli backpackers find not only a convenient stopping-off point, but a haven and a home. At any given moment, several dozen Israeli youngsters are in the area, going to and fro between the Internet café and the kiosk offering cheap international calls, between the fabric shop and the motorcycle repair shop. They all follow the same route, tread the same path, and each of them believes that he, she, or they are special, that they're the first to discover India and fall under its spell.

I took Maya to one of the many Israeli buffets scattered throughout the Main Bazaar. A young Indian boy coaxed us to enter. "Food like home," he said in Hebrew. "Everything fresh and cheap."

"You speak Hebrew?" Maya asked incredulously.

"Sure, sis. Awesome. Come."

"Can we take a look around first?" she whispered to me.

I laughed. The Mossad agent was gone, replaced by the typical Israeli girl, fastidious and apprehensive. We walked past a long oil-cloth-covered table that held an array of large bowls, all full despite the late hour. There were bowls of hummus, tahini, pita bread, spaghetti, and fries, as well as Indian dishes. Won over, Maya shamelessly filled her plate to overflowing. The lady had an appetite.

We found empty seats, feeling somewhat out of place among the dreadlocks, sharwals, and Hebrew army slang all around us. Everyone was talking about the events in the north. More Israelis kept coming in, each one bringing with them the latest report they'd gotten off the Internet. A young backpacker sat down beside us and announced, "I just read the blog of the Israeli girl in Manali."

"What does she say?" I asked.

"It's bad, bro. Bodies on the road from Old Manali. She says there are bursts of gunfire all the time. The terrorists are surrounded. Yesterday they threw three bodies out a window. She says she can't stop crying."

Maya put down her fork.

"We're getting together for a little party at the Rishi guesthouse to raise morale around here," the backpacker said. "Why don't you come?"

He rose and walked to the Internet terminals at the far end of the restaurant. They were all occupied by youngsters typing messages and speaking on Skype. He found a free station and sat down. I followed him and saw him pull up an Israeli news site. "Okay if I read over your shoulder, bro?" I asked. He nodded.

The site contained the Manali blogger's latest entry.

Israelit-manali@gmail.com

It's awful. We're feeling helpless and miserable. We're watching from a distance, but there's nothing we can do. Shefer is the most frustrated. He was a commando in the army. Last night when it got dark he went and tried to get the bodies. They shot at him. He says you can tell they're well-trained. They only fire when they've got a good target in their sights. They're saving their ammunition. Shefer sat up on the roof all night and said the Indians didn't make any attempt to launch an attack on the terrorists. Not even once. He's furious with them. He says they don't have the right equipment. A police officer showed up today and went from room to room telling everyone to stay inside because they're planning a rescue operation. I guess they think there are still hostages alive in there.

Maya's head appeared beside mine.

"Can you go back to the headlines?" she asked.

The youngster did as she requested. Most of it was the usual political bullshit. India announced it was suspending peace talks with Pakistan. Pakistan, in turn, declared that if India redeployed its forces, it would do the same, and they weren't intimidated by the threat of a nuclear attack. Besides, they had nothing to do with the events in northern India. Islamabad claimed the terrorists were homegrown jihadists, the products of India's discriminatory policies toward the Muslims. According to the Pakistani interior minister, "As long as Delhi continues to treat its Muslims like second-class citizens, events of this sort will inevitably occur. Since the partition, India has displayed intolerance toward anyone who is not Hindu. Is that the true legacy of Gandhi?"

I asked him to bring up the *Times of India* site. There was an op-ed written by the leader of the opposition calling on the government to resign because of what he termed its "policy of weakness." He claimed it was time that India took action and sent its army into Pakistani Kashmir to clean out the terrorist nests once and for all. "We are the greatest power in the region, and we act like an ostrich burying its head in a pile of buffalo dung," he raged.

I'd seen enough. I went out into the darkness of the Main Bazaar after closing time. The street had changed almost beyond recognition. The riot of colors had been replaced by the somber, ominous face of India. Shadowy figures hurried down the street, an abandoned dung fire was still smoking, a single cow appeared and disappeared like a primordial apparition, a dog sitting in front of a shuttered store raised its head, barked, and curled up again.

Maybe it was the cold or the menacing atmosphere, but Maya kept very close to me. We walked back to the hotel, our bodies lightly touching from time to time. When we got there, Gupta was still sitting in his chair chewing paan. "Two men were here. I did not like them. They asked about you," he said.

"What did they look like?"

"Like most young Indian men. They were dressed in Western clothes from the bazaar and smelled of cheap cologne." His tone was plainly disdainful.

Maya and I exchanged looks and turned toward the stairs. We were standing at our doors when she broke the silence. "Tomorrow we start at the hotel where Willy was killed. A detective named Singh will be waiting there for us at ten. He's heading the investigation."

"Good," I said. "Just don't expect to find all the answers there."

We could have said "good night" and gone into our rooms, but we didn't. We just stood there, prolonging the moment. Neither of us knew what to say. It was all in the look she gave me and my urge to reach out and relive the sensation of the accidental touch of our bodies in the street. But we were both professionals and we had a job to do. In the end, we each uttered a rather forced "good night."

I went inside, rolled out my mat, and prepared to meditate. I took a deep breath, but my head was somewhere else. I tried to push the thoughts away by exhaling sharply, but it didn't do any good. My mind went off in its own direction.

CHAPTER 19

Moving slowly and cautiously, Benny descended toward the riverbank a few hundred feet below Ram Jhula. The bridge was silhouetted against the dark sky. From time to time the moon emerged from among the passing clouds, sending a beam of light onto the river. Above him was a broad banyan, the sacred tree. He knew the tree very well. And he knew the river. Holding onto the banyan's aerial roots, he slid toward the water.

Benny had arrived in Rishikesh several years ago and had fulfilled his dream of running a guesthouse for Israelis where they could live the Indian experience. First thing every morning, he immersed himself in the river, contented with his life. "I start the day with the sun and a billion Indians," he liked to say to the youngsters who gathered around him, their wide eyes crazed from too many bongs. Now alone and frightened, he realized that nothing would ever be the same.

He tightened the straps on his sandals and gazed up at the sky, praying that Chandra, the moon, would not give him away. Then he took a deep breath and waded into the cold water. The current seized him instantly, swinging and tossing him about, hurtling him against the rocks, drawing him down to the bottom and throwing him back up. *Fuck, I'm going to drown*, he thought.

He managed to grab hold of a rock, but he couldn't hang on. The swirling current pulled him back in. Very soon he was exhausted, gasping for air. The current was too strong and his arms were too weak. He could no longer tell if he was on the surface of the water or on the river bottom. Just when he had accepted his fate, a tall woman rose up in front of him. Her wet sari clung to her body, revealing all her charms: long thin arms covered in bangles that tinkled in the water, firm round breasts with delicate pink nipples, a narrow waist and broad hips. She reached out to him with an inviting smile. Benny smiled in response and stopped struggling, submitting himself to Ganga, the goddess of the river, and allowing her to carry him away. Deep down he knew she was a mirage, that there was no woman there, that he was drowning and his brain was playing one last trick on him. Again, the current swung him around, spinning him up and down among the rocks. When he saw a yogi in nothing but a loincloth he knew it was the end. But then the yogi stretched out a very real hand, pulled him out of the water, and lay his battered body on a rock.

It was a while before Benny's mind cleared. When he finally grasped what had happened, he realized his savior had disappeared. It was a miracle he was alive, and all thanks to the laughing yogi who lived on the banks of the Ganges. He was known throughout the region as the only person who could swim the river whatever the conditions, even when it was teeming with raging waters in monsoon season. Benny made his way up the bank to the road. Not far away, the lights were still on in a row of shops. He headed in their direction. Seeing the yellow sign over a kiosk advertising a phone for international calls, he went inside. The owner gave him a questioning look.

"It's bad," Benny said. "Your worst nightmare. Terrorists in Rishikesh."

He called his parents in Kfar Saba.

"Hi, Dad. Listen, we're being attacked by terrorists. Call the Foreign Ministry. It's horrible. They killed some of the Israeli kids who were staying in my guesthouse."

Benny's voice broke and the tears flowed from his eyes like never before.

"Are you somewhere safe?"

"Yes, Dad," he sobbed into the phone.

"Hang in there, Son. Get a grip. You have to be strong."

Benny couldn't stop crying.

"I'll make the call," his father said. "Can you hear me, Benny?"

A column of military vehicles was rolling toward him. Benny wiped his tears. "The Indian army's arrived. I have to go, Dad."

Still soaking wet, he ran out into the middle of the road and waved his arms frantically. The lead truck halted. A young officer jumped out and walked up to him.

"The terrorists are over there," Benny said, pointing in the direction of the bridges.

The officer listened patiently while Benny described everything that had happened, and then picked up the radio and repeated what he'd heard. "Can you come with us?" he asked Benny when he finished giving his report.

Benny paused before responding, weighing the tempting option of staying where he was safe. Then he nodded and got into the truck with the soldier. As he wrapped himself in a thin army blanket, he told him about Dorit on the other side of the river. "There is another force across the river coming up from Haridwar," the officer said. "She will surely see them."

* * *

Dorit watched Benny until he entered the river. She saw him hesitate for a moment, and she saw his body stiffen when it encountered the cold water. Then he disappeared into the darkness. "God be with you," she whispered. She'd never felt so alone and helpless. She was immobilized by fear, unable to decide what to do or where to go. All she wanted was to sink to the ground and stay there forever.

Something wet rubbed against her bare feet. It was licking her. She looked down and saw a tiny puppy energetically swiping its tongue over her lacerations. He was the scruffiest creature she'd ever seen, even for India. The icy paralysis that had seized her started to thaw. She bent down and picked up the puppy. She could see a thin beam of light in the distance and began walking toward it, moving as quickly as she could.

The first thing she saw was a tall clock tower. Then she caught sight of a white gate. As soon as she passed through it, she found herself in a different world. Cradling the dog in her arms, she traversed a beautiful garden. She realized she was in the ashram. She'd been here before, had even taken a few yoga lessons here. At that time, she was very critical. To her, the compound looked overly ornate and synthetic with its new marble statues and manicured courtyard. She felt no personal connection, either to the ashram or to its spiritual leader, Swamiji, who spent the day ambling through the garden in an orange robe. She looked deep into his glowing eyes and felt nothing. But now the place was empty, devoid of any human presence. Dorit's senses were heightened by the trauma she had been through, and yet, to her surprise, she felt an unfamiliar aura of fullness and completeness. Looking around her, she sensed compassion issuing from every corner. She remembered standing alone on her last visit here, keeping herself apart from the Westerners gathered in a tight circle around Swamiji, and hearing him say, "I am a believer of God, I am the son of the gods."

Holding the mangy puppy tighter, she entered the ashram feeling calm and serene.

CHAPTER 20

"WHERE ARE YOU off to?" Gupta asked the next morning. The man had to know everything.

"GB Road," I said.

He started gagging. For the first time ever, I was actually afraid he was choking on his paan, and that's not a common sight. After prolonged coughing, he finally spat out the remainder of the paan and declared, "GB Road? And you are taking the lady with you? Not possible."

"Why not?"

"Very dirty place."

I wasn't surprised by his remark. As a brahmin, Gupta spent a good part of the day purifying himself. I'm not talking about simply washing his hands and splashing a little water on his whatsit before and after, but a lengthy cleansing ritual that would have put a surgeon to shame. When he referred to GB Road as dirty, he didn't just mean it was grimy. He meant it was impure.

"What business do you have there?" he asked.

"I'm investigating a murder. An Israeli man was savagely killed."

"Was he a friend of yours?"

I moved my head in a gesture indicating something between a "yes" and a "no." That's only possible in India.

"And you want to find out who killed him?"

This time I gave him a clear Western nod. I knew what was coming. Along with the standard cautions, Gupta always had an appropriate quote to offer. He was an avid reader of Hindu texts. He was particularly fond of the Bhagavad Gita, the Song of God.

"Do you recall what Krishna said to the Pandava prince, Arjuna? I have told you many times."

I remembered. Just when he is about to triumph over his foes, Arjuna spots his former friends and teachers in the enemy camp. He halts the fighting, preferring to accept defeat than to cause injury to people who were close to him. What follows is a dialogue between Arjuna and Lord Krishna, who has served as his charioteer in the war. It is one of the most remarkable expressions of moral principles in the history of mankind.

"Yes, Master Gupta," I said. "The most important thing is dharma, the supreme law by which every human being has a destiny and a purpose."

Gupta blushed, flattered by my use of the title "master."

"Just so," he said. "Do what you must. You are a warrior and so it is your duty to do battle."

"Yes, Master."

When Maya came down, ready to start a new day in Delhi, she found us laughing.

"Did I miss something?" she asked.

Gupta immediately became a fawning mass of blubber. He called for his son, who emerged from the kitchen with his mouth full, and shouted, "Go get Jai Baba."

I tried to persuade Gupta we were in a hurry, but it was a lost cause. I knew we wouldn't be leaving anytime soon. Jai Baba, who lived under the stairs outside, was already there. He tottered in on his scrawny deformed legs, arranging his lungi to make sure his genitals were properly covered so as not to embarrass Madam

Gupta. The tray he carried held an aging coconut and a bowl of prasadam, a kind of sweet rice pudding, which also looked well past its due date.

Gupta asked Jai Baba to apply a tilak to Maya's forehead. The old man grinned from ear to ear.

"What's that?" Maya asked.

Gupta hacked vigorously. Knowing that what would come next was a serious wad followed by a philosophical lecture on Hinduism, I jumped in ahead of him. "It's a bright red mark that represents the third eye, the eye of the soul."

Gupta had to put his two cents in, too. "And it is a sign of your divine beauty."

"Cut the bull," I said, throwing Jai Baba a few coins. He went back to his place under the stairs.

I saw them as soon as we went outside. Two men standing across the street pretending not to notice us. They were dressed in an appalling version of trendy fashion India-style. One had on ludicrously tight gray trousers and a black net shirt. He was combing his hair, which gleamed with at least a gallon of oil, with exaggerated indifference. The other, in a pale pink nylon shirt and black trousers that seemed to be made of some kind of plastic, was digging into his ear with a long nail, a popular Indian pastime. I knew they had a long day ahead of them keeping on our tail. I'd have time to take care of them later.

"Are we walking?" Maya asked.

"Morning constitutional. Do you mind giving them a workout?"

"On the contrary. I don't know how you slept, but that mattress was the death of me. I've never before set foot in such a poor excuse for a hotel."

We walked through the Main Bazaar in the direction of the train station. It was still early, but the morning bedlam had already begun.

The fruit stands were heaped with mangoes, bananas, and apples from Manali. The buses filled the air with exhaust fumes as they sped down Qutub Road, stopping with shrieking brakes to deposit clumps of passengers along the way. The conductors hanging from the windows shouted out the name of the next stop and clapped their metal coin holders like castanets.

We reached the train station, where sleeping passengers were crammed together on the floor. The only way to maneuver around the large hall was by stepping over the human hurdles. Maya, with the trepidation of a newcomer to India, moved gingerly, but to her horror, in her effort to keep up with me she sometimes found herself treading on a stray hand or foot. We headed toward the upper bridge. The swarm of abandoned station kids caught sight of us immediately. "Babuji," they begged, a skinny little hand emerging from tattered garments. "Mama," they cried, grabbing at Maya's clothes to get her attention, "chewing gum, chocolate."

Maya was in shock. Not frightened, but very uncomfortable. I knew what she was feeling. On the one hand, she wanted them to go away, but on the other hand, they tugged at her heart. Following my normal practice, I pulled out a stack of small bills and handed each child a five-rupee note. It would buy them a meal at the samosa stand outside.

One of the boys was particularly daring and independent. I'd run into him many times in the past and felt a certain affection for him. Coming up to me, he pulled at my shirt and said, "Babu, bad people are following you."

I winked. "I know." Handing him a bill, I added, "Stick close to them."

The boy laughed and tried to wink back at me. He couldn't really manage to pull it off. A moment later he was hassling the two creeps. The station cop started chasing the urchins away with his long baton. His timing was perfect. He didn't mean them any harm. They had their karma and he had his role to play.

We climbed the stairs to the bridge that crosses over the station. Looking back, I saw the two guys still following us and the kid holding on to the trousers of the one in the pink shirt, which was already dripping with sweat. Picturing the sweat streaming down his legs under the plastic pants, I burst out laughing.

"What's so funny?" Maya asked.

"Only in India," I said.

She looked at me askance. We stopped for a minute and watched the trains rolling down the tracks below us and the endless throngs of people everywhere we looked. After descending the steps at the far end of the bridge, we crossed a large parking lot and we were at our destination: GB Road. For many in the traditional, conservative world of India, the street of the brothels was a place to let their hair down occasionally. For Willy, it was the last stop.

CHAPTER 21

MUHAMMED SAJID'S HOTEL was not far from where Abdul Aziz Wani had taken me. It gave me a bad feeling.

"This is it?" Maya asked, examining the building.

I could imagine what she was thinking. What on earth was Willy doing in a place like this? He could have afforded a suite in any five-star hotel in the city. The sign on a shop across the street read "Tanwar's Bakery." I remember what Willy had written: "Besides the cakes and the swarms of flies, there are two nasty looking characters in the shop."

We went into the hotel and found a dozing clerk sitting behind the reception desk and a cleaning lady lackadaisically passing a mop across the floor. The reception clerk opened his eyes reluctantly. "You need a room?" he asked. "How long?"

He looked at Maya appreciatively. We laughed. It was like he didn't know how to say anything beyond those two questions.

"No room," I answered. "I want you to tell me what you know about the man who was murdered here."

"Are you a relative? A friend?"

"Something like that."

"Well, it is a thousand rupees for a relative, five hundred for a friend."

"How much for a cop?" Maya asked, pulling out one of her imposing business cards.

The clerk took the card and scrutinized it closely. "How much did you pay for these?" he asked. "I have a friend who can print you a thousand for a hundred rupees."

I lay a hundred rupees on the desk. The jerk closed his eyes as if he were going back to sleep, leaving them open just a crack. I added another hundred and the crack grew a little bigger. Three hundred more and he opened his eyes wide and shoved the bills in his pocket. The cleaning woman gave him a meaningful look.

"I need another fifty, for her," he said. "Otherwise the owner, the great Mr. Sajid, will get it all."

I handed him another bill.

"How long did he stay here?"

"The time he was killed?"

"Why? Were there other times?"

"Yes. Whenever he came to visit the Tibetan whore."

"Did you see her?"

"Once. Another hundred rupees will buy you the name of the place she worked."

"No more," I said.

The clerk didn't look happy, but he was obviously the type that was never happy. "You do not happen to have a bottle of whiskey or a packet of Marlboros?"

"No."

"Too bad. The Tibetan girl worked for Madam Pushpa. Her girls are all from Nepal or Kashmir or Tibet. She gets the customers who like the exotic ones."

"Did you see anyone go up to his room?"

"Not really." He creased his brow in a phony show of concentration. "I was in the kitchen eating rice and dal when they came. That is all my stingy boss gives me. But they knew which room he was in."

"Did you see them?" I repeated.

"I got just a glimpse. I told the police. One of them was Tibetan and I think the other was Kashmiri. He had on a gray fur hat."

"You didn't hear anything?"

"No. He was in the top room, like always. Major Singh is waiting for you there."

We went upstairs.

Denial is a terrible thing. I felt it full force when we stood in the doorway of the only room on the top floor. My stomach turned over and the veins in my forehead started pounding. I realized that I hadn't wanted to admit to myself that I had played a role in Willy's death. I hadn't actually done anything, hadn't even told him to go to India, but I was still part of the karma that had ultimately brought him to this dingy room.

Major Singh was standing by the window. He was dressed in a meticulously ironed olive-green uniform and a Sikh turban, and was holding a long wooden baton. He acknowledged our presence with a nod, but didn't offer to shake hands.

"Our crime scene technicians have completed their work here. I have been waiting for you."

"Can you tell us what they found?" Maya asked.

"You can read the report as soon as it is ready. I will make sure there is a copy in English."

It wasn't that I didn't trust the Indian techs, but I wasn't expecting their report to contain anything earth-shattering. I started my own examination of the room. The rug was worn and sent clouds of dust into the air with every step, except in one spot where a large gelatinous stain was covered entirely by a buzzing swarm of black flies. The stain spread from the rug onto the floor, forming a dark viscous pool by the window. A lot of blood had been spilled here.

The sight of Willy's blood strengthened my determination. I wanted answers fast, and the only way to get them was to do things my own way. There was a single chair in the room. It stood at the edge of the rug near the window, in the very center of the drying blood. That must have been where Willy was sitting, looking out on the two men who were about to kill him. I took off my shoes and socks and set them aside. Then I took one long stride and sat down on the chair, placing my feet in the thick pool of blood. Maya gaped at me in astonishment, but this wasn't the time for explanations. Major Singh understood. I could see it in his eyes. I knew he would wait patiently for me to return from the journey to death on which I was embarking.

Death meditation is meant to be practiced in solitude in a quiet place, not in a hotel room in Delhi. But I had faith in the power of my soul and I knew I could safely make my way there and back. It is a dangerous journey. Not everyone returns from it.

I placed my hands on my knees, closed my eyes, and breathed deeply, reciting the word "om" over and over. Once my breathing had settled into a slow, regular rhythm, the image of Kali, the Hindu goddess of death, rose up before me with her bloody twisted smile and the chain of skulls around her neck. I let the image sink in, becoming absorbed deep inside me as my body grew heavy, slack, and motionless. Then I focused on the physical: inhale, stomach out; exhale, stomach in. Gradually, I slowed my heart rate. Forty, thirty, twenty, ten beats per minute. I held it there, standing in the dark corridor. I knew that at the far end was the light to the other side. I conjured up the image of the Willy I had known. Alive and well, as God had created him.

He was sitting across from me in his chair with his back to the window. Sitting and waiting. His eyes were wide open. They passed right through me. All of a sudden, his head was detached from his body. Blood spurted wildly from the stump of his neck, like a picture on a Mayan death relief. It was a sign that I still hadn't gone deep enough. I had to move closer to the edge of death to see Willy whole again. I slowed my breathing even more, sinking to the deepest depths of consciousness where the body no longer exists. I was in my own death.

Willy was in front of me again. Whole and unharmed.

"Willy," I called out to him through my consciousness.

He was still sitting on the chair, watching. I knew he was looking out, contemplating his death.

"I'm not afraid," he said.

I nodded, but I saw what he couldn't see. The word "death" was carved on his forehead. It is carved on the forehead of each and every one of us, but we don't see it. It scares us, so we ignore it instead of looking it straight in the eye.

"Death has no meaning," he said.

I smiled. I was glad he had achieved a state of utter peace and lack of fear.

"You see, I yearned for death. The guilt was eating me up inside. It was time to put an end to it."

I kept silent.

"I tried to fix it, I swear. Everything I did was an attempt to fix it. But I just caused more suffering. So much suffering."

I continued to maintain my silence.

"Maybe it was too late." He sounded thoughtful.

"It's never too late," I said. I was trying to make him strong. I didn't want him to be eaten up by doubt. I wanted him to heal, to be whole again.

The trace of a smile hung on his lips, and he vanished.

I didn't really want to come back, but I owed it to Willy. I took a deep breath and opened my eyes. Maya and Major Singh were staring at me. Maya glanced at her watch. "Half an hour," she said. "You didn't move a muscle for half an hour. You were like a dead man."

"I came pretty close."

"Close to what?"

"To death," I answered.

I stood up carefully, my limbs stiff from lack of oxygen. With every movement I made, I gradually returned to normal. I exited the pool of blood. Thanks to Singh, a basin of water was waiting for me with a bar of soap and a towel beside it. I stepped into the basin and let the water wash the dried blood from my feet. Then I scrubbed them with the soap, cleansing myself of the blood of the dead, and wiped them with the towel. Maya was still staring at me quizzically.

"Willy knew he had to pay," I said.

"You're saying that Willy just sat here waiting to die?" she asked.

"He knew there was nothing more he could do. Sooner or later they'd hunt him down and kill him."

"He didn't put up a fight?"

"No."

"Why not?"

"That's what we have to figure out."

We left the room, Major Singh walking beside me. After a while he asked, "Did you get any information from him that can help in the investigation?"

"You know that sort of conversation isn't rational. All I can tell you is that he knew they were going to kill him. He might even have known his murderers."

We went outside. I felt a tug at my trousers, and looked down. It was the same legless beggar from my adventure with Abdul the night before. Automatically, I pulled a note from my pocket, but he didn't reach out for it. I gazed at him in surprise. Looking up at me with dull eyes, he said, "You are a good man. He was a good man, too."

"What did you see?" Singh asked.

"I saw a great deal. I saw the Tibetan girl leave. She was walking quickly. She was carrying a large cloth bag as if she was going on a journey. I saw him, too. He was standing at the window watching her. I saw the hotel clerk come out with an envelope. He stood there and watched until the clerk came back. Then he sat down at the window and waited. And I saw them, the Tibetan and the Kashmiri who came to kill him. They went upstairs and a few minutes later they came out and ran away. The sword is over there," he said, pointing to a heap of garbage.

I gave him the bill in my hand and added another. Major Singh ordered the two cops he had brought along to go through the garbage. It wasn't long before one of them stood up waving a huge curved sword he was holding with the help of a plastic bag.

My heart was heavy. I couldn't rid my mind of one simple fact: at the end of the day, Willy had made a bad judgment call.

CHAPTER 22

WE ENTERED THE police morgue. If I had an ounce of sense, I would have turned around, gotten my bag from Gupta's no-star hotel, boarded the first flight home, and forgotten I'd ever made the stupid bet with Willy.

But I didn't. Why not? Because I was so cocky I thought there was no puzzle I couldn't solve? No, that's not me. And I know very well that sometimes you just have to let it go and walk away. Not get involved. There are moments when a window opens like a wormhole in the cosmos. In defiance of every law of physics, if you step through, you find yourself in a different universe. Our entry into the morgue was that kind of moment. I realized it as soon as I came through the door, but I went in anyway.

I've seen a lot of violence in my day, but the sight of a bloody corpse still makes me sick to my stomach. And that's nothing compared to what we saw there. It was a large, moldy storeroom with no windows and an ancient cooling system that wheezed. Bodies, or what used to be bodies, were strewn on the floor in various stages of decomposition. The stench was indescribable. Two men stood beside the single autopsy table in the room, an orderly in a blood-stained gown and his assistant.

"We do what we can for the living," Major Singh said, with no hint of apology. "And our resources do not suffice even for that."

Maya held her nose, using her other hand to get a handkerchief out of her bag. She covered her face with it, leaving only her eyes exposed. They spun around the room wildly, taking in the appalling scene. I glanced over at her. Her tough exterior was about to crack. I've seen a lot of things in India that are hard to look at, but nothing like this. It was even worse than the burning of bodies on the banks of the Ganges. At least there, despite the crowds, the people peddling wood and sawdust, the attendants poking the fires, and the dogs picking at the corpses, the cremation ritual affords some kind of understanding of death and enables the spectators to come to terms with the end of the physical body. The only thing the morgue afforded was the sense of a slaughterhouse.

A heavy black body bag lay on a table next to the wall.

"I do not think the lady will wish to see this," Singh said.

The lady stiffened and walked silently to the table. "Horrible," she said when she'd pulled the zipper down a short way and looked inside.

"Horrible" is much too feeble a word to describe the brutality of Willy's decapitation. Anyone who has ever seen a clip of a beheading on YouTube knows how it turns your stomach and awakens your deepest fears. Willy's head was lying beside his body. His face was frozen in an expression that indicated he knew what was about to happen. His eyes were bulging.

Maya's face was expressionless. She stood there like a block of ice, staring at the body. "Can you open it up?" she asked Singh.

"Boy," Singh barked.

The orderly appeared beside him and pulled the zipper down carefully. Maya made a slow circle around the table.

"Ask him to turn it over," she said.

Willy's hands were tied behind his back. I pictured them forcing him to his knees and making him stretch his neck out. I hoped he'd had time to make peace with his maker.

"Where are his effects?" Maya asked.

The orderly brought her a bag. Inside were a wallet stuffed with bills and Willy's Israeli passport. Nothing seemed to be missing. Robbery wasn't the motive. The men had come to his room for one purpose only—to execute him.

"Can I take the passport?" Maya asked.

"Be my guest," Singh said.

"I'd like to look through his wallet," I said.

"Of course."

The wallet held rupees, dollars, euros, and a single business card. I recognized the name: Maayan Austin Sufi. Without a word, I returned the wallet to the bag and handed it to Singh. But the major was nobody's fool.

"The name on the card means something to you?"

"It's an Israeli name, but it's rather unusual."

"And . . . ?"

I decided not to tell him I knew her. She might have had some connection with Willy, but with his murder? No way. I thought it was better to keep quiet. There was no address on the card. Finding a particular Westerner in Delhi was like looking for a flea on a stray dog.

We went outside into the bright sunlight of Old Delhi. A huge flock of pigeons filled the blue sky, twisting on the air currents on their way to the large courtyard of the Friday Mosque, where they would feast on the seeds scattered by visitors. Life around us went on as usual. It was a typical Delhi street scene: a man selling cigarettes and paan under a broad tree; a street barber waiting by his chair and mirror; people peddling notions of all sorts; nail cutters tending to customers; piles of scissors, leather belts, and plastic sandals for sale on the ground.

We followed Singh to his green jeep, which was waiting in the shade. The driver stretched and opened the door for his commander.

Before getting in, Singh paused and stroked his large mustache. "Stay out of it, Dotan. Let us do our job."

"Is that an order or a suggestion?" I asked.

He gazed at me with his dark eyes. "It is a piece of friendly advice, with warm regards from Colonel Krishna," he answered, climbing into the jeep. The driver leaned on the gas and the tires screeched as the vehicle merged into the heavy traffic.

When Maya finally broke her silence, what she said took me by surprise. "I have to eat. I don't like to say it, but I need meat. I want to stuff myself until I explode."

I still hadn't figured out how her mind worked, but I knew she was trying to find a way to fill the empty feeling inside, to block out the horrors of the morgue.

I decided to take her to Kareem's. It's a place you have to go to, praying to the gods of meat and knowing that flies and dirt only exist for those who go looking for them. Like pale-skinned Westerners concerned for their digestive system, for instance.

CHAPTER 23

To get to Kareem's, we went through the Friday Mosque.

"I didn't know a mosque could be so beautiful," Maya said.

Amid all the turmoil and atrocities, we were becoming immersed in, she didn't miss the beauty. I liked that.

I showed her the gallery of columns, pointing out the graceful elegance maintained throughout the building, despite its massive proportions. I drew her attention to the play of light and shadow on the white marble and red sandstone, to the arabesques on the black marble. I told her about the emperor, Akbar the Great, who sought to create a synthesis of Hinduism, Islam, and Christianity, with a few other creeds thrown in. He worshipped the light and the sun as the Persians did, kissed the Old Testament, took a Christian wife after meeting with a Jesuit preacher, and refrained from intercourse and alcohol under the influence of the Jain monks.

"One thing he said really resounds with me," I told her. "He became a vegetarian, and declared, 'My stomach will not be a tomb of animals.'"

She gazed at me and giggled. "Wow, you sure know a lot." Then, to my surprise, she took my hand and announced, "Now we get some food. Akbar or not, I want meat, please."

Descending the southern steps of the mosque, we found ourselves in front of a sign reading simply "Kareem." As usual, there was a long line of locals waiting outside, Muslims and non-vegetarian Hindus unwilling to forego the pleasure of the best kabab in town. They all turned to stare at us, or more precisely, at Maya, undressing her with their eyes. There wasn't a single square inch of her that wasn't scanned, ogled, and fantasized over. And she had a lot of inches worth fantasizing over.

I ignored them openly as I went to peer inside. Not that I could see much. The windows were covered in millions of fly droppings. Kareem didn't have time to clean. Muhammed, one of his sons, caught sight of me and came out. "Dotan Babuji," he said with a big grin. "Come in, come in."

No one in line voiced any objections. They simply made way for the foreigner being treated with deference by Kareem's son. I followed him in, with Maya right behind. I could see the rather uneasy look in her eyes as she glanced around.

Muhammed used the dirty black towel on his shoulder to clean a table for us, throwing the crumbs on the floor and shouting for a boy, who passed an even filthier rag over the surface. The flies fled momentarily, but they were back in a minute, resuming their place of honor on the table.

"Will I survive this?" Maya asked.

"It's all in your mind. Forget the flies and the dirt and you'll find yourself on the doorstep of the true heaven, the place where only believers go. In the eyes of the men who eat here, the virgins awaiting in paradise are only for suckers. These carnivorous delights are much more satisfying."

She surveyed the plain wooden tables, the sawdust on the floor, the young men with flashing black eyes stealing a glance at her. Their eyes were salivating, and it wasn't because Kareem's sauces were hot. I asked for small portions, telling Muhammed that the lady didn't have much of an appetite. I knew what would happen if I told him she was hungry.

To start with, I ordered mutton bora, chunks of tender fatty mutton baked in the oven. What arrived at the table were small cubes of seared meat surrounded by blobs of yellowish fat that gave off a pungent odor. Maya was about to stick her fork into a piece of meat when she decided to examine it first. She wasn't pleased with what she saw. She got a tissue from her bag and wiped it vigorously before using it to pick up the chunk of meat. She chewed slowly, enjoying every bite. Then she took a deep breath, and another, and said, "I never had such tender mutton."

I could tell that the harsh scenes of the day were beginning to fade from her memory. The hotel, the morgue. She had already tucked away several pieces of meat when one of the kitchen boys brought us a straw basket of hot khamiri roti, thick slightly sweet flat bread, something like a soft puffy pita. Maya tore off a piece and used it to soak up the yellow fat on her plate.

"Amazing," she declared.

I debated what to order for our main course. I rejected the option of the mutton raan leg roast. It was so gigantic it would take five starving loggers to polish it off. Instead, I ordered a single portion of badam pasanda, boneless mutton cooked in yogurt, almonds, and spices. When it arrived, she dived right into it. "Slow down," I said. "And leave room for dessert."

Ignoring me, Maya tore off pieces of roti, soaked up the sauce, and stuffed them into her mouth. I've never seen anyone eat like her. Kareem peered out from the kitchen and came to stand beside us, beaming with pleasure as he watched her wolf down his food.

"She eats like a man," he said. I wondered if she realized it was the greatest compliment he could pay her.

He didn't bother to ask what we wanted for dessert. He himself brought us kheer benazir, the furthest thing possible from the Polish version of rice pudding. From her response to the first spoonful, it was clear that Maya had been introduced to the delights of the delicate blend of cardamom and cinnamon, the first stage of the entry to paradise.

She leaned back in her chair. "I'm going to burst," she said with a smile, slowly passing her hand over her bloated tummy. "The only thing I can think about now is bed." Grimacing she added, "Actually, what I really need is a five-star hotel. What I wouldn't give for stiff white sheets that crackle when you slide onto them. Somewhere I could forget about K.K. Gupta for a while? Is that possible?"

The intimate tone in which she voiced her lament was a cue. I knew she wouldn't be put off. That she wouldn't mind. That it was worth trying. I took her hand in mine, almost—just almost—unwittingly, and stroked it gently. I could hear the collective breath of the other diners catching.

Maya looked around and leaned toward me. "They're devouring me with their eyes," she whispered.

I ran my fingers down her long arm. A rustle of impending release passed through the restaurant. She realized what was going on and didn't like it. Sitting back abruptly, she changed the subject. "I had to erase the pictures from my mind. It was bad."

"Very," I said, taking my hand away.

Muhammed placed glasses of black tea in front of us. A touch of cloves gave it a pleasing aroma.

"How well did you know Willy?" Maya asked.

"There was something about him that was intriguing enough for me to keep up our friendship," I said. "But I also knew what a hard-nosed bastard he was."

We left the restaurant. There's only one word to describe the weather outside: broiling. The sun wasn't making its way slowly through the sky; it had gone from morning to noon in one leap.

Trying to breathe was like trying to drink boiling hot tea, just without the water. I knew it was only the beginning of the hot season. In the next stage, the asphalt roads would start to melt, the lawns in the squares would turn yellow and then bald, the soil would dry out and disintegrate into dust, the smoke would stand in the air without moving, and the people would doze off at any given moment, whether they were sitting, walking, or driving.

Maya's face turned bright red. That's what happens to light-skinned people with freckles. "I'm going to faint," she said. The combination of a heavy meal and the heat of Delhi was beginning to take its toll on her. The river of Indians flowed in and out of every alley, merging and splitting off in infinite patterns.

"Maniac," she yelled. I stopped and turned around.

"He pinched my butt. I can't believe it," she fumed, pointing to a young man walking away quickly. "He just pinched me. Hard."

While she was preoccupied by the perpetrator, I turned my attention to two other young men who had been following us since we left Kareem's. I'd seen them before. The kid in the black net shirt and his friend in pink. They'd shown up out of nowhere. I steered us in the direction of the main road and flagged down the first cab I saw. The two clowns got into another one.

"Where are we going?"

"You talk too much," I said. "Give me a minute to think."

Maya gazed at me. "One minute you're the nicest guy in the world and the next you can be a real bastard." Turning away, she stared out the window, becoming a tourist again.

I instructed the driver to turn into a side street and stop. Then came one of the song-and-dance numbers without which no Bollywood action film is complete. Every twenty minutes, like clockwork. And I wanted them to start singing.

By the time the second cab pulled up behind us, I was already outside waiting for it. I made a fist and punched it through the open window straight at the neck of the man nearest to me. It was the one in the black net. My fist met his Adam's apple, rendering him unconscious. His companion opened the far door and started to pull out a gun. Rolling over the hood of the cab, I landed right beside him screaming "ahhh," a word known throughout the world. But apparently, he didn't speak the language.

The idiot insisted on trying to point the gun at me, but by then I had already grabbed his arm. I twisted his wrist back so that the barrel of the gun was pointing at the sky. His whole body followed, bending backward until his spine was contorted into an improbable arch. I heard a crack. There was no doubt in my mind that, at the very least, he'd need a vigorous massage with a lot of hot oil. Lucky for him, they don't cost much in India.

He let go of the gun.

"Who sent you?" I asked

No response. I gave his wrist another twist. It was about to break. That worked. "Babuji," he whispered, addressing me by the honorific, "I know nothing."

I twisted harder and heard a snap. Just a crack, not a full-blown fracture. The kid was breathing heavily. "Babuji, we do not know. We get a phone call and soon we go to get the money."

"Where?"

He groaned in pain. "Please stop. You are breaking my arm. I will tell you."

I let him go.

"Near the Nizamuddin Auliya mosque."

"Who?"

"A tailor."

Hesitating, he glanced at his companion. His head was thrown back and he was wheezing loudly.

"What's his name, this tailor?" I asked, threatening to grab his arm again.

"Ravi."

I shoved him back in the cab. I could see the fear in the driver's eyes, along with admiration for the wild foreigner. I knew he'd have a story to tell later in his local chai shop.

"What did you learn in school today?" Maya asked derisively.

To my mind, there was no call for her to be nasty. I took a deep breath before responding. "We have another visit to pay."

CHAPTER 24

I CHECKED MY watch. One thirty. Very good. The best time of day for a visit to the Nizamuddin Dargah, the mausoleum of the Sufi saint Nizamuddin Auliya. We hailed a cab. When I gave the driver the address, I caught the quizzical look on Maya's face.

"It's a small Muslim quarter with a unique medieval character," I explained.

The driver got lost near the entrance to Humayun's Tomb. I told him to stop, and we got out. Gesturing toward the garden-tomb of the second Mughal emperor, I said, "When it's all over, I'll take you here. It's my favorite place in Delhi."

She examined the building in the distance and then turned to me with a look that held a question mixed with yearning. Not a bad combination. I was wondering myself. Was it just a slip of the tongue or did I mean it?

We entered the Muslim quarter on foot. Small one-story houses lined the narrow streets where life went on peacefully. It was like an ancient village accidently trapped inside a big city, but not allowing that fact to interfere with its quiet routine. The Nizamuddin Dargah complex is located in the center of the quarter. I've sought refuge there more than once after long days on a case. I like to come at midday after the prayers, when it's hot and the place is nearly empty. No tourists. No music. No noise. Just wandering Sufis and mysterious dervishes, pious people who come to contemplate the mystical. I lie down on the cold white marble and close my eyes, glad for the chance to be alone with myself for a few minutes, and that's no easy task in India. I knew this time Maya and I would have to earn that kind of peace some other way. The hard way.

The girl was sitting on the invisible line between the women's section and the large courtyard reserved for men, just as she was every day, as she was every time I came. To the best of my knowledge, Maayan Austin Sufi was the only Israeli who was ever drawn to India by the mystical doctrine of Sufism. She followed in the footsteps of the Sufi master Ibn Arabi, who said, "My creed is Love; wherever its caravan turns along the way, that is my belief, my faith."

In Israel, she was a joke. People kept asking what love had to do with Islam. So she left to search for insight elsewhere. At some point, she found the works of Amir Khusro, a Muslim Indian poet and musician. His poetry sent tremors down her spine. She knew right away that this man, who died seven centuries ago, was meant to be her spiritual guide. It was he who had written: "I am a pagan, a worshipper of love . . . if there is no pilot in our boat, then we do not need one. God is in our midst, we do not need a pilot."

She made her way to India. When all the other Israeli kids went to the ashrams in Punna, Dharamsala, and Rishikesh, she went to the city they all fled from—Delhi. As they moved along the standard seasonal axes of winter in Goa, spring in Hampi, and summer and fall in the Himalayas, she trod the same path every day, in the broiling heat of summer and the freezing cold of winter, walking from her small room in the Muslim quarter to the tomb of Amir Khusro. That's where I'd first met her, sitting and softly beating a tabla drum to herself.

We went over to her. As I sat down opposite her, she raised her eyes and smiled. She looked ethereal: long white dress, red hair in frazzled dreadlocks falling on her shoulders and framing an angelic pale face lit up by her signature broad smile. She brought her palms together in a Namaste greeting.

"I've missed you," I said.

"He means he missed God, not me," she said with a small laugh to Maya, who was still standing, and added, "Come sit down."

Maya sat down beside me, curiously eyeing the strange unkempt Israeli girl who had chosen to spend her life beside the tomb of a Muslim saint in remote India.

"Why?" Maayan asked, as if she had heard the unspoken question. "It's simple. I follow in the wake of love. That is my belief, my faith."

She shut her eyes and then opened them again, looking at me. "Much has changed since you were here last. The neighborhood isn't the same as it was. It's sad. New people have come and they frighten me."

"Like who?"

Her eyes flitted left and right. "I don't know exactly. There's talk of connections to Kashmir, Pakistan, Muslim extremists. The sort of talk you never used to hear. The quarter used to be a place of tolerance and love. Something's disturbing the peace and quiet today."

"Yes, I know," I said. I paused before dropping the bomb. "Maayan, what was your name doing on a business card in Willy Mizrachi's wallet? What's he to you?"

Maya was stunned. Her eyes darted from one of us to the other and back again. We sat and stared at each other. Finally, Maayan sighed deeply and said, "Everything comes out in the end, doesn't it?"

"I'm sorry, but I've got to know."

"I do volunteer work at a women's shelter in Old Delhi. You know how they treat women in India. It's shocking. Young widows are thrown out onto the street, girls are sold into prostitution, little orphan girls become slaves in rich people's houses. Willy was look-ing for somewhere to hide a Tibetan girl. He showed up at the shel-ter, and I helped him."

"Tashing? You mean the Tibetan girl who worked for Madam Pushpa on GB Road?"

"Hold on a minute," Maya broke in. "What's going on here? Who's Tashing?" She glared at me, furious. "Anything else you're keeping from me? Is that what you call sharing information? Did you know about her when you questioned the reception clerk?"

I kept silent. Explanations, if I had any to offer, would come later.

Maayan passed her eyes from Maya to me before going on. "Willy had a crazy plan. He thought Tashing was the way to get his son back."

The bet, I thought. *That fucking bet.*

"Did you know about that?" Maya asked.

All the trust that had been built up between us was gone in a flash.

"That's why Abdul took me to that place," I said. "At the time, it didn't seem credible."

"I'm your partner," Maya fumed. "You're supposed to tell me these things."

She was hitting below the belt, but she was right.

"What else do you know about her?" she asked Maayan. Her tone wasn't the friendliest I've ever heard, but I didn't interfere.

"She was different, not like the other women at the shelter. I think she chose to prostitute herself. I'm not sure why. She must have had a reason. Maybe it had something to do with the Tibetan issue."

"Who was Willy hiding her from?"

"I don't know. He said from the police, but I don't think that was the whole truth, if it was true at all. I think Tashing was mixed up in secret webs that Willy knew nothing about and didn't take into account."

"What makes you say that?"

"When Tashing was staying at the shelter, we got close. She's an amazing girl. Very beautiful, and special. It was things she said, bits and pieces, never anything specific. She led me to understand that her life was in danger and she trusted Willy."

"When was this?" I asked

"A few months ago."

"Have you seen her since then?"

Maayan seemed reluctant to reply. Finally, she said, "I ran into her once, by accident."

"When?" Maya asked.

"Two or three weeks ago."

"Where?" I asked.

"At the central bus station. She was getting on a bus to Ladakh."

Ladakh. A high desert region with a sparse population and diverse landscape: windswept valleys, rushing rivers, canyons, isolated villages, remote monasteries, one road, and one major city called Leh. A world within a world. I knew it would be like looking for a needle in the Himalayas.

"Did you speak to her?" I asked.

Maayan nodded and fixed her eyes on me and then on Maya. "She was pregnant. She had a huge belly, the end of the eighth month, beginning of the ninth. We spoke. When she first saw me, she looked scared. But after that she calmed down. I saw the quiet confidence in her eyes. She said, 'I'm going back to the Himalayas. I'm going to have my baby at home, in my Shangri-La, where nobody can take him from me.'"

"Did she say who the father was?" I remembered what Willy had said to me in his office: "Exactly one year from today, same time, same place, you're putting a bottle of Talisker on my desk and Itiel is standing here with his wife and kid and a big grin on his face."

"No," Maayan answered. "Does it matter?"

"She didn't say anything about Willy?"

"No. We didn't talk about him. And I didn't ask her any questions."

"A tailor by the name of Ravi. Does that mean anything to you?" I asked her.

She stared at me for a long time before saying, "Yes. I live across from his shop."

"And . . . ?"

"I know he's involved somehow with Muslim extremists. Whenever something happens that sparks more tension between the Hindus and Muslims, people gather in his shop. They don't bother to hide their anger anymore. They flaunt it, proudly waving their green flags. Lately, they've suddenly remembered I'm Israeli, which didn't used to matter to anyone around here. As long as I'm still under the wing of Amir Khusro, nobody would dare to do me harm."

"What else do you know?"

"Very little. But I think Ravi has connections to the Muslim underground in Kashmir."

"How come?"

"I was at a large Sufi assembly. Thousands of believers came from all over India. I saw Ravi using the opportunity for his own purposes. He met with lots of people, mainly young troublemakers, the kind who don't have any interest in the love of God and mankind."

"What was Willy's connection to all this?"

"I don't know. I've thought about it a lot. I got the impression he had some trouble with them."

"What gave you that idea?"

"I saw him here in the neighborhood."

"When?"

"A few weeks ago. He came in a black Mercedes with a skinny little Kashmiri guy. They went into Ravi's shop. I heard shouting. Then they came out and drove off. That's all I know."

We got up to leave and she drew the tabla closer and began drumming gently, letting her long slender fingers run across the taut skin. I saw her retreating back into her own world. She closed her eyes and began singing in Hindawi, the root of Urdu and Hindi: "Darya prem ka, ulti wa ki dhaar. Jo utra so doob gaya, jo dooba so paar," the river of love runs in strange directions. One who jumps into it drowns, and one who drowns, gets across.

CHAPTER 25

A GENTLE RAIN started falling. It did little to relieve the blinding heat, but it wrapped the dust in a thin layer of moisture and brought it down to the ground. Countless snakes of water began slithering through the streets, picking up along the way the filth that had collected in every corner, crack, and crevice: leaves of the sacred banyan tree, withered flowers, the feces of dogs, cows, and humans, a plastic sandal. And then all of a sudden it stopped. The rivulets vanished, the moisture evaporated, and within minutes the heat was as blinding as ever.

We walked through the streets of the Muslim quarter. Ravi's shop was in the center of the bazaar. It was easy to find given the big green flag with a Muslim crescent flying over the entrance. We took off our shoes and placed them next to a pair of plastic sandals beside the doorway. I saw the question in Maya's eyes, something on the order of "Won't they get stolen?" It made me laugh. Pushing aside the dirty white curtain, I went in, Maya following behind me.

We were in a small dimly lit space. The floor was covered by a large thick mattress that might once have been white. Along the walls were old wooden shelves piled high with fabric. The tailor was seated cross-legged in the far corner, a large Koran open in front of him. He was a short chubby man dressed in a cheap European-style suit without the slightest distinguishing marks, save for his eyes: round cold black stones that sent a single message—hatred.

"You're Ravi?" I asked.

"Foreigners have no reason to be in my shop." The ferocity in his voice intensified with every word he uttered. And he made no attempt to hide it. He sat there shaking with rage. It was a rage that didn't ask to be controlled, the rage of loathing. This was his shop, his territory, and we were defiling it. He wanted us gone—now.

"Leave, you filthy pigs," he spat.

But we hadn't come to buy Benares silk for a sari or fine cotton for a long kurta or filmy organza for a special occasion. Even before Ravi had finished spewing out his words and fury, I was on top of him. With one hand, I pulled him out from behind the low table and with the other I gave him a resounding slap. Maya looked on in shock.

"Is there anything else you wanna say about foreigners?"

The stumpy man kept silent. His hate was greater than his fear.

"Willy Mizrachi," I said, still gripping him by the collar and slapping him a second time. "What was he doing here?"

No answer. I gave his collar a twist and his face began to go red.

"Willy," I repeated. "He came with Abdul Aziz Wani. Talk, or I twist it tighter."

Ravi's eyes were starting to pop out of his bright red face. His lips moved and I released my grip a little. I felt his spit on my face. "I don't talk to heathens," he said.

I wasn't really mad, but I picked him up and held him in the air until he started convulsing. When he lost consciousness, I let go and he fell to the mattress like a sack of potatoes. Something was wrong. Maya saw it, too. She crouched down and pressed her finger against his neck, looking for a pulse. "No," she said quietly.

It hadn't been my intention to leave a trail of corpses in my wake. It was too early for that. I laid him on his back and punched his chest, knowing my fist could wake the dead. There's a certain window when it can work. If it doesn't, you leave behind a corpse with a crushed chest. It wasn't the prettiest sight in the world, but his heart responded as if it had been shocked. He was breathing again.

"Wanna go again, or do you have something to tell us?"

He dragged himself backward and leaned against a large cushion at the edge of the mattress, as far away from us as possible. "A Zionist dog and his weapons. What did he think, that he could decide where they went?"

I was itching to hit him again. Sensing my temper rising, Maya grabbed my hand and pulled me outside. "We're not in the business of leaving bodies behind," she said.

I stuck my head into the shop next door. "Go look in on Ravi, please. He's not feeling so well."

The shopkeeper gave us a piercing look, but didn't reply.

When we got back to the hotel, Gupta was sitting in front of the television with his wife and eldest son. Our friend Major Singh was being interviewed. "What can you tell us about the terrorists?"

The police officer replied incisively, "Their fighting methods would not put the most elite army units to shame."

"What do you mean?"

"They only shoot to kill. Reports from troops in the area say they are determined and ruthless. And although they are outnumbered, they have no fear of going head to head with our security forces."

"Where did they get these capabilities?"

"We have no doubt that the terrorists were trained in Pakistan."

"Where does your information come from?"

"I cannot share that with you at this time. You will have to wait until the incidents are over."

"Why do you think they are targeting Israelis?"

"Their aim is clearly to strike a blow at the friendly relations and military cooperation between India and Israel. Our two countries are fighting hand in hand against Islamic terrorism at home and abroad."

The interviewer was distracted for a moment, adjusting his earpiece before returning his attention to Major Singh. "One last question. The terrorists in Mumbai were armed with weapons used by terrorists throughout the world, not only Islamists. Mainly AK-47s. But we have just received a call from a viewer saying that in the news photos of the current attacks, he can see that one of the weapons is a TAR-21, an Israeli assault rifle known as Tavor. Can you relate to this information? What does it say about our close military cooperation with the Israelis? Could it be too close?"

"I do not know what you mean by 'too close.' We cooperate closely on many levels. In regard to the information itself, I can only tell you that we are looking into it. If it is true, I would have to assume that Israeli weapons that were meant for our security forces fell into the hands of negative elements. Unfortunately, there are many."

The interviewer pressed harder. "Does the fact that the terrorists are using Israeli weapons have anything to do with the murder of the Israeli arms dealer Willy Mizrachi a few days ago in Delhi?"

Major Singh didn't reply immediately. "The matter is still under investigation," he said finally. "We are looking into every possibility, including that one. But I cannot give you any more details at this time."

Maya broke my concentration. "Do you think Major Singh knows more than he's saying?"

"Yes," I answered, distracted. Gupta switched to INTV, a young dynamic English-language channel that was broadcasting from the streets of Delhi.

"The winds of war are already blowing," pronounced an eager young reporter. "An angry Hindu mob is on the warpath, attacking their Muslim neighbors. It does not seem to have taken long for the slogan of the last elections, 'forgive and forget,' to be forgotten."

A series of reports followed. Muslims locking themselves in their homes until the riots died down. A Muslim cab driver being dragged from his taxi and beaten mercilessly. A Muslim fabric shop in the Chandni Chowk bazaar set on fire. An interview with Ahmed Buchari, the imam of the Muslim quarter adjacent to the Qutb Minar, who declared angrily that "the Muslim public is sick and tired of becoming a punching bag whenever there is an increase in tension on the border with Pakistan. Where is the vision of Gandhiji? In the country we were born into, it did not matter if you were Hindu or Muslim."

"Yes," the interviewer agreed. "But lately we have been hearing the word 'jihad' throughout India."

The imam wasn't fazed. "In Islam, true jihad is the struggle against the nafs, the ego, a term every Hindu can readily understand and identify with. Those who distort the meaning of jihad are doomed to eternal torment in hell. Allah will never pardon them."

"Is it true that the Muslim quarter around the Nizamuddin Dargah has become a breeding ground for terrorist groups?"

The imam didn't respond. The viewers could see him repressing his fury, forcing himself to maintain his composure. "The root of Muslim extremism," he said in a calm voice, "can be found in the mutual hatred that has grown up in our society since the partition."

I imagined that many of the viewers, both Hindus and Muslims, were nodding their heads in agreement. Especially the older generation, who had known a life of tolerance and friendly relations with their neighbors.

Gupta was even more adamant. "India will never go back to the way it was."

CHAPTER 26

I FELT WE had gotten as much as we could out of Delhi. I wasn't particularly pleased that we hadn't managed to learn more. I told Maya I was going out to get a shave.

"You're going to get shaved in the street?"

"Why not? They take very good care of you. You even get a head massage. And all for a hundred rupees at most."

She didn't reply. Ever since our conversation with Maayan Austin Sufi, there had been a sour note between us. We both sensed that we were treading water, and I imagined Maya herself had been trodden on as well. All those great minds in Jerusalem who think they can operate in India by remote control. Remote control, my ass. I sometimes had the impression that the country might have Internet and cell phones, but the population was still making its way along the caravan routes on bulls and camels. Nothing moved.

I found a barber's stall near the metro station. The barber switched the blade on the razor. I checked to make sure it was unused. I didn't feel like getting AIDS. I leaned back and let him lather my face with his brush. He used so much foam that it got in my nose and somehow found its way into my ears. Then he started shaving from the throat upward, contrary to all logic. But that's India for you. He moved the blade around gracefully, wiping off the foam with a towel draped over his arm. There was a short pause, and then

I felt the blade pressing too hard against my Adam's apple. Much too hard.

I opened my eyes. It was an ugly situation. Tarik, Aziz's goon, was holding the razor to my throat. His face was right up against mine. He was so close I could see the deep craters around his nose left by pimples. He smiled, revealing the diamond set in his front tooth.

"That's a nice piece of plastic in your mouth," I said.

I knew I'd hit home. He closed his mouth and pressed down on the blade. I assumed that any second now I'd feel it cutting into the skin, but he suddenly pulled it away and held a piece of paper up to my eyes. Then he dropped it onto the barbershop bib, folded the razor, and put it in his pocket.

"Next time I cut," he said.

"Next time I'll rip the plastic outta your tooth."

Without replying, he turned and left. I followed him in the mirror as he got into the black Mercedes and drove off.

The barber apologized profusely. "A massage on the house," he said.

I gestured my agreement and he set to work. Soon my face was burning from all the slapping, kneading, polishing, and creams. He moved on to my head with the same zeal. I stopped him before he could pour on half the contents of the multicolored bottles on the shelf. I left gleaming like a baby's bottom. Then I took my first look at the note. It said "Lobsang Jigme," along with a cell phone number.

A young man was sleeping on the street next to two public telephones. I woke him with a slap on the shoulder and asked him to dial the number for me.

"Hello," a voice answered.

"Lobsang Jigme?"

Silence.

"Hello?"

"I'm listening."

I introduced myself and told him I'd gotten his number from Abdul Aziz Wani. "Can we meet?" I asked.

"Don't know. Call back in an hour." The line went dead.

I sat down to wait in one of the grimy little restaurants where Israeli backpackers feel at home, and ordered tea with lemon, ginger, and honey. It's good for the brain. I knew I had to decide on our next step before I went back to the hotel. The questions spinning through my head were mostly about the girl, Tashing. What happened between her and Willy? Did he take her to meet Itiel? Was she involved in his murder? Why was she so scared? Above all, whose child was she carrying?

The tea arrived. It tasted strongly of ginger.

A grungy Israeli came in, looking like one of the kids who've been in India too long. It was the clothes, the dreadlocks that reached to his waist, the embroidered bag hanging from his shoulder. And he was barefoot. To my surprise, when he turned in my direction, I recognized him. Valium. It had been quite a while since the Sigal Bardon affair and the drug smuggling charges in Bangkok, but he hadn't changed.

"Valium?"

He came closer, took a bite out of a chapati, looked at me with red eyes, and said, "Do I know you?"

I nodded. He sat down across from me and then forgot I was there, concentrating on the food.

Valium was a victim of the datura inoxia, also known as the Devil's Trumpet. It's an innocent-looking plant with white bell-shaped flowers that actually contain alkaloids from the atropine family, a poisonous plant that can be fatal if its consumption isn't carefully controlled. It typically causes memory loss. The Hindu sadhus use a few drops to make a drug they take for their deepest meditations.

You have to be a no-brain Israeli to imagine you can handle on your own what the sadhus have learned from thousands of years of meditation, hallucinations, delirium, and asceticism. But Israelis like to push the boundaries.

Valium got his nickname from his habit of pleading for valium whenever he went into withdrawal. You can buy it in every pharmacy in India, no prescription necessary. Despite his condition, I assumed that, like other Israelis who have been in India for a long time, he probably knew things that could be of use to me.

"You want something to eat, Valium?" I asked.

A boy brought a large plate of dal and rice. He pounced on the unexpected bounty, finally wiping up the last bits of sauce and tapping his stomach with obvious pleasure. I ordered him a glass of masala chai with a lot of sugar. He sipped the boiling hot tea with much blowing and wheezing.

"Valium?" I asked. "Where can I get a gun? Anyone selling guns in Paharganj?"

"I don't know, man," he said, getting fidgety.

"Who?" I insisted, adding in nearly the same tone, "Want some more tea?"

"Sure. Order me a Kingfisher beer, too."

I didn't miss the sly look. Laughing, I ordered another glass of tea.

"Look, man," he said, "I can tell you who sells the best hash, acid, or opium. But that's it. Guns aren't my thing."

When the tea arrived, I grabbed the tall glass, holding it out of his reach. His hand hung in midair. "Ram's guesthouse. All sorts of freaks hang out there."

I'd heard of the guesthouse before. Wherever there are backpackers, there's some dump like it. A place where they eye the naïve travelers greedily. And after the looks come the deeds. I let go of the tea.

Valium hurriedly picked up the glass and took it with him to a dark corner of the small restaurant.

The hour was over. I went back to the phones.

"Lobsang Jigme?"

"Yes," he answered shortly. "What do you want? I have no business with you."

"I want to meet with you."

"Why?"

The conversation was going nowhere. I decided to take a chance.

"I'm trying to find out what happened to Willy Mizrachi, the Israeli arms dealer."

"He is dead."

"That much I know. It wasn't pretty."

"I always told him he should read our Book of the Dead. His journey was keeping him from enlightenment. He used to laugh and say you do not die every day. You only die once."

That sounded like Willy.

"I would advise you to forget him and his business affairs." There was a hint of threat in his voice. I didn't like it.

"I can't do that. It's my job now."

This time the pause was shorter. I could hear the wheels turning in his head. "If I were you, I would go back where I came from, and take the blond Mossad agent with you. The Himalayas are my turf."

If he was trying to push my buttons, he succeeded. It was obvious he was involved in whatever Willy was up to. He wasn't just making idle threats. He had something to hide. Suddenly, it was clear to me. The next step was to find Tashing, and maybe as an added bonus, to twist Lobsang's Tibetan balls along the way.

"I look forward to seeing you," I said, and hung up.

CHAPTER 27

RAM'S GUESTHOUSE WAS one of the most dilapidated I'd ever seen. Probably one of the cheapest, too. Which is why a steady stream of Israelis were going in and out the door. "Five dollars a night." When I went in I ran into a Scandinavian guy as agitated as a propeller. "Don't stay here, man," he said when he saw me. "The place stinks. I got head lice."

He threw his backpack down on the floor in front of the skinny Indian reception clerk and declared that he had no intention of paying. The clerk smiled uncomfortably, causing the Scandinavian to scream, "I'm not paying. You oughta pay me. After staying here, I have to find a barber and get my head shaved."

He really did have a fine head of hair. Long and blond, it was tied back in a ponytail.

Despite blushing in shame, the clerk replied, "I am sorry, sir, but you must pay. It is only two hundred rupees. It is not much money, sir."

The Scandinavian was about to say something when an unshaven young thug with a Star of David hanging from a gold chain around his neck appeared. Speaking English with a heavy Israeli accent, he yelled, "What's your problem? Pay up and get the hell outta here."

He reached for the tourist's backpack. The Scandinavian threw a ten-dollar bill on the counter, spat at the clerk, and then spun on his heels and left without waiting for his change.

The Israeli noticed me leaning against the wall opposite the reception desk. "What's your story?" he asked.

I stared at him in silence.

Scratching his whiskers, he repeated, "Whaddaya want?"

"I need a gun," I answered. Straight to the point.

He looked like someone who'd gotten up on the wrong side of the bed and hadn't had time to roll his first joint. First the Scandinavian, now me. All of a sudden, his eyes cleared. "Hey, I know you. You're the great Dotan Naor who does favors for the rich and famous. You get their snot-nosed kids outta jail. But I know exactly what you really are. A dirty rat who works for the Mossad and the Indian police. That's what you are."

"Look who's suddenly holier than thou. I asked if you had a gun to sell me, I didn't come for a job interview."

"A gun? Who would dare get that close to you?"

I pulled out a bundle of dollars held together with a rubber band. The money Willy had left me. It seemed odd to be using an arms dealer's money to buy a firearm. I peeled off five hundred-dollar bills. "I need two handguns. The rest is your commission."

His eyes were shining with greed, but his fear was greater.

"I don't have anything for you. Get outta here."

I peeled off two more bills. Seven hundred dollars. That's a lot of money in India. It would feed a whole family for a few months, or buy a kilo or two of the best hash. "Take it," I said. "Unless you'd rather steal five dollars a night for the shit hole you're running here."

"You think? And tomorrow the Indian police show up and want to know what you were doing in my shit hole. Go on, get out."

He came closer, preparing to shove me out the door. That was crossing the line. I kicked him in the knee. I knew he'd have to go back to Israel to get it fixed. They don't do platinum implants in the public hospitals in India. Since I was pretty sure his Israeli passport had expired long ago, I'd messed him up bad. With a scream, he collapsed on the floor. But despite the pain, which I imagined was unbearable, he didn't give in. "Out," he managed to mouth at me.

I left.

* * *

Colonel Krishna's office was in one of the colonial buildings with arches and well-tended gardens that were once kept a pristine white. Today they are so neglected that the plaster is falling off. The sign on the gate read "Homeland Security." I showed the armed guard my passport and went in.

I found the colonel in his office, a somber spartan space not unlike an army tent. A single picture hung on the wall behind a simple metal desk: Mahatma Gandhi smiling. When Krishna saw me, he smiled, too.

"I can give you ten minutes. Then I must leave for a meeting with the minister."

"I need the lowdown on the FFFT, Fighters for a Free Tibet."

"They are a group of foolish and dangerous lads. They are capable of destroying everything the Dalai Lama has been working for years to build, as well as fouling our diplomatic relations with China. The hooligans are taking advantage of the border dispute to turn the whole region into a powder keg. They know that China is demanding the entire territory of what they call Greater Tibet. They want to use that as an excuse to set the region on fire. They believe their only hope lies in a full-scale war between China and India, which will end with Tibet being granted at least partial independence. They became more extremist after the speech of Barack Obama. In their opinion, he ruined any other chance of an independent Tibet by kowtowing to the Chinese and declaring that Tibet is an integral part of China."

"Where do they operate?"

"The most recent incidents were on the border in the Tawang district of Arunachal Pradesh. But they are mainly active in the area of the Rumtek monastery."

Rumtek? Where had I heard that name before? And then I remembered. I saw Willy bending over his computer screen and bringing up a map from Google Earth. Rumtek was the Buddhist monastery where Itiel was staying.

"Do they have weapons?"

Krishna hesitated for a moment before saying, "Yes."

"Where do they get them?"

"Good question."

"Where does the money come from?" I asked. "I can't believe any Tibetans in India would transfer funds to them through one of their charitable organizations. They'd be going behind the back of the Dalai Lama."

Krishna got up and went to stand in front of the window. He stared out at the street for a while and finally remarked, "It is amazing how things can get more complicated instead of becoming simpler."

"You need money to buy weapons, a lot of money."

"That is true," the colonel said. "I have asked one of my officers to join us. He has information that may be of interest to you."

A chubby bespectacled young man entered holding a thin file. He pulled a document from it.

"What's that?"

He waited for Krishna's approval before answering. "This," he said, "is a bank transfer in the amount of fifty-five lakh rupees from Pakistan to the account of one Lobsang Jigme in the Leh branch of the Bank of Kashmir. We presume it is not the first."

I did a quick calculation. A lakh is worth a hundred thousand rupees. So we were talking five and a half million rupees, or over eighty thousand dollars. I let out a quiet whistle. A tidy sum. When the officer left, I stood and went to stand next to Krishna. "What does it mean? That the Tibetan group is collaborating with the Islamist extremists in Pakistan?"

"It is starting to seem so."

Krishna turned his eyes to the picture of Gandhi. I knew exactly what was going through his mind. India had changed. Gandhi's vision of a country where all people and all faiths enjoyed equal rights was fading quickly.

My ten minutes were up. Shaking my hand, Krishna said, "Let me know what comes of your meeting with Lobsang Jigme in Leh."

So he knew, I thought, although I didn't say it out loud for obvious reasons. Krishna had presented me with a gift: a connection between the two men who had decapitated Willy and Tashing and Lobsang Jigme. Naturally, I couldn't thank him. All I said was, "Why don't you talk to him yourself?"

He let go of my hand, looked me straight in the eye, and said, "I would like to very much. But the gentleman is hard to find. The Himalayas extend over a very large area, and the last thing we wish is to turn them into a battleground. For all Indians, the mountains are the Shangri-La of the soul. We would not like to destroy that, would we?"

CHAPTER 28

SRINAGAR, KASHMIR

FLIGHTS TO LEH in the Ladakh region, the "land of high passes," leave early in the morning. They have to land in a narrow window before the airport is covered in fog.

The departure board showed three domestic flights to Leh. Ours, on Air India, was the first, with an estimated departure time of six thirty. Estimated, because in India you never know when, or even if, a flight will actually take off. Surprisingly, we boarded on time. It was clear they were under pressure to keep to the schedule. The propellers started turning even before the air stairs were detached.

The flight path twisted among the Himalayan peaks, above the raging rivers flowing to the Ganges Delta. It's a dramatic landscape, harsh, but also transcending. Halfway through the flight, we hit weather. The plane bounced up and down from one air pocket to the next. The flight attendants hastily gathered up our cups and strapped themselves in. It seemed to me that some of the girls were looking a little pale under their heavy makeup. Maya's hand inched over and grasped mine. Then the pilot announced that due to bad weather we would be landing in Srinagar instead of Leh.

"That's gonna fuck us up," I said. If only I knew how badly.

"Why? What can happen?" Maya asked.

"What? Anything. We'll be in Srinagar, the heart of Kashmir. It used to be the Garden of Eden of the Mughal dynasty, the summer playground of the British. Now it's a sewer of all the Muslim hatred for Hindu India."

At the Srinagar airport, we came face-to-face with the familiar Indian pandemonium, just more chaotic. As usual when plans go awry, everyone wanted to know what was going on, what they were supposed to do now, how and when they would get to Leh. And as usual, no one had any answers, and those whose job it was to know were reluctant to take responsibility. The weather simply added to the chaos. Rain was pouring down, and water was trickling, dripping, and streaming everywhere. Heavy dark clouds swept over the mountains, moving like swarms of locusts toward Kashmir Valley. Earlier, when we had just landed, we'd been able to make out the mountain peaks, but within minutes, they were completely hidden by thick gray fog.

The small carousel labored to spit out the luggage. The message was clear. No flights to Leh would be departing today. We found our backpacks and left the terminal.

"What do you want to do?" Maya asked.

I paused before replying, but it had to be said. "This is your last chance to turn around and go back."

She looked at me apprehensively. "Are you kidding?"

"No. Not a bit. From this point on, there's more than a fifty-fifty chance that something will happen that we didn't plan for. We're going to be moving through hostile territory without any backup. Everyone here is Muslim. And they're all informers for one separatist group or another. The mere mention of the word 'Israel' is enough to light them on fire, and the potential for a lynching is always around the corner."

She considered my words before speaking. "You don't know the real reason I'm here," she said. "You never asked."

"I come from a generation that doesn't ask those questions."

She gazed at me in silence for a long time, her hesitation reflected on her face. Finally, she came to a decision. "You remember the terrorist attack at the Dolphinarium club in Tel Aviv in 2001?"

"Sure."

"I was there. I was at the club when it happened. I didn't cry when I saw the mangled bodies. My best friend was killed right before my eyes. It could have been me, I could have died that night. I knew she'd never finish high school, never be kissed again, never join the army, never get married, never be a mother. But I did go to the army, determined to do whatever I could to protect kids like her, like the girl I used to be."

I wanted to take her in my arms, but it wouldn't be appropriate. So I just kept silent. What could I say? I got it only too well. That was our life, and not just in Israel. In general.

Maya pulled herself together and changed the subject. "So what do we do now?" she asked.

"We keep moving. We hire a jeep. There's no point in hanging around here without knowing when we can fly out."

"Whatever you say."

The jeep drivers were huddling under an improvised plastic awning. "Hey, mister. Where do you want to go?" one threw at us, but none of them moved. They knew the less competition they had, the higher the price they could demand. One driver was standing alone at a distance from the others. As we walked toward him, I tried to assess the state of his vehicle. A Mahindra jeep. Not new, but it looked in pretty good shape. It wasn't as comfortable as the new 4X4s, but I'd seen others like it doing what no fancy jeep could on India's tough roads. The young driver was clad in the simple clothes of a Kashmiri villager. Despite the cold of the morning, he was wearing sandals. Something about him conveyed gravity and trustworthiness.

"Good jeep," he said with a bashful smile, placing his hand on the hood. "And I am good driver."

I checked the tires. Worn. They'd never pass the annual safety inspection in Israel, but here in the kingdom of universal recycling, they were still usable. I bent down and examined the asphalt under the vehicle for oil leaks. There weren't any.

"We want to go to Leh," I said.

The driver looked up at the clouds. "No problem," he said.

I asked if he came from the mountains or the valley. Laughing, he answered, "I am from Srinagar." That was a relief. Too many accidents happened on the steep Himalayan roads because of bad judgment on the part of drivers from the valley who were suffering from lack of oxygen. The rusting carcasses on the mountainsides spoke for themselves. I asked him how long he thought it would take. He wasn't quick to reply.

"You know, sir, it is a long and difficult road."

"Still."

He thought for a moment, counting something on his fingers. Finally, he answered, "It is nearly two hundred kilometers to Kargil, sir. To get there, we must cross the Zoji La Pass. It is the only road, but military convoys have priority. So we may have to spend the night in Kargil. After that we have another one hundred and seventy kilometers to the Alchi Monastery, and then ninety kilometers more to Leh. Two or three days, if luck is with us."

Maya was astounded. "Two or three days to cover the same distance as a ninety-minute flight?"

"You heard the man."

"So why not just wait for a flight tomorrow?"

"Who says there'll be one? We could be stuck here for a week. It's better to keep going."

I told the driver I'd give him an extra fifty dollars a day if he made it in two days. We shook on it and I asked him his name.

"Pankaj, sir."

* * *

Maya kept her eyes glued to the window, as fascinated by the sights around us as she had been on her first day in Delhi. On the southern side of the valley rose the Pir Panjal mountains, maybe not the highest in the world, but definitely the most dramatic. To the north were the mighty Himalayas gleaming in their eternal snow. Nothing compares to that sight. The road ran past apple and walnut orchards, vineyards, and rice fields, some already flooded before being hoed and others blossoming in green. They were interspersed by fields of saffron, as well as marijuana.

"Incredible," Maya exclaimed. "It's so beautiful. I thought all India was like Delhi."

"You were wrong. No other country anywhere has so much diversity. Mountains, forests, deserts, fertile plains, massive rivers, pristine beaches. Should I go on?"

"No need. I get the picture."

We drove for a few minutes in silence before she repeated, "Incredible."

"Yup. It's hard to believe that this beautiful valley is at the heart of the conflict that has everyone shaking in their boots these days, the war between Islam and the rest of the world."

"We can't escape it," Maya said sadly, uttering out loud the words that were going through my mind.

I thought about the amazing landscape all around and how even here everything was so fucked up. I felt closer to her than ever. Taking her hand, I squeezed it gently, sensing the depth and strength of our union. Whatever happened, she would always be there.

We reached a military check post, one of thousands scattered throughout Kashmir. There are over half a million Indian soldiers and police officers in an area with a population of less than ten million. One for every twenty inhabitants. An armed soldier was standing at the barricade. His comrades, a short distance away beside the single army tent, were busy making lunch. The soldier peered into the jeep, saw two Western tourists, and raised the barrier, nodding to Pankaj.

We hadn't gone more than fifteen miles before we were stuck in a huge traffic jam. Three lanes of trucks, buses, jeeps, and cars, each of which had already tried to overtake the others. We stopped. Pankaj turned off the engine. Several drivers were sitting by the side of the road or standing beside their trucks, smoking. We sat there for half an hour until I couldn't take it anymore and decided to find out what was going on. I approached a tall local police officer talking to a truck driver and asked what was causing the holdup.

"The road is closed."

"Why?"

"They are conducting a search for hostages. Everything from here to the east, until Pahalgam, is closed."

"Do you have any idea how long it'll be?"

He looked me in the eye, stroked his mustache, and asked sarcastically, "Do I look like the chief of the army?"

I went back to the jeep. Reaching for the map case I always carried with me, I took out a topographical map of Kashmir and found an alternative route that bypassed the roadblock. It linked up with the road to Kargil from the northeast.

"Pankaj, turn around," I instructed, explaining what I wanted him to do.

"I know that road. A very good idea, sir."

"Do you think the search has anything to do with the Israeli couple that was abducted?" Maya asked.

"I'm sure it does."

Pankaj made a U-turn and we sped southward, heading back in the direction of Srinagar. When we arrived at the check post, there was a convoy of police jeeps parked along the side of the road, their motors running. The soldiers were standing near the tent with their hands in the air, surrounded by policemen. The one who had previously manned the barricade was now in handcuffs, and a police captain was screaming at him in Hindi. We didn't need a translator to know that he was shouting profanities. I told Pankaj to stop. By the time I reached the captain, he was already beating the soldier senseless.

"Captain, sir, may I have a moment?"

He looked at me, stupefied. "Do you mind?" he said. Naturally, what he meant was fuck off.

"Captain? Sir?"

"You do not see that I am busy? I have no time for tourists."

I pulled out Colonel Krishna's letter of authorization and waved it in front of his face. When he saw the letterhead, he nearly saluted. I asked him what was going on.

"We believe these clowns allowed the vehicle carrying the hostages to pass. One of them may be a collaborator," he said, pointing to the soldier.

I gestured toward the jeep and Maya got out and joined us. The captain almost fainted at the sight of her blond hair. There was nothing he wouldn't do for her. That's how I was able to use his radio to contact Colonel Krishna.

"Yes, my friend," the colonel answered with cosmic serenity.

I told him what was going on and asked if there was any chance I could obtain a gun in some unofficial manner.

"There is no unofficial manner," he replied.

Silently cursing his abominable British inflexibility, I thanked him politely. Then I took out the phone with the Indian SIM card I had bought at the bazaar in Delhi and punched in a number. I knew that Ran "El Pashtun" always kept his cell phone on.

"Where are you?" he asked.

I gave him as precise a picture as possible of the events and my location.

"What now?"

"Any way you can get me some firepower?"

"That would mean asking certain people in Srinagar for a big favor, maybe too big. The fact that Israelis are involved makes it particularly sensitive. They're not great fans of Israel, but they are businessmen."

"I understand," I said.

"An hour, at the turnoff to the road you mentioned. Get out and lean against the jeep."

"Thanks. How are things where you are?"

"At the moment, shitty. I think there may still be some people alive inside Chabad House. One of my men caught a glimpse of the rabbi's wife through his binoculars. Tonight is the moment of truth."

"What are you planning?"

"That depends on the Indians. If they launch an attack, I'll leave it to them. It's their territory. Even I have to obey the rules sometimes. But if they don't do anything, I'm going in. Which means I'll be playing all my cards. After that, I'll have to get out of here and start over somewhere else. You have any openings?"

We were still laughing when he disconnected.

"Who was that?" Maya asked.

"A friend. The type you can count on when you need him. There aren't many like that."

We walked back to the jeep. "Poor kids," I said. "Their abductors know the area. And they know the search is on for them. They're going to head for the Pakistan border as fast as possible. We have to keep our eyes open."

"You think we'll run into them?"

"Not likely, but you never know."

Maya fell silent. I knew what was going through her mind. I waited. She had to get there on her own. Finally, she said softly, as if speaking to herself, "I'd like to help them."

Pankaj started up the jeep and we continued down the road. At the turnoff to the bypass, I told him to pull onto the shoulder and switch off the engine. I got out, leaned on the hood, and waited, gazing at the mountains above Kashmir Valley.

I thought about the fate of the two Israeli kids. Right now they must be feeling all alone in the world.

CHAPTER 29

TWO DAYS AFTER PASSOVER EVE
KASHMIR VALLEY

OREN AWOKE FROM a restless sleep. He was cold, but that wasn't what had brought him awake. The silence of the night had been broken by an unexpected noise. A motorcycle engine. He heard voices not far from the hut. He went back to sleep, pressing as close to Yael as he could. She was sobbing in her sleep.

They were awoken early. As they stepped outside, they saw figures wrapped in Kashmiri blankets standing around a fire, smoking and drinking from steaming cups. The outlines of the weapons they were carrying were clearly visible. As usual, none of them paid them any mind. The men crossed their arms over their chests and began to recite the prayers. When they were done, the female terrorist ordered the young couple into the jeep. Oren could sense the tension in the air, and wondered if it had anything to do with the motorcycle he had heard during the night. Nor did he miss the boxes of ammo and hand grenades being loaded onto the vehicles.

He was surprised to see changes in the seating arrangements this morning. They were ushered into the lead jeep, with the terrorist chief, whom everyone referred to respectfully as Mullah Sayeef-Allah, beside the driver. One member of the crew got in opposite them, an AK-47 on his lap, and the rest piled into the second jeep. They set off on a rugged track that climbed toward the mountains. No one spoke. The jeep rolled down into a broad channel of water that split off into dozens of surging rivulets spread out like a system of capillaries. The driver advanced cautiously to avoid being carried away by the current, as the mullah issued a stream of instructions. The silent threesome in the back was thrown from side to side. Oren looked over at Yael and knew he had to do something. The only weapons at his disposal were words. He prayed their abductors were not devoid of any trace of humanity, that they would not be totally immune to mercy or suffering. As they climbed slowly out of the water, he addressed the mullah.

"Can I say something?"

The mullah turned around. "Speak."

"We're worth more to you alive than dead."

"How much do you think you are worth?"

Oren hesitated. There was nothing in the mullah's tone to suggest he was making a joke. On the other hand, the man was unpredictable and intimidating. Very intimidating. Glancing at Yael, he took a deep breath before answering, "A lot. Israel doesn't turn its back on its citizens. We're worth a lot. Money, prisoners. I'm certain Israel would release quite a few Palestinian prisoners in exchange for our return."

"How much money?" the mullah asked.

"Millions of dollars." From the look the mullah exchanged with the driver, Oren knew he had inflated the figure. By going too far, he may have sealed off the tiny window of hope he'd managed to pry open.

"How many Palestinians?"

"Hundreds, maybe thousands," he replied, deliberately overstating again. He realized he was making a tactical error, but exaggerating the strength of his homeland buoyed his confidence. For a brief moment, he felt more powerful than these fanatic Muslims. They knew, too, that even though Israel was far away, it had a very long reach. He tried to remember how many prisoners had been released in exchange for the captured businessman Elhanan Tannenbaum, and how many in the earlier Jibril deal in exchange for three Israeli soldiers. It gave him hope. If he wasn't mistaken, four hundred and fifty Palestinians were exchanged for Tannenbaum, and even more were released in the Jibril deal. He decided to take his chances. "The Germans would probably broker the deal," he said.

They drove for a while in silence. Then, to Oren's surprise, the mullah began asking about his family. He told the truth.

"You in the army?" he asked finally.

"Like every Israeli." Oren knew what the next question would be.

"In Gaza? Lebanon?"

"I was in computers."

He was relieved he hadn't taken part in Operation Pillar of Defense in Gaza.

"You are all responsible for what happened in Gaza," the mullah said coldly. "At this very moment, we are slaughtering every Israeli in India. The gallant soldiers of Himalaya Mujahideen are spilling Zionist blood in Manali, Rishikesh, Pushkar, Delhi, and Mumbai. People all over the world are seeing the pictures. True Muslim believers everywhere are celebrating, in Gaza, Nablus, and Damascus. A TV crew is on the way. We will give them a good show."

"Allahu akhbar," the driver said in acclamation, and the terrorist opposite them added, "Din Muhammad besayeef"—the religion of Muhammad is the sword.

Oren turned to Yael and felt an icy knife cut through his belly. She was paralyzed with fear. *So that's it*, he thought. *They're going to kill us to show the world what they're capable of.* He took her hand and squeezed it in an effort to reassure her, in utter contrast to what he was really feeling.

In the late afternoon, they reached an isolated mud house and were led into a small, bitter cold room with a tiny barred window. Through it, Oren could see the high mountains, snow-covered and threatening. Yael sat down on the frigid floor, as lifeless as a rag doll. His heart ached with pity. *Our life together will be very short*, he thought. *We'll never lie in a warm bed and fantasize about the future, never have children, never grow old together.* Yael was trembling, whether from fear or cold or both. He went to sit beside her and put his arms around her. That was all he could do. He suddenly realized that she hadn't said a word all day, hadn't even looked at him or touched him. She was in shock.

An hour or so later, they heard a car coming. Oren rose and looked out the window. A dusty black Mercedes pulled up outside and came to a stop just a few yards from their prison cell. A slight man got out and spoke angrily to the mullah, who stood there calmly and complacently. A goon, armed with dark glasses despite the fading light, was leaning on the car. "You fuck it all up," he heard the stranger say to the mullah before continuing in a language Oren didn't understand. All he caught was the word "Pakistan" repeated several times. Whatever he was saying, it didn't seem to faze the mullah. In response to his indifferent reply, the little man's voice rose. A few members of the mullah's crew came out of the house and lined up along the wall. The man by the car straightened up, took off his sunglasses, and picked up the short-barrel assault rifle that had been lying on the hood.

"Listen to me," the stranger said in English. "Do not take them to Pakistan."

The mullah stood there, his arms crossed on his chest. "Abdul," he said, "you are a believer. Do not forget that. Their fate is neither in your hands nor in mine. It is in the hands of Allah."

"The price we will have to pay is too high," said the man he had called Abdul.

Sayeef-Allah shrugged his shoulders. "Perhaps. But is it not worth it to us to redeem the land of Kashmir from the Hindu heathens? With the help of Allah, Kashmir, Pakistan, and Afghanistan will be one united Muslim land."

"A-salaam, a-salaam, a-salaam—that is all I hear, and then in the next moment you are talking about guns and ammunition. Where will the money come from?"

"Trust in Allah."

"You are a fool. Kashmir has no interest in peace, only in who is stronger. Can you not see that it is we who will lose?"

"You have no patience. We will continue to fight until Kashmir is free."

Abdul gave him a look of contempt. "You are too naïve."

He turned and began walking back to the Mercedes. The goon opened the door for him and got in behind the wheel. He started the engine and they took off, raising a cloud of dust. Oren remained glued to the window until the dust settled. He wondered who the man was and why he had come.

Over and over in his mind, he replayed the brief moment when Abdul had glanced toward the small window and their eyes had met. It lasted no more than a split second.

CHAPTER 30

I REMAINED LEANING on the jeep, as Ran had instructed, watching the traffic go by. Trucks loaded way beyond their capacity, open jeeps full to overflowing, a couple of buses, their roofs crammed with baskets, sacks, and passengers.

A beat-up Suzuki approached from the direction of Srinagar, passed us, and then made a U-turn and came back. A kid stuck his head out the window and ordered, "Follow us."

As I got back in the jeep, Pankaj gave me a searching look. I understood his concern, but didn't volunteer any explanation. We turned onto a side road and drove for about two hundred yards, stopping behind a stand of poplars that would provide cover. Two youngsters got out of the car. One went to the trunk and untied the rope that was holding it closed. We climbed out of the jeep and joined him.

"We brought what Ran asked," the kid said. His tone was less than friendly.

I looked into the trunk. It held an AK-47 with five full magazines, an M-16 with three magazines, a box of additional ammo, and an RPG-7 grenade launcher with six rockets.

"That's all?" I asked.

The two men exchanged looks. "It is all we could get on short notice," one of them answered. It wasn't an apology, merely a statement of fact.

"If it was not Ran who asked, we would not do it," added the other, fatter, kid.

We gathered up the weapons. They closed the trunk and started off. After no more than a few yards, they put the car in reverse and came back. The passenger rolled down the window and handed me a Glock and two full magazines. I knew each held thirty-three bullets. Things were looking up. The handgun was a substantial addition to the firepower we would have at our disposal if and when it became necessary.

"This is so Ran will not say we screwed you," he said as they drove away.

We put the weapons in the back of the jeep and covered them with a blanket. Pankaj looked worried. "I have a family," he said.

"I know. I don't want to get you in trouble. I'm hoping we won't have to use them."

He was still concerned.

"We'll pay you an extra hundred dollars a day, on top of what we originally agreed on. And we'll cover any damage to the jeep."

I knew it was a fortune in his eyes, the kind it was worth taking a risk for. The decent thing would be to let him go; the right thing was to tell him what we were planning. "Pankaj," I began, "I want to give you the facts, at least as we know them. Two Israelis were abducted from Lake Dal. We believe they're being taken to the Pakistan border. I don't know what'll happen or what we'll have to do, but I don't want you to be in the dark."

He listened in silence. Finally, he gave me his characteristic bashful smile and got back in the jeep. There was no need to say anything more. We turned onto the bypass. After a few miles, Pankaj stopped at the entrance to a narrow dirt track that ran north.

"Sir," he said, "I know a shortcut to Lake Wular. The road to the lake is good. From there, if you wish, we can take another shortcut. The terrain is rougher, but it will take us to the road to Sonamarg."

Before I had a chance to answer, my cell phone rang. The reception was lousy. I got out and climbed a small rise beside the road, hoping for a better signal. It was Colonel Krishna.

"We have satellite pictures of two unidentified jeeps to the west of Lake Wular," he informed me. "The people are armed. We are working on the assumption that they have the Israeli couple. Our troops in Srinagar are preparing a rescue operation."

"How big?"

"Very big. We are also sending a special forces unit from Delhi to help in the release of the hostages. They will arrive in two helicopters. Other forces in the area are already on the move."

I didn't like the idea of choppers. There was a good chance the terrorists would hear them coming and be ready for them. I started walking back to the jeep, gesturing to Maya to get out the map. "Can you give me the coordinates?" I asked Krishna. "Lake Wular isn't exactly a puddle."

While I waited for an answer, Maya and I bent over the map. I pointed to the large lake, the source of constant friction between India and Pakistan over water rights.

Krishna cleared his throat. I knew he was considering whether or not to give me what I wanted. It was obvious to both of us that as soon as I had the information, the race would be on to see who would get there first, who would make the first move and how. Our friendship won out. He gave me the approximate coordinates and disconnected. We continued to scrutinize the map.

"They headed straight north to put as much distance between themselves and Srinagar and Lake Dal as possible. And they're moving much faster than we thought," I said. "They've had two days to make their way north without any interference. As I suspected, they chose the less populated route through Kashmir. Now they're going to try to go west, more or less parallel to the road to Muzaffarabad, the capital of Pakistani Kashmir. To the north are high mountains with not many passes. They know how easy it would be to block them."

"Our window of opportunity is closing," Maya said. "I have to report in."

I was amazed to see her pull a small sat phone from her bag. Switching it on, she moved away from me. I could see her eyes examining me. Serious, not smiling. Truth is, I understood. Unlike me, she didn't have the luxury of a freelance relationship with the world. She was part of the system. I couldn't hear what she was saying, but from the expression on her face, it seemed the conversation wasn't going well. When she came back, she couldn't look me in the eye.

We continued our journey in uncomfortable silence. Finally, Maya turned around. "I'll get the handgun," she said. I heard her rummaging through the pile of weapons. "I don't believe it," she said, handing me the Glock. "Look."

I checked out the gun. Tiny letters engraved into the left side of the barrel read: "To A.A. Wani from Willy." I froze. Truth may be stranger than fiction, but here, in the middle of the huge region known as Kashmir, in the heart of an even bigger region known as the Indian subcontinent, I was holding a pistol presented by an Israeli arms dealer, my friend Willy Mizrachi, to his Indian partner, Abdul Aziz Wani. Clearly, it was more than a mere coincidence. With all due respect to karma, the gun didn't show up in my hand by accident.

"Abdul," I sputtered. "That man is like an octopus. His tentacles reach everywhere."

I wondered what the hell was going on, who had woven the complex web that linked Willy to Abdul, Abdul to Ran, and Ran to God only knew who. Around here, arms were a basic commodity, just like rice, oil, and salt, just like drugs.

The paved road gave way to a dirt track that wound toward the mountains, some parts more passable and others narrow and tortuous. At a certain point, Pankaj steered the jeep confidently into a large ravine. We were starting the climb up the muddy bank on the other side when I saw it. "Stop!" I shouted, startled.

Beneath a thorny bush was a small bag made out of squares of brightly colored fabric with small Ragistani scenes embroidered around the edges. I got out, retrieved it, and looked inside. It held two packs of Israeli-made daily contact lenses. "Poor kids," Maya said, a spasm of rage contorting her beautiful face.

I put my hand on her shoulder. "We're getting closer."

"She probably can't see a thing. Maybe it's better that way."

"How do you know they're hers and not his?"

"I'm guessing," Maya said.

I took out the map, trying to figure out where they might have gone.

"What are you thinking?" Maya asked.

"I'd put my money on this route," I said, pointing to a wide ravine that led to Pakistan. "If their jeeps are in good enough shape, they can make it from the lake to the border in one day. The Indians can't seal it off hermetically."

I asked Pankaj to pick up the pace. "We have to go eastward, through the ravine."

A group of turbaned men dressed in blue suddenly appeared at the side of the road. They were walking quickly, heading north. Barefoot, they each carried a heavy lance or scimitar. Not one of them so much as glanced our way as we drove past. They simply kept walking, maintaining their rapid gait. Maya watched until they disappeared from sight.

"Who're they?"

"An order of Sikhs."

I was just about to explain the meaning of blue in their faith when we were again surprised by the sight of naked men running along the ravine. Their long hair was twisted into a gigantic knot around their heads, and their bodies were smeared with mud. As they ran, the strands of wooden beads around their necks bounced up and down on their chests and their genitals swung back and forth.

"And them?" Maya asked, pointing in astonishment.

"Naga sadhus, holy men who came down from the mountains."

What's going on? I wondered. *They're like characters out of the ancient epic the* Mahabharata, *as if they've all been summoned to the final battle between good and evil.* I knew I was getting carried away, that the idea was ridiculous, but that's what it felt like. Forces from the underworld had risen to the surface. In our attempt to find out what happened to Willy, Maya and I had been sucked into something much deeper and mightier than we had planned.

It suddenly struck me: this is what the day of reckoning will look like, when forces stronger than us summon us to meet our fate. A cold shiver ran down my spine. The adrenaline began rippling through my veins. I didn't know what lay ahead for us, but I knew that whatever happened was meant to happen.

CHAPTER 31

Kashmir, Day Three

Yael and Oren stood beside the jeep in the dark. It was freezing cold. This time there was no fire and no tea. They didn't dare exchange words or even a touch.

All of a sudden, headlights appeared in the darkness, bouncing on the rugged road as they drew closer. A few minutes later, a jeep pulled up. Mullah Sayeef-Allah yelled something at the driver, who immediately killed the lights. Two men got out, glanced at the hostages, and walked toward the mullah. One turned around and went back to the jeep for a video camera, positioning it on his shoulder. Oren shuddered. *What are they planning to show the world?* he thought. *How we looked just before they killed us?*

The mullah ordered them back into the jeep and within minutes the small caravan was on the move, their jeep in the lead, followed by the TV crew and the rest of the terrorists bringing up the rear. They crossed an asphalt road and continued along the rocky terrain on the other side. Finally, they saw the glimmer of first light. The convoy entered another ravine. Slowly but steadily they made their way through the mountains, until it felt as if the mute walls of granite were closing in on them. Oren gazed at the breathtaking landscape around them. *If we have to die,* he thought, *at least we'll be surrounded by this stunning beauty.* He was looking at Yael, sitting rigid and mute beside him, when he heard it. The noise broke through the silence. It was the sound of chopper engines growing louder the closer they came.

The convoy halted instantly. The terrorists jumped out and took up battle stations. Mullah Sayeef-Allah signaled to one of his men, and he dragged Yael and Oren to the wall of the ravine. The TV people spilled out of their jeep, the camera at the ready. And then there appeared two light attack helicopters high in the sky above them. They flew past and vanished.

A thundering noise rocked the granite walls. Yael and Oren covered their ears, but not before they heard the mullah shout something to his soldiers as a chopper reappeared in the narrow canyon and descended, ready to attack. It fired, the missile hitting the rear jeep where it stood in the middle of the ravine. The vehicle rose in the air and burst into flames. Lying on their backs, the soldiers of Himalaya Mujahideen fired their light weapons at the chopper before it vanished again.

Mullah Sayeef-Allah took advantage of the lull to run to his jeep and return with an RPG launcher. "We will send them a message written in blood," he shouted, his threat echoing over and over again off the canyon walls. Yael and Oren were petrified. The mullah stood erect in the middle of the ravine while one of his men loaded a rocket into the RPG before hurrying back to take cover. The cameraman got ready to film the scene from behind a large rock.

The second chopper returned, descending toward them from the opposite direction. Sayeef-Allah responded instantly, shifting position as if he were turning on an axis. He was ready. The moment the chopper released a rocket, the mullah fired. The TV crew's jeep took the hit. A wheel flew off, decapitating the cameraman who had risen to film the action. The terrorist's missile struck the chopper's tail rotor. Yael shrieked as the helicopter began spinning, finally striking the canyon wall and crashing to the ground. The cheering of the Mujahideen soldiers sent chills down Oren's back. He drew closer to Yael and could hear her muttering to herself hysterically. *Something's wrong with her,* he thought. He held her tightly in a desperate attempt to comfort her.

They heard the other chopper land at the entrance to the canyon. Sayeef-Allah signaled to his men and they started running toward it, armed with a heavy machine gun. A lone terrorist remained behind with the hostages. He took cover behind a rock, his back toward them as he stared in the direction of his comrades. The other TV guy tore the camera from his dead colleague's body and followed the terrorists as they ran through the canyon and took up positions for the decisive battle.

CHAPTER 32

WE HEARD THE choppers approaching. They flew over us, riding low in the sky. A few minutes later came the sound of shots fired. *We've got 'em*, I thought. A deafening explosion split the air not far away. "A chopper's down," I said, pointing to the column of dark heavy smoke rising from within the canyon.

I told Pankaj to speed up. As he leaned on the gas, the second chopper flew over the canyon, circled a patch of flat ground at the entrance, and set down. A dozen soldiers leapt out and began running toward the canyon. I did a quick calculation. Two jeeps plus two hostages. No more than eight terrorists.

"The Indians have a small numerical advantage," I said to Maya, "but they're vulnerable because they have to climb up the canyon."

We scanned the unfamiliar terrain. A pale goat track ascended toward the edge of the canyon closest to us. "That way," I instructed Pankaj.

The chopper rose in the air, caught sight of us, and flew in our direction. I knew it was targeting us. They had no way of knowing we were on their side. Hurriedly, I looked around in the jeep for something that would tell them who we were. All I could find was my orange shoulder bag and Maya's sat phone. Getting out of the jeep, I waved both objects wildly in the air, hoping that Buddha would smile on me and the pilot would catch my meaning before he fired at us. The chopper descended, passing only a few feet over my head. The copilot gave me a thumbs-up. I breathed a sigh of relief.

After a short rise, the goat path began to descend. *Here*, I thought. I signaled to Pankaj to stop and jumped out, grabbing the AK-47. Moving just as fast, Maya got the M-16, locked in a magazine, and shoved two more into her pants pocket. Then she got the Glock, loaded it, and stuck it in her belt. I slung the RPG on my back.

"Ready?"

She nodded. "I don't know how this is going to play out," she said, "but I want you to know that even though you're an arrogant bastard, I wouldn't like to lose you."

"Thanks," I answered, "I love you, too."

The circumstances notwithstanding, she gave me the sweetest smile in the world.

We made our way in zigzags, moving at a quick pace. When we reached the entrance to the canyon, we lay on the ground and peered in. The battle was being waged right below us. A number of terrorists were taking cover behind rocks, their backs exposed to us as they kept their eyes on the Indian troops climbing toward them from the opposite side. A few bodies were strewn on the ground.

We exchanged a look. I took the RPG off my back and stretched out beside Maya. She already had one of the terrorists in her sights. "Fire at will," she said, even managing a wink.

Our shots were economical and precise. Two terrorists fell in the first barrage. It didn't go unnoticed. The others identified the source of the shooting, and one started running toward us with a machine gun. I decided it was time to try out the RPG. Rising to a kneeling position, I placed it on my shoulder and nudged Maya with my elbow. She got my meaning. Crawling backward, she loaded a rocket and gave me a tap on the shoulder when it was ready. It was too easy. The terrorist didn't even have time to aim before the rocket found its target.

Two of his comrades took off at a run, a tall bearded man with a white turban and a slim woman. Getting to my feet, I shouted to Maya, "Cover me! They're going for the hostages!" She moved closer to the edge and emptied the last M-16 magazine while I slid as fast as I could down the steep canyon wall.

My legs seemed to remember the days when I was younger, when I used to go on extreme hikes through the Negev wadis and the Judean desert, running down the rocky slopes without stopping, letting my feet find the best foothold, shifting angles, halting for no more than a second, and then turning in a new direction, going faster and faster without a break. I hadn't done that in years, but my legs hadn't forgotten. And then abruptly, they stopped moving.

I wasn't the only one who froze in shock. So did the two terrorists and Maya, who had followed me down and was holding the Glock out in front of her, as well as three Indian commandos who appeared out of nowhere. What had brought us all up short was the sight of a girl with unruly hair and a pale face raising a huge stone in the air. Before any of us had time to react, she brought it down hard on the head of a terrorist lying on the ground behind a rock with his back to her. Again and again, she struck at the shattered head, emitting a terrifying scream that echoed off the canyon walls. It was the scream of someone whose mind was clouded, but had cleared for the moment it took to save the body.

A second later I heard a shot from the Glock and saw the female terrorist fall. I ran forward, shooting from the hip. Bullets from my AK-47 and the commandos' rifles struck the bearded terrorist in the limbs and the back. He fell facedown. Two commandos instantly cuffed him, despite his injuries. He was the only one left alive. Maya stood beside the body of the female terrorist and turned it over warily with her foot to assure herself that she was dead.

Two figures stood a short distance away. One was still holding the large stone in her hands. The man next to her put his arms around her. "It's over, Yael," I heard him say.

I gazed at them in silence. They needed a moment alone. I felt a hand take mine and squeeze it hard. Maya.

"Good job," an Indian officer said as he walked toward us. His insignia showed him to be a major in the special operations unit. Although he was addressing me, his eyes were on Maya.

"This is Maya," I said.

"Maya? Is your name really Maya?"

She smiled, and then burst out laughing hysterically in much-needed release.

"Good job," he repeated.

Suddenly a man holding a camera appeared from among the rocks. The major was the first to react. Raising his TAR-21, he fired. The journalist's collapse was accompanied by the sound of the camera smashing. "You people make excellent weapons," he said. He spoke into his radio and a few minutes later the chopper landed at the entrance to the canyon. I went over to Yael and Oren. He was cradling her in his arms.

"Are you okay?"

Oren nodded, looking worriedly at Yael. Nothing more needed to be said. Maya responded instantly. "The helicopter will take you to Delhi, where the Israeli embassy will look after you. We'll make sure they notify your families," she said, keeping her tone businesslike.

We escorted them to the chopper. A moment before they got in, I remembered. I reached into my pocket for the wrinkled embroidered bag and handed it to Yael. For a second, her eyes conveyed a glimmer of understanding.

"It'll be okay," I said.

With everyone in the chopper, it rose, leaving us covered in dust. Another cloud of dust engulfed us when Pankaj pulled up, doing an impressive doughnut. Maya got the sat phone out of the jeep and dialed.

"It's over," she said into the phone. "The hostages are free. They're safe and sound, on their way to Delhi in a military chopper. You can inform the families."

She looked over at me, nodded, and handed me the phone.

"Take good care of her," a voice said.

I gazed at Maya. I liked everything I saw. "To tell you the truth, I can't stand her," I said before disconnecting, "but I think we've still got a long road to travel together."

Without asking for permission, I dialed his number. I knew he would be waiting by the phone. I could picture him in his favorite spot at the window, looking out at the unending flow of Indian life. Krishna picked up immediately. He listened silently as I gave him my report. Finally, he asked, "What now?"

"Now Willy."

"Remember the *Mahabharata*. I know you have read it more than once. Before the big battle, Krishna appealed to Karna, the great warrior of the enemy camp, to switch sides. Krishna said to him, 'Your loyalty is understandable, but it is destructive, unnatural. You must distinguish between the good and the bad.' Dotan, my friend, that is also true for you. Your friendship with Willy does not promote the good. On the contrary. You are supporting actions that will enable bad events to transpire. That is undoubtedly what led to his death."

I took a deep breath. Krishna wasn't the type to waste words. Before I had the chance to consider the full meaning of what he had said, he added, "I have news for you that is both good and bad in equal measure."

My heart skipped a beat.

"Early this morning the hostages in Manali were rescued. The rabbi and his wife and daughter are safe. Four commandos were killed, as were two Israelis. One of them is Ran. I think you knew him quite well."

I handed the phone to Maya, unable even to say good-bye. The wave that washed over me was too strong. I was deluged by the moments that had brought Ran and me together over the years. He had chosen a different path than I had, but we had remained fast friends to the end, in every sense of the word. I had never judged the choices he made. It was none of my business. Who am I to pass judgment? It goes without saying that he was fucked up, but aren't we all, in one way or another? There was one thing I was certain of. Ran knew what happened to Willy. Maybe he was even involved in the circumstances that led to his death. But I wouldn't get answers from him anymore. Not in this life, anyway.

The clouds over the Himalayas dispersed, leaving the sky unusually clear. Pure glowing light touched the rocky slopes, the snow-covered peaks, the eternal glaciers, and was reflected back into space ten thousand times over. The landscape was open, empty, naked. Just like me. I sat in the jeep, void of any trace of consciousness, stripped bare, clad only in my true nature. All masks were off after the battle.

The road to Leh was open.

CHAPTER 33

Tashila Retreat, Rumtek Monastery, Sikkim

Itiel awoke out of a dream. It was the same dream that had brought him awake every night for the past few weeks, and it left him deeply troubled. Something happened to him in the dream. It felt like he was having a stroke, like a flash of lightning was passing through his nervous system.

Night after night he was startled awake, his heart pounding in fear. Night after night he tried to calm himself. Night after night he lay on his hard bed, steadied his breathing, and began to meditate. He knew there was nothing physically wrong with him. His consciousness was simply playing tricks on him. It had started when Tashing left. Just walked off saying she would not be back. Since that terrible day, he had become much harder on himself, spending long hours in meditation in a sitting position, lying flat, or even walking. But he couldn't get Tashing's smile out of his mind. The many months of Buddhist discipline did no good. Her smile was still there, etched permanently on his brain.

Itiel rose, put on the orange robes he had been granted not long ago, and splashed his face with water from the bowl on a stool in the bathing corner of his small room. He washed his hands, dipping them over and over in the water, scrubbing them obsessively with a sliver of rough soap to make sure they were free of the red stains that came and went relentlessly in his mind's eye. When he was done, he dried them on the ragged towel hanging above the bowl, slipped his feet into simple plastic sandals, opened the wooden door, and went out into the darkness toward the retreat's main meditation hall.

Several tallow candles were burning in the empty hall. Itiel sat cross-legged on one of the embroidered cushions facing a large statue of Buddha. He joined his hands in a Namaste greeting, took a deep breath, brought his hands down in front of his heart, and closed his eyes. Then he exhaled, placed his hands on his knees, and tried in vain to sink into a meditative state. The memories were whirling around in his head. He struggled to create some kind of order.

*   *   *

It began with his father, Willy, who had simply shown up at the retreat one morning. Itiel hadn't been surprised. That was his thing, showing up in the most out-of-the-way places. Using his usual materialistic arguments, he tried to persuade his son to leave the retreat. "You can do the same thing in Israel," he said.

"No, I can't."

"I'll build you a retreat just like this one, wherever you want. In the Negev near Arad. You can look out on the Edom Mountains and the Dead Sea. Just say the word."

"I don't think so."

"We'll talk again tomorrow."

Willy stayed the night in one of the simple pilgrim hostels in the village below the retreat. He was fine wherever he was. Itiel wasn't worried about him. The man was as stiff as an old playing card. Before he left, Willy climbed back up to the retreat. After a further failed attempt to win his son over, he said, "I want you to know I'm not giving up on you." When he left, Itiel was torn. He was angry at his father, but he hated himself.

The following day he went down into the village to buy food for the retreat. After filling his bag with all the items on his list, he hung it on his back and walked out into the street. That's when lightning struck.

A young woman was sitting on a small wooden bench near the hostel. She turned her eyes to him. She was dressed in traditional Tibetan clothes, her black hair was wound around her head, and a large string of corals hung from her neck. Itiel tried to look away, but he couldn't take his eyes off her. Slowly, he raised his head and gazed at her again. She was the most breathtaking sight he had ever seen. She smiled at him. He felt as if he were drowning in the light that radiated from her eyes. He smiled back. The grin didn't leave his face the whole way back to the retreat.

* * *

That memory. That pain. *I made this whole journey for nothing*, he thought. *I've come all this way and it hasn't changed anything.* He opened his eyes. Norbu Rappa, the head of the retreat, was standing in front of him in his red robes. The Western monk sat down cross-legged on a cushion. His thick hair was held in place on top of his head with a piece of cloth, and his long beard was gathered up under his chin. He watched Itiel in silence.

Deep inside Itiel's head, the sweet melody of her voice continued to resound. *I am thinking of you. You are far away from here. We are separated by high mountain ranges. But the same moon shines down on both of us and the same wind blows over us.*

Itiel breathed a heavy sigh. Norbu Rappa said nothing. Merely gazed at him in silence.

He tried to raise his eyes to the head of the retreat, but all he saw before him was Tashing's smile. If he could only cover his eyes. As

Buddha is his witness, he tried. But he couldn't do it. She had cut him to the very core. She had distracted him. It was entirely his own fault, and he had been paying for it every day during the long and tortuous spiritual journey at Tashila Retreat.

Again, he attempted to look at Norbu Rappa, but again he failed. Her voice, deep within him, quenched him like rain on an arid field, filling his spirit more than any form of meditation he had practiced. That only infuriated him more. *How was it possible*, his soul raged, *that the minute the gift of that small voice fell into my beggar's bowl, it shook my world, the world it had taken me so much agonizing effort to build?*

Norbu Rappa sat facing him, seeing everything, saying nothing. He was waiting.

Curse the moment I fell in love with that corporeal creature called Tashing, Itiel thought.

Finally, Norbu Rappa spoke. "Like the world around you, you are entitled to love," he said, his voice barely above a whisper.

Itiel breathed deeply and closed his eyes.

"Do not concern yourself with the past," Norbu Rappa went on in his clear, soothing voice. "Do not dream of the future. All you can do is focus on the present."

Behind his closed eyes, Itiel imagined a pale pink lotus flower growing amid broad leaves and then blossoming, opening itself to the world, flawless, immaculate, pure. He opened his eyes. Norbu Rappa continued. "The most compelling object of passion is form."

Itiel sighed again. How right he was. Form was the greatest obstacle. Her long body, her voluptuousness, her broad face with its high cheekbones, her almond-shaped eyes, her full red lips. He didn't want to envision it anymore. The illusion of form only pushed him further away from everything he had sworn to achieve at the retreat.

He had arrived at Tashila gripped by a desire to free himself from the chains of the past. From the wasted years he had spent grasping at the vanities of the world: the law degree, the sought-after internship. His contempt for his father's occupation as an arms dealer hovered over everything he did. There was always blood on his hands. Whatever he got from Willy—money, possessions—was stained with blood. Even if his own hands were clean, he felt as if he could never wash it off. And then he found Buddhism. It would be his salvation. When he first made the pilgrimage to the retreat, he didn't know what to expect. He met Norbu Rappa, who had just completed a meditation cycle of three years, three months, and three days in darkness.

"How?" he asked in amazement.

Norbu Rappa smiled. "It can be done. You must prepare yourself."

Norbu Rappa's smile was everything Itiel was looking for at the time. The quiet. The serenity. The detachment from the world.

He got up, leaving Norbu Rappa with the burning candles, and climbed to the roof of the temple. Dawn was breaking. The Himalayas became painted with bands of bright gold, and the high desert around shone in pastel shades of pink, blue, and yellow. He sat down cross-legged in the middle of the roof and began chanting the most powerful mantra of all, "Om mani padme hum"—oh, jewel in the lotus. He placed his hands on his knees, the palms facing upward toward the sky, and took deep, rhythmical breaths.

Itiel sat there, not moving, until it grew dark. From time to time he took a sip of water from a bowl one of the apprentice monks had placed before him. When the sun sank below the horizon, he allowed his eyes to close. The green valley of the temple was covered in darkness. The mountains disappeared from sight. An hour later, the moon began to rise.

And then once again he heard the bell-like voice of Tashing saying, "The same moon shines down on both of us." With her voice came the memory. They are lying on a snowy white bed, the window open and moonlight falling on her beautiful, pure, naked body. He passes his hand over her small belly that has begun to swell. Smiling, Tashing nestles in his arms.

"You will love him like you love me, yes?"

"I already love him like I love you," Itiel confirms, kissing her stomach gently.

"Our child is special. I saw a white elephant in my dream."

A shiver passes through his body.

"I have many dreams about him," Tashing goes on. "I dreamt that he was not born here," she says, taking his hand and placing it on the most sensuous place on Earth, "but here." She moves his hand to her right side. Itiel's heart is pounding. Impossible, he thinks. He knows that Tibetan women often dream of white elephants and hope their unborn child will be a famous monk, maybe even a reincarnation of Buddha, who is said to have emerged from his mother's side.

Itiel sat on the roof detesting himself, the moon, and especially her. All his meditation had been worthless, the long journey he had made far from everything he had once cherished—his home, his family, his secure future—had been for nothing. The sublime meaning of his quest vanished the moment he imagined the sound of her voice, the sight of her body. He remembered a haunting line of poetry from the famed Bengali poet Rabindranath Tagore: "Deliverance is not for me in renunciation. I feel the embrace of freedom in a thousand bonds of delight."

He sees himself sliding down beside her, gently moving aside her long hair and embracing her ear with his lips. She sighs in pleasure. "Oh, jewel in her ear," he says. For the millionth time, his brain teems with excuses and justifications. There is no jewel greater or rarer than Tashing, no place holier than inside a woman, no prayer akin to a woman, no meditation that ever has been or will be comparable to a woman. Tashing was the ultimate lotus, the flower that lay on a snowy white bed waiting to be plucked.

He heard the Tibetan monks chanting in the hall below. He was very familiar with the words:

All forms are ephemeral.

All forms are subject to suffering.

All forms are devoid of materiality.

Itiel felt pulled in different directions. Which light should he follow? He had come to the retreat to distance himself from the material world and found himself drowning in the deepest sensual passion he had ever known. He made his decision: he'd meditate for one night and one day. No more. Just one night and one day.

He began reciting mantra after mantra. Again and again, he chanted, "Totally and eternally I am awake."

CHAPTER 34

KARGIL, JAMMU DISTRICT, KASHMIR

WE MADE THE last leg of our journey to Kargil in darkness. The jeep wound its way along the sinuous road, climbing to nearly nine thousand feet. Moonbeams danced like magical fingers of light on the snowcapped mountains and played on the rushing water of the river below. We rode in silence, each of us occupied by their own thoughts. Pankaj drove cautiously, ever mindful of the deep chasm beyond the edge of the road. The worn rear tire played catch with the cliff on the other side.

We entered Kargil. The city's lone gas station was deserted. A handwritten sign on the pump read, "Sorry, closed due to power outage." We didn't see a living soul, save for a stray dog that awoke and reluctantly toddled away from the puddle of oil where it had been sleeping.

"You don't have another jerry can?" I asked.

"No. We will have to wait for morning to get gas."

"I don't know about you," Maya said, "but I'm filthy. Right now, I'd be happy with any smelly dump that had a bucket of hot water."

We found a small hotel, Tourist Bungalow, at the edge of town. I tore my clothes off and threw them into the pail in the corner of the room. Then I stood under the stream of hot water and let it wash off the squalor of the battle. Feeling better, I put on a set of clean Indian clothes and stepped onto the small balcony that looked out on the garden. The balcony ran the whole length of the floor and connected my room to Maya's. I knocked softly on the glass door of her room. She opened it. Her hair was wet. We sat at the little table and gazed quietly at the moon casting its light on the Himalayas.

"Extraordinary," I said.

She gave me a searching look.

The sat phone beside her rang, cutting off what hadn't been said. She picked up the phone. "Yes," she said. She listened, looked at me icily, and said, "It's for you."

It was Tammy from Channel 10. "How's it going, baby? Did you know the whole country's talking about you?"

"Me?"

"Of course. The story about the hostage rescue came out today. They weren't giving much away until finally the Foreign Ministry issued a statement saying they'd been freed by Indian forces and an Israeli specialist. They meant you. I want to put you on the air. You're a hero."

I didn't respond.

"Everyone in the media is trying to find you. The newspapers are frantic, Channel 2 is driving the Israeli embassy in India crazy. They interviewed the security officer there, a guy by the name of Hanoch, who said there was no question you were the best man for the job, but he refused to elaborate."

I still didn't respond.

"So, what do you have to say for yourself? We're ready to put you on air right now, a special bulletin. We're not even gonna wait for the evening news."

"I don't think so."

"You're killing me," she said, begging. "We're already running a banner promising an upcoming bulletin. The whole country's waiting for it. Ynet put up a piece about you, including your famous photo with Putin. The Maariv website uploaded an item from its archives under the headline, 'Everything but the Foreign Legion.' You don't understand what's going on here."

"Actually, I do. But the answer's still no."

Silence from Tammy's end. Finally, she said, "You've got a girl with you, right?" I could practically hear her face scrunch up.

"Uh-huh."

She hung up.

"How did she get this number?" Maya asked. "It's a secure phone."

"TV producers know how to get what they want."

"Always?"

"Most of the time, not always."

Deciding to let it go, she took a deep breath. I stroked her hand. She looked piercingly into my eyes. Within seconds, the moonlight was shining down on boundless lust. We came together, touched, felt, searched. I had no idea who was leading who, which one of us was urging the other on. I tore her clothes off, she pulled my shirt off. I clutched wildly at her breasts and then, as if by mutual decision, we slowed down and passed our hands over each other unhurriedly. The fold of her neck, the soft skin under her arm—slowly, very slowly, I found each of her most sensitive spots. Her fingers traced the contours of my tattoos. She drew the tiger on my chest, kissed the dragon on my back. We were intoxicated by passion, igniting fire and light. At times we were ruthless animals, at others merciful angels. And then she stretched out her hand and touched me down there with infinite tenderness. I kissed her nipples lightly and they stiffened. I kissed harder. She came with a monumental explosion. When she was calmer, she pulled me on top of her and said, "Come."

An hour later we were lying peacefully in each other's arms on the rumpled bed. The moonlight played on her blond hair, casting shadows on her magnificent body. Then a knock on the door and a voice said, "Dinner is ready, madam." A few seconds later we heard the man knock on my door and deliver the same message. We burst out laughing. I gave her a gentle kiss.

"I'm starving," she said.

I pulled her closer.

"Not for that." She laughed. "I'm really hungry. I need food. I could devour God knows what right now."

"You can devour a lot of rice and potatoes and lentils. Maybe a little chicken."

While I dressed, Maya went to take a shower, but first she turned around, came closer, and looked me in the eye. "Is this a one-night stand?" she asked

"No."

I took her in my arms. I was in love with her. I was in love with her hair, the smooth skin on her neck. I was in love with every inch of her. Kissing her lightly, I said, "I'll wait for you downstairs."

I went out to the balcony and the moonlight.

CHAPTER 35

THE STEEP CLIFF above Leh glimmered in the bright sunlight. As we drew closer, the light softened, endowing the royal palace that extended out from the rock face with a hint of its ancient glory. The streets gleamed with the icy water flowing down from the mountains into the rough stone gutters, which carried it to the barley fields in the valley below. The city was dotted with inviting signs: ayuvedic massage, tension-relieving treatment, Internet café, nail salon, Yak & Tail Hotel, "Silk Route Travel—Expeditions, Treks, Bus tickets, Reliable service." A peddler hawked cheap knockoffs to bright-eyed tourists.

The sun was beginning to set, painting the broad sky, so close you could almost touch it, every color of the rainbow. In Leh, the usual kitschy sunset casts a spell, creating an aura of holiness that envelopes everything it touches—buildings, windows, signs, streets, vehicles, and human beings. The tourists stopped in their tracks to watch; the locals streamed to the Buddhist temple of the Cho Khang monastery in the center of town.

I told Pankaj to stop in front of the temple. "Come on," I said.

We went in. Maya halted at the entrance to the compound, gazing wide-eyed at the sights around her, the mandalas on the broad stones of the courtyard, the pilgrims circling the temple clockwise, passing their right hands over the large prayer wheels. We joined their slow progression around the temple. Something in the expression on Maya's face told me she got it. Together we cleansed ourselves of jaded energies and prepared for what was to come. I was hoping this was the place where we would close the investigation into Willy's death. I prayed for a new beginning.

Leaving the temple, we went out into the crowded street.

"What now?" Maya asked.

Good question. Thinking out loud, I answered, "If Colonel Krishna's information is correct, we have a good chance of finding Lobsang Jigme here. Maayan Austin Sufi told us that Tashing was also on her way to Leh. Lucky for us, it isn't a big city."

"Where do we start looking?"

"In the bazaar. You always start in the bazaar."

We walked a short distance to the small jewelry market and found ourselves in a narrow-covered passage flanked by stalls selling Tibetan jewelry, both new and antique. Going from stall to stall, we asked if they knew where we could find Lobsang Jigme. We were met with empty expressions. No one answered, not even yes or no. They simply ignored us. Finally, we reached a stall occupied by a young girl. She was obviously disconcerted by our question. "You know him?" I asked.

"He is not here."

"So where can we find him?" I pressed.

Her eyes darted uneasily left and right.

"We need to talk to him," I said.

"I do not know anything. Speak to his sister."

"His sister?" Maya asked. "Who's she? What's her name?"

"Tashing."

"Where is she?"

"She is sick."

"Can you take us to her?"

"I cannot leave here," she said, her eyes continuing to scan the other vendors. None of them was paying any attention to us, save for one young Tibetan in a red cap who was leaning on his stall, watching.

"A friend of yours?" I asked, angling my head toward him.

She nodded.

"When do you close?"

"About one more hour. At seven."

"We'll be back."

We went into a café opposite the stall and chose a table on the balcony where we could keep an eye on her.

"Tashing? Are you sure it's her? I can't believe we found her," Maya said.

"Don't get too excited. Tashing is a common Tibetan name. We don't know yet if she's Willy's Tashing."

An hour later the girl covered her stall with a large blanket and stood beside it, waiting. Without exchanging a word, we followed her through the narrow streets of Leh. The farther away we got from the center of town, the fewer signs of Western civilization we saw. Gradually, we found ourselves in a typical Tibetan village. An elderly man was leading a yak to its enclosure, pulling it by a rope tied to a nose ring. The asphalt was replaced by mud and sewage. A cow lumbered slowly toward its barn. Oil and kerosene lamps appeared in the windows of the small houses. Meager light, copious darkness.

We reached a house at the edge of town. Our guide stopped and knocked on the little wooden door. An old Tibetan woman, her face carved with deep wrinkles, opened it a crack. They exchanged a few words until finally the old woman agreed to let us in.

Inside, the house was almost bare. A small fire was burning in the middle of the single room. Above it hung an iron pot emitting a strong aroma. A girl in a red silk Tibetan dress was sitting on one of the beds. A long, thick braid fell on her shoulder. Only her hands, hiding her face, were visible. The light of the flames played on her long fingers. She didn't move.

"Tashing?" I said quietly.

Slowly, she lowered her hands, sat up straight, and turned to look at us.

I was looking at the most beautiful face I had ever seen. Broad and dark-complexioned, it displayed high cheekbones, perfectly symmetrical arched brows, and full, sensual lips. The magnificent sight was completed by turquoise-studded earrings and a matching necklace with a large natural turquoise in the center. But it was the impeccable almond-shaped eyes that took my breath away. Reflected in them was only one thing: heartrending anguish, the bottomless grief of loss and pain.

I sat down on the bed opposite her. The old woman brought a large thermos jug and filled small cups with salty, oily Tibetan tea. Maya took a sip and screwed up her face. The improbable liquid was a mixture of tea, milk, yak butter, salt, and bicarbonate of soda churned into a fatty foaming drink. Under different circumstances, I would have teased Maya about it.

"Where is Lobsang Jigme?" I asked.

She looked me in the eye. "He took my baby."

The pain in her voice was intense.

"They say my baby is the next Dalai Lama. He showed all the signs. He was not afraid of the buffalo head they put in his bed. He laughed at the skeleton masks. I should be a proud Tibetan mother, but I am not. They took him away."

"Who's 'they'?" I asked.

"Lobsang Jigme and his friends."

"Why did they take him?"

"They want to keep him with them, far from the eyes of the teachers in Dharamsala and Leh. They want to raise him to know how to use a gun. He has a destiny. When the day comes, he will lead the rebellion to free Tibet from the tyranny of China."

"Why him?" Maya asked.

"Because they believe that the merging of Tibetan and Israeli blood will rejuvenate our bloodline. They say we have become docile, drained, and enfeebled. They believe he is a miracle, the only hope."

"Where did they take him?" I asked.

"They are hiding him in a remote village. I heard them speak of Nako."

Tashing gazed at the dying fire. After a few minutes, which seemed like an eternity, she raised her eyes to me again. In a cold voice dripping with hate, she said, "I am of no interest to anybody. Everybody used me. They sent me to work in Delhi to get cash to buy weapons. Many girls are sent from the poor villages of Ladakh to the brothels in Delhi, Mumbai, or Calcutta. I was not the only one. And then Willy came and gave me hope of a different life. But in the end, I was just a pawn in his cynical game. He came to Delhi, and the Kashmiri arms dealer introduced him to my brother."

"The Kashmiri arms dealer? You mean Abdul?"

"Yes. He told Lobsang that Willy was looking for a girl to make his son leave the monastery, and my brother knew I could do it. Willy fell into the hands of my brother and his friends like a ripe fruit. A rich arms dealer with an obsession, to save his son. For them, it was as if Buddha himself had sent him. They hid their true intentions behind much Buddhist wisdom. They lit many candles and incense, burnt much yak butter."

"What was he for you?" Maya asked quietly.

Tashing turned to her. Something passed between them. They understood each other without the need for words. I decided to let Maya take the lead.

"At first I thought he was like the other rich foreign clients. That he would give me gifts."

"What happened later?" Maya asked.

"He asked me to travel with him through India. I thought it would be nice."

CHAPTER 36

So she went on a road trip with Willy.

In the heart of the old city of Gangtok, just a few miles from the Tashila retreat, Willy paid for two rooms in a traditional-style hotel. Then he went out and left her alone. Tashing felt strange. For the first time in years, she was back in the Tibetan world, but now she was in an unfamiliar hotel with a Western man. Behind her was bustling Delhi and the oppressive life she had accepted without complaint for a higher purpose—the Tibetan people.

She spent the whole day in the hotel room, not eating, only gazing at the snowcapped peaks of Kangchenjunga, the third highest mountain in the world. From her window, she could see the five peaks spread out like an open hand—the hand of Buddha turned to her in blessing. The mountain was enveloped in fog, and then the fog lifted and the slopes glittered with thousands of points of light breaking on the snow. She remembered the past, thought about the present, and wondered what the future held for her. The memories of the past were not pleasant. All those men who touched her, defiled her with their foul penetration of her body. No immersion or purification could wash away the filth, but she took comfort in the sunlight seeping into the room, as if it purged her a little.

She knew she would do whatever Willy asked. But so far, he had not asked anything of her. Tashing wondered if he desired her. She saw him lust after other girls, but with her he was gentlemanly, restrained, and considerate. She knew that wasn't his nature. She could see the untamed violence that seethed within him, as if he was at war with the whole world. Instinctively, she sensed the primeval darkness that dominated him. But with her, he was different. She called it Willy's "Buddha nature." And she waited.

He returned in the late afternoon and knocked on her door.

"You stayed inside all day?"

"Yes," she answered, smiling, and saw how her smile smoothed out the angry wrinkles beside his mouth.

"I'm going to take a shower and then we'll get something to eat."

He left. She could hear him moving ponderously in the room next door. Then she heard him speaking on the phone, struggling to suppress his anger. Since she did not understand his language, she blocked out the sound and continued to gaze at the snowy mountain and wonder what lay ahead for her.

*   *   *

In his room Willy put down the phone. He took a quick shower and dressed smartly. He went out and knocked on her door.

When she opened the door to him, he stared at her and immediately caught himself. "You are incredibly beautiful," he said softly.

Willy gazed at her broad shining face, the mesmerizing oval eyes, the cherry-like mouth, the white teeth that revealed themselves when she smiled, the long braids wound around her head. Totally unadorned, save for a small golden nose ring, she was dressed in wide red Tibetan trousers and a tight matching blouse. His eyes traveled over her breasts. Again, he caught himself and looked away, cursing quietly, but all the while still smiling at her.

She was everything he wanted, but not for himself.

They went downstairs to the hotel's small dining room. She ordered the Tibetan vegetable dumplings known as momos and a small portion of rice and dal. He ordered chicken tikka, well done, and a large bottle of Kingfisher Premium.

It was time to tell her, but Willy didn't know how to begin. He poured himself a glass of beer, examined the foam, and took a long swallow. Finally, he said, "I saw my son today."

Feeling upset, he sighed deeply.

"The first thing he asked is what I'm doing here."

Tashing remained silent. She seemed to understand how hurtful the question was. She waited for him to go on.

"I told him I'd come all this way to see him. He didn't seem pleased. It was like I was disturbing him. As if my very presence shattered his peace, unsettled him."

Tashing must have known that he was working up to something. Going round and round, gradually peeling back the layers of something that concerned her.

"When I got there, he was sweeping. My son was holding a broom and cleaning the courtyard of an old temple." Willy sighed again, envisaging the picture he was describing.

She let him be, evidently not knowing how to console him.

The waiter arrived with their order, placing the hot plates of food on the table. He stood a short distance away, watching the unusual couple who had become the talk of the Tibetan streets around the hotel.

Willy slowly ate the chunks of tikka chicken, periodically washing it down with a sip of beer.

"Tomorrow we're going to move to the hostel near the Tashila retreat," he said. "It's not as fancy as this hotel." As if reading her mind, he asked, "Do you trust me?"

"I made the decision to trust you, and that is enough for me."

He slumped in his chair, as if the blunt answer only increased the weight of the burden he was carrying. In the last few days he had begun to wonder if he was doing the right thing. India had changed him. Everything he had always thought was white now looked black. Nothing was as it appeared to be. This Tibetan whore he had bought in Delhi had turned out to be the only light in the darkness. He decided to wait for the next day to tell her what he had been about to reveal. They finished their dinner and he said, "You can go back to your room if you like."

* * *

Tashing resumed her seat by the window, gazing out at the mountain. Its face was covered by a blanket of darkness. A single ray of moonlight shone on the rocky peak until it, too, was swallowed up in the dark. She heard Willy climb heavily up the wooden stairs, go into his room, and talk angrily on the phone.

This time he was speaking English. She could hear every irate word he said through the thin wooden wall.

"That's impossible, Abdul," he raged. "There's no way the Muslim extremists got hold of the weapons. I can't believe it. What are you telling me, that we're supplying arms to terrorists?"

There was a pause while he listened.

"They're out for blood," Willy said. Another pause.

"How much do they want?"

A pause.

"Two million dollars? And then what? How can I be sure they'll leave me alone?"

She heard Willy laugh. "Yes, I'm a businessman, but I'm not that rich. Give me a little time to finish what I came here for and then I'll get back to Delhi, and we can try to make a deal with them."

There was one last pause before she heard him say, "What will be, will be."

*   *   *

When Tashing came down for breakfast, she found Willy drinking coffee and reading the *Darjeeling Daily*. Smiling at her with a face free of any worries, he said, "I've been waiting for the day I can have a normal cup of coffee in the morning. Next time I come to India, I'll bring an espresso machine and teach you how to use it. A cup of coffee and your face—no better way to start the day. You light the place up like sunrise on that mountain out there."

Tashing giggled. "You are very cheerful this morning."

"Yes, for the meanwhile." A cloud passed over his face. "Can you be ready in an hour?"

"I am ready now."

"Great."

They drove along a narrow road, their eyes taking in the mountain range, the forest, and the tea plantations that spread across the terraces. Finally, they arrived at a modest hostel. The owner showed them to their rooms on the second floor, which looked out on the hand of Buddha peaks. On the opposite side, they could see the monastery compound.

When Willy invited her to join him for a cup of tea in the garden, she knew. Her future had come.

"Tashing," he said in a hoarse voice. He took a sip of tea, cleared his throat, and went on. "You know I want you, but not for myself."

She sat in silence.

"I want you for my son, to be his wife."

Tashing raised her eyes to the hand spread out in the mountains. The five peaks gleamed in the sunlight. There wasn't a cloud in the sky, which was very rare. With a heavy heart, she wondered if it was a sign.

"But he is a monk," she said. "A Buddhist monk. How can I do that?"

"You've done worse things in your life," he said, but once the words were out of his mouth, he followed with, "I'm sorry. I don't know why, but from the first time I saw you, I knew you were meant for him. You're the one he'll fall in love with."

She felt a tear forming in her eye. She gazed at him, at the mountains, and then back at him.

"I will try," she said.

"I know it'll work. I've paid for your room for three months. Take this," he said, handing her a thick envelope. "There's enough here to keep you for a few months." He opened his briefcase and took out a document. "I've opened an account for you in a Delhi bank. You'll be taken care of for the rest of your life—you and the child I want you to have with my son."

"Child?" she said, her voice barely above a whisper.

"Yes, child. And there's something else. Itiel—that's my son's name—doesn't have to know everything. There are certain things I wouldn't mention, especially where it concerns how I earn my living. Things like Abdul and the weapons."

"And how I earned my living?"

Willy laughed. "That you can tell him. It'll warm the cockles of his heart. He thinks every holy man needs a whore to wash his feet. Or maybe it's the other way around, he should wash her feet. I can't remember exactly. Think of Jesus, or Siddhartha. Besides, he's no different than any other man. It'll just make you even more desirable."

"You enjoy humiliating women."

"Sometimes. I apologize. It's an old habit. I'm not good with emotions."

They sat in silence. After a while, Willy said, "This is the first time in my life I've ever envied anyone. I wish I could be in my son's place. But that won't happen in this life."

Tashing knelt down in front of him, took his right hand in both of hers, and kissed it.

She didn't imagine she'd never see him again.

CHAPTER 37

"Willy left the next day," Tashing told us. "That was the last time I saw him. He called me a few times at the hostel in the village, but after a while he stopped calling. When I met Itiel, I told him about it. I think he did not want to interfere."

"How did you meet Itiel?" Maya asked.

Tashing lowered her eyes and stared at the glowing embers. She sat in silence for several minutes before answering. "I did what every whore knows how to do. I seduced him. I learned he liked to meditate in the afternoon at a certain place in the woods, under an old tree. I dressed in my finest clothes and painted my eyes to look like an innocent Tibetan girl. Every day I walked by the tree."

She started giggling. It was the first time we heard her laugh.

"What's so funny?" I asked.

"I allowed myself to believe I was a pure village girl again. I was mistaken. It was clear to Itiel that I was a daughter of the demon Mara sent to distract him from his meditations. I knew he noticed me, that he followed me behind his closed eyes. Each day I distracted him a little more. It took two weeks until he came to my room at the hostel. We did not speak, only sat on the bed and stared at each other. Then we began to touch, slowly, gently. We discovered what we already knew, that we fit together perfectly. Itiel was so moved that he trembled. I had only to hold him, to warm him with my body, for him to grow calmer. Then we came together. It was like a holy union."

"Tantra," I whispered to Maya. "Spiritual eroticism." What a lucky son of a bitch Itiel was, I thought. What a gift he'd been given, without even knowing it. As usual, Willy had nailed it. I stared at Tashing for a long time. Finally, I said, "We're going to look for your brother tomorrow."

"I want to come with you."

We said good-bye to Tashing and the old woman, and took the hilly path back to the hotel. The evening fell softly, the shadows gradually veiling the tea-filled terraces as the pickers slowly climbed the upward tracks with straw baskets heavy with tea leaves on their heads. It got chilly. Maya wrapped herself in the woolen shawl she had bought at the bazaar, moved closer to me, and said, "I'm cold. Hold me."

We walked on with our arms around each other. Later, when we were sitting on the balcony, she asked, "What do you think happened between Tashing and Itiel? Why did she leave?"

"I don't think he could handle the head-on collision between two worlds. For him Buddhism was a way to rebel against the material world he despised at home. Until Tashing showed up, he was maintaining a precarious balance. It all came crashing down on him when he fell in love with her. He couldn't keep living a double life. He had to choose. Staying with Tashing meant going back to the world he loathed, and I guess that feeling was even stronger than love."

A chill ran through Maya. She moved her chair closer to mine and took my hand, almost aggressively. We both liked the buzz it gave us. After a while we got up and, without exchanging a word, each went to our own room. We were swamped by emotions aroused not only by the events of the day, but also by what was happening be-tween us.

I was in bed when I heard her through the wall. "Are you asleep?"

"No."

"Can I come?"

"Uh-huh."

"What does 'uh-huh' mean?" she asked irritably. "Yes or no?"

"Yes."

She entered through the door to the balcony, wrapped in a sheet. She let it drop and stood in front of the window, a sensual silhouette in the dim light. Then she slipped into my bed. We battled. There's no other word for it. We battled all night, angry, violent, needy. Offense and defense. I made her squirm, howl, and groan under me. At a certain point, she whispered in my ear, "You're slaughtering me." The bed shook. It was like a life or death battle. Sex that de-manded that every last drop be drained out of it, out of us.

"I want us to come together," she said.

I came with her. We were joined. We were one.

CHAPTER 38

WE WERE ABOUT to embark on a demanding drive through the Himalayas. I knew Lobsang had a big head start on us. And he didn't travel like a tourist. He'd be moving like only the Indians can, without a break except to fill up on gas when he had to.

In order to cover more ground, Pankaj and I took turns driving, switching every couple of hours. He wasn't thrilled with the idea to begin with, but he warmed to it after my first session behind the wheel. We got into a rhythm. Maya and Tashing sat silently in the back. A few hours into the drive, Maya broke the silence. To my surprise, she asked Tashing, "What's your son's name?"

I turned around to see Tashing's reaction. She was gazing out the window, hiding her longing and pain. "I named him Pema Choden. Do you know what it means?" she asked, turning to me.

"No idea."

"Itiel told me that in Hebrew his name means 'God is with me'. I wanted a Tibetan name with the same meaning. 'Pema' is the lotus flower and 'Choden' comes from 'Chohanden,' which means 'holder of dharma.' It is a nice name, is it not?"

"Lovely," Maya said. "What's dharma?"

Tashing and I exchanged a look. "In this context it means someone who carries on Buddha's teachings, a disciple, maybe even a reincarnation of Buddha himself," I explained.

The journey from Leh was uneventful. We crossed the Tanglang Pass at an elevation of 17,480 feet, and drove through the Morey plains, a strange desert-like terrain where Tibetan yak herders minded their flocks. Packs of wild asses darted through the broad plains. By the time we arrived in the district capital of Keylong, it was late at night. I was pleased by how far we had come. If we had managed to cover so much distance in one day, there was a good chance we could make it all the way to Nako the next.

We were exhausted, utterly sapped. The small hotel had only two rooms. The girls took one and Pankaj and I shared the other. He was lying on the bed smoking one last cigarette when he suddenly asked, "Mr. Naor, sir. What will you do with the child when you find him?"

I stared at him in the dim light. It was the first time he had ever questioned me so directly. Something was bothering him. "What do you mean?"

"I am Muslim, but I am Indian first. I respect the law of dharma. I understand the child has a destiny. You can not interfere with it."

I sat looking at him in silence. The kid surprised me. Naturally, I had thought about it, but I preferred to set the issue aside until we met up with Lobsang. If we ever did. I'd invoked every excuse in the book: we were on the hunt for Lobsang Jigme to find out what happened to Willy, who killed him and why; Tashing wanted, at the very least, to see her baby. Each of us had their own reason for being here. And then all of a sudden, this young Muslim raised the most critical question of all—what moral right did we have to interfere?

"You're right, of course," I said. "When we started out on this journey, our only goal was to solve the murder of my friend. We didn't expect to find ourselves entangled in a web of so many different people and causes. I don't know what's going to happen."

I'm not sure my answer satisfied him. I'm not even sure it satisfied me. When I switched off the light, his breathing was already deep and rhythmic.

CHAPTER 39

THE FIRST RAY of sunlight shimmered like a golden ribbon on the Himalayas, the majestic sign of a new day. Itiel, asleep on the roof of the temple, awoke to the sound of the morning prayers. He realized he must have dozed off. He hadn't achieved the goal he had set for himself: to meditate for one night and one day. Dazed, he sat cross-legged on the roof, his head bowed, sunk in thought.

He remembered the day he was informed by monastery headquarters in Dharamsala that his father had been murdered in Delhi. Ever since, he had been unable to keep from reliving their last meeting during his father's single visit to the retreat. For the first time in his life, he had seen Willy squirming, indecisive. They sat in silence, highly conscious of their disappointment in one another, of their estrangement, and especially of the fact that nothing could bring together the different worlds they had chosen to live in. The past stood like a wall between them. Neither believed in the possibility of a shared future.

Willy broke the heavy silence. "You know that I just want you to be happy, don't you?"

The soft tone of his voice took Itiel by surprise. Willy didn't wait for an answer. "The truth is, I don't care anymore what you do with your life, I don't care if you're a prominent lawyer or not. It took me a while, but recently I've come to understand a thing or two. I just want to see you happy. I know you, I know who you are inside.

You're my son, after all. Believe me when I tell you that you won't find happiness here."

Itiel listened. Every word was a stab in his doubting heart.

"You'll only be happy when you feel real love. Not love for the world or for any Buddha," Willy said, pointing to the statue under which they were sitting. "I'm talking about loving yourself."

Itiel almost got up and walked away. Away from the words, away from the chance that they might be true. And he almost answered his father. But he knew he could never share with him the quietude of his own experience, the intimate comprehension of things as they really are. He kept silent.

"Actually," Willy went on, "everything I did, in my clumsy way, was so you could be happy. I wanted to see you tied by bonds of love, a husband and father, so you could keep on growing."

He got up and gave his son a penetrating look. "I never gave up on you. And you know me well enough to know I'll do anything to get what I want."

That sounded all-too-much like a familiar threat. Itiel rose and looked his father in the eye. Willy tried to put his arms around him, but he flinched and stepped back. He saw an expression of hurt flit across Willy's face, instantly replaced by the look of determination he knew so well. The one that said he didn't give a damn about any-one else. Without another word, his father turned on his heels and strode quickly out of the temple.

Itiel also remembered Tashing and her swelling stomach. For the first few months, he found it wondrous. He loved to pass his hand over it, place his ear against it and listen to the life growing inside. Over time, the wonder was replaced by apprehension. The closer they got, the more he pulled away from her, withdrawing first emo-tionally and then physically.

It had been several weeks since he had gone down to the village or meditated under the sacred tree. One morning he was sweeping the compound when Tashing appeared at the entrance to the retreat. She stood in the center of the courtyard, her large belly seeming to send tremors through the quiet space. He caught his breath. Slowly, she came closer, each step like a knife in his heart.

"I am not angry with you," she said. "You are the only man I ever wanted and the only man who ever said 'no' to me. I am leaving because you do not wish to share with me the thing of greatest importance to me. Our child."

He stood in front of her, his eyes fixed on the ground.

"I am leaving so I can have our baby in a safe place."

What was she talking about, he wondered. He raised his eyes and saw her fear, but didn't ask. He had imposed withdrawal on himself. Withdrawal from what was happening in her body, in her mind, in her soul. He knew that if he asked any questions, the agonizing wheel would begin to turn again. He brought his eyes back down to the ground.

Still, she tried. "I cannot stay. Lobsang Jigme knows I am here."

The name sent a shiver through Itiel. When they first met, Tashing told him about her brother, the leader of a desperate Tibetan underground organization. He had plotted the course of her life with only one purpose in mind, to free Tibet. Itiel was horrified by the thought of her being in danger, but he chose to remain silent. *Whatever happens is what was meant to happen*, he repeated over and over to himself.

Watching her leave tore him up inside. He knew she wouldn't be back. Knew he would never see his son. Not ever.

Itiel sat on the roof, his mind no less muddled than it had been before. Nothing had changed.

He sat and thought, until he made his decision. As if in a trance, he reached for the shoulder bag he had brought with him, moving so slowly it seemed to take forever to get it open. He found the box cutter and pushed up the thin blade, checking to make sure it was sharp enough. Grasping his left eyelid with his left hand, he stretched it outward. With a quick stroke, he sliced it off and threw it over the roof. A few seconds later, the right eyelid landed beside it on the garbage heap, where the temple chickens were pecking for food. The blood flowed down his face and stained his clothes. But he didn't feel a thing. He continued to sit there until he sensed the rays of sunlight striking at him, and then he began to laugh.

Norbu Rappa found him sitting there grinning, his face covered with dried blood.

"What have you done?" he shouted.

Itiel replied in a whisper. "My problems are gone. Nothing will interfere anymore. It was only the weakness of the body that made me fall asleep. Now nothing will distract me from meditation, from the path."

As the sun rose in all its glory, a fireball in the sky, the grin remained on his face. No images disturbed his mind, no voices called to him. He saw only one thing—the jewel in the lotus.

Norbu Rappa summoned the monks who placed Itiel on an improvised stretcher and carried him down from the roof. They kept a vigil at his bedside, not leaving him alone for a second. During his shift, Norbu Rappa thought he heard Itiel mumbling something. He brought his ear closer and heard him whisper in pain.

"Tashing, Tashing."

CHAPTER 40

NAKO

NAKO, A TINY ancient Tibetan village, seemed to have been planted in the heart of the high Spiti Valley. We were greeted by harvested rice fields, with the village houses, surrounded by high stone walls, spread out behind them. Brightly colored Buddhist flags fluttered in the strong wind. We made out a few figures among the fences and the buildings. An old woman carrying a heavy bundle of twigs on her back. Two women beating rice, and then abandoning their wooden flails and going into a house, closing the heavy wood door behind them. There was a strange stillness all around, highly unusual for a busy Tibetan rural community.

The sound of kettle drums came from the center of the village, where the roof of the gompa, the Tibetan temple, rose into the sky. Making our way along the slate paving stones, we headed toward it. The deep echo of the drumming grew louder and was joined by the sound of the long Tibetan horns that accompany the prayers.

The path opened onto a large square. In front of us was the imposing ancient gompa. Beside it, a new wooden temple was nearing completion. A single car stood in the square. I recognized it immediately: Abdul Aziz Wani's black Mercedes.

"What the hell is he doing here?" I wondered out loud.

A cloud passed over Tashing's face.

"Do you know who that car belongs to?"

"Abdul," she muttered.

Something in her expression made me pull up short. And that's when I got it. All at once, the penny dropped. The facts that had been swirling around in my head, the pieces of the puzzle, all fell into place. Willy, Abdul, Lobsang, Tashing, and especially—mainly—the child. I realized there was no time to lose. We had to move fast. I sped up until I was nearly running. Maya and Tashing hurried after me.

We entered the large hall of the ancient building. Two rows of Tibetan monks in red robes sat facing each other on small cushions, reading devoutly from long prayer scrolls spread out before them. I recognized the text: the rebirth sutra that reveals the arrival in the world of a new Buddha, one who will not abandon mankind but will remain among us until he has put an end to all suffering. Suddenly, I understood exactly what that meant to them: it spoke of their own suffering, the suffering of the Tibetans, the misery caused by estrangement from their heritage, both physical and spiritual. That was at the heart of all of this.

Aside from the monks, there was no one else in the gompa. *We're in the wrong place*, I thought, spinning around and heading back toward the entrance. Suddenly, two bursts of gunfire rang out from close by. The noise echoed through the valley between the towering mountains and then ricocheted back, striking the temple. The horns and drums fell silent.

Tashing's scream was harrowing. In a frenzy, she took off at a run.

We ran after her. The moment we entered the new temple, we saw them. Abdul was lying on a heap of bare wooden planks. Blood was issuing from his chest. Tarik, his loyal driver and bodyguard, was standing next to him, smoke rising from the barrel of the Uzi in his hands. Opposite them, two young Tibetans were sprawled on an old carpet, their weapons beside them and the blood spreading out beneath them.

Tashing screamed again. She ran toward the men on the floor and wrapped her arms around the head of one of the youngsters.

"Lobsang," she cried out.

He opened his eyes and gazed at her.

"The baby has to stay here. This is where he belongs," he wheezed. Red froth began bubbling from his mouth as his chest rose and fell laboriously. He was struggling to speak. We saw him stroke Tashing's hand. Just before his eyes closed, he muttered, "Stay here with the child. You are Tibetan."

I bent over Abdul. He didn't have much time left.

"We'll get you out of here," I said.

The hint of a smile came over his face. "Where to? Leh? Manali? You know as well as I that I have little time left. Let us not waste it."

He coughed. His eyes wandered over the paintings on the ceiling depicting the stages in the life of Buddha, beginning with his mother's dream of a white elephant. Following in chronological order were portrayals of her meeting with the Brahmin who declared that the infant would change the course of the world, the birth, and the child's life as a prince in his parents' royal palace. Then came the most significant scene—the young man's discovery of suffering. The future Buddha encountered four sights: an old man, a sick man, a dead man, and a monk who had renounced the pleasures of the flesh. Overwhelmed by what he saw, he was carried on a wave at whose crest he grasped the full nature of human life.

"I should have kept the child with me. I should not have let her leave," Abdul muttered, his eyes turning to Tashing, who was still kneeling beside the body of her dead brother. "That is what Willy asked of me. He was right."

Abdul coughed again, spitting up blood. Then he looked at Lobsang. For the last seconds of his life, he was filled with rage. "That Tibetan dog cut off Willy's head."

"Why did Lobsang kill Willy?" It was the only question I asked, the only one that troubled my mind, the only one for which I didn't have an answer.

Abdul cleared his throat, struggling to reply. "You still do not understand?" I shook my head.

"Strange. I thought you knew him better than I did. But he even managed to fool you."

Blood was staining the wood beneath him. His breathing was labored. All of a sudden, a smile appeared on his face. "In the end, that ruthless bastard was the only one of us who acted humanely. All he really wanted was a stable loving family. What he did not have himself he wanted for his son. He wanted to see Itiel with his wife in one hand and his son in the other. That was the nature of your bet, was it not?"

I nodded.

"He made a very unwise choice. A Tibetan whore. Typical of Willy, no? But he could not know that the odd union of an Israeli monk and a Tibetan prostitute would result in a child the Tibetans would declare the next Buddha. How can they give him up?"

Again, Abdul coughed, bringing up more blood. He began to mumble, the words becoming less comprehensible. Without warning, he grabbed my sleeve and pulled me closer. He was trying to tell me something. I leaned down and clearly heard him say, "Karma is a strange thing, is it not?" Looking up at me, he whispered hoarsely, "We do not have the right to judge another person. We do not know their past or what the future holds for them. Only what is in the present, and that . . ."

The light in his eyes went out and his face relaxed into a peaceful smile.

Tashing rose and walked toward us. Tarik remained sitting, numb, beside the body of Abdul Aziz Wani, a Muslim arms dealer whose soul had returned to Allah in a Tibetan Buddhist temple. Without speaking, we went through the old temple and back out to the square.

The village had returned to life. A column of Tibetan men and women was making its way along the narrow path to the temple. In the lead was an elderly barefoot monk in a tattered robe with a huge grin on his face. He was carrying a red woolen blanket from which a small head emerged. Then we heard a baby crying. Tashing began to shake. We stood riveted in place, watching as the monk came closer.

The drums and horns started up again. A chorus of monks broke into a chant. The sounds were carried to the mountains, the mighty Himalayas, heralding the new king.

CHAPTER 41

"WHAT HAPPENS NOW?" Maya asked.

We were sitting in a village house not far from the temple, sur-rounded by a flurry of activity. But our small circle—the elderly monk, Tashing, Maya, and I—was strangely subdued. Tashing was cradling the baby in her arms.

"I will stay here in Nako," she said. "It is my duty. I will help the monks raise him, although they know their job well. He is not the first lama they have raised from infancy."

"Won't you miss your life in the city?"

"Miss what I was in the past? Not at all. When my son grows up and becomes a monk, I, too, will shave my hair and join a monastic community. There is such a place for women not far from here, on the shores of the Chandra Taal Lake."

We sat in silence, gazing at the tiny infant. I thought of the up-heaval he had sparked and wondered how many lives would be lost before he took his first step. Tashing seemed to read my mind. "In the end, Willy understood that the child growing in my belly had special meaning for Lobsang and the Tibetan freedom fighters," she said. "He wanted to protect me. He came back for me in the vil-lage below the retreat. He did not know that Lobsang had already found me, that he, too, had come to the village to persuade me of the baby's importance for Tibet. He said I must give him up. Willy brought Abdul and Tarik and other men with weapons. They took me away and hid me in Abdul's villa. That is where I gave birth to Pema Choden."

"So that's what happened?" I asked. "Lobsang followed you and killed Willy because of the child?"

Tashing nodded.

"It's so sad," Maya said. "The uncle murdered the grandfather, ideology killed the family. And for what?"

I should have offered some words of wisdom, some pithy saying from an ancient Eastern philosopher. But I didn't.

Tashing handed her son to the monk, who placed him on his lap. Studying the infant, I prayed that this child, whose birth had already caused so much blood to be spilled, would grow up to be a man who chose the right path. I prayed that Pema Choden would not do as Lobsang had wished, would not lead an armed revolt, but would bring hope to his people. That he would follow in the footsteps of his predecessors who had chosen the path of looking inward in order to realize the potential for wholeness within each of us.

My musings were interrupted by the noise of an approaching chopper. A few minutes later, Colonel Krishna appeared in the doorway and gestured for Maya and me to follow him outside. We stood at the edge of the square, watching the colonel's soldiers going in and out of the two temples, the old and the new. The village was still again, wrapped in stunned silence after the events of the day.

"We found Itiel," Krishna said. "He is in a small retreat near Rumtek. He is in very bad shape. I would like for us to fly there. Then we will go on to Delhi where we can complete our business and close the case."

I looked at Maya.

"That works for me," she said.

I sought out Pankaj, waiting just off the square. It was hard to say good-bye to the young Muslim.

"See you later, partner," I said.

His eyes gleamed with pride. Taking my outstretched hand in both of his, he said, "I am yours, Dotanji." With a bashful smile, he took leave of Maya, climbed into his jeep, and drove off.

We went in to say good-bye to Tashing. "I know where you are going," she said, taking off her mala bracelet of Tibetan prayer beads. "Please place it on his wrist."

As we got into the chopper, we saw her standing in the doorway of the village house.

She was crying.

CHAPTER 42

TASHILA RETREAT

WE SAT IN silence for the whole of the long flight to Sikkim. We each had a lot to think about. Maya kept her head turned to the window, looking out on the Himalayan slopes rising to the Tibetan Plateau to the north. The shadow of the aircraft looked puny against the peaks to the east and west of us.

We landed just outside the retreat and were greeted by a Western monk. "Norbu Rappa," he said, introducing himself, "head of the Tashila retreat."

"We have come to see the Israeli," Colonel Krishna explained.

Norbu Rappa nodded. "I'm afraid he isn't well."

We followed him into a small cabin where candles were arranged around a lone bed. A monk sat beside it, tenderly wiping the patient's face with a moist towel. He rose, making room for us by the bed. I came closer and was horrified by what I saw. It wasn't the Itiel I knew, the boy with the infectious grin. The face of the young man in the bed was sunken and tormented. His open eyes looked unnatural, frightening.

I gave Norbu Rappa a questioning look.

"He did it to himself," he said. "I am to blame for not seeing that the battle raging in his soul was too great for him to bear."

"What do you advise?" Colonel Krishna asked me.

I didn't reply, not knowing what to say. There was no doubt in my mind that Itiel would get the best medical care in Israel, but I wasn't sure that's what he needed. Norbu Rappa answered for me. "I believe it would be best to leave him here with us. He will get the spiritual comfort he needs. We understand the places where his soul is wandering. Slowly, step by step, we can bring it back to him. It will take time, a very long time, until he is ready to return to the world."

I looked at the monk. His eyes conveyed sincere concern.

"He's right," I said. I bent over, picked up Itiel's scrawny limp hand, and slipped Tashing's mala bracelet on his wrist. After that I was ready to leave.

*   *   *

The first leg of the flight to Delhi passed in shocked silence. At some point, Krishna got a thermos from the pocket of the seat beside him and poured us out cups of tea with milk.

"Straight from the monastery," he said. "It will refresh you."

Gratefully, we sipped the hot sweet tea. I still had a few loose ends to tie up. I gave Krishna an inquiring look.

He got my meaning and replied with his characteristic smile. "Conclusions? You Westerners always want conclusions," he said. "You can make plans to achieve what it is you wish for. It will transpire, but not as you expect."

It was a moment of clarity that encapsulated the very essence of everything that had happened. Krishna went on. "None of you ever understand that, and perhaps you are incapable of understanding it. Willy had good intentions. He wished to help his son. But in reality, he sold Israeli weapons, not knowing they would be sold on to Muslim terrorists. Lobsang imagined a future when Tibet would be free, and he was willing to kill, to commit murder, to realize his dream. Their actions ignited a series of terror attacks. What did they achieve in the end? Only suffering."

So that's the story, I thought. Israeli arms meant for the Indian army and anti-terrorism squads were sold to a small Tibetan underground movement and from there they landed in the hands of the most savage brutes. Those hands spilled the blood of innocent Israelis. It was a very heavy price to pay. Oh, Willy, what a shitstorm you started.

Krishna asked the pilot to fly low over the Ganges. The course of the river from the Himalayas, the home of the gods, to the low-lying delta in the Bay of Bengal symbolizes the course of human life. The brown river flows slowly, heavy with silt.

"There is something we must do," he said.

The chopper circled over the muddy water, the main rotor raising ripples in the river, momentarily arousing it from its lackadaisical progress. The colonel reached for a white burlap sack filled with orange chrysanthemums, rose petals, and white jasmine flowers. Maya turned to look at me.

"To say good-bye," I explained, "just good-bye."

Krishna opened the narrow window next to him and we each followed his lead.

The image of Willy and our last meeting in his office swam up before me. "Willy bet me that within a year his son would meet a woman and they'd have a kid," I said to Maya. "Everything he wished for came true. Just not the way he wanted. It's presumptuous of us to think we can interfere in God's plan, isn't it?"

As far as I was concerned, that insight put a period to everything that had happened to Willy. And to us.

We tossed handfuls of flowers into the water, watching as they floated, eddied, disappeared beneath the surface and reemerged, rising and falling, until they vanished forever and became one with the river. Ma Ganga, the mother of all beginnings and of the end. It was a fucking great way to say good-bye. We took our leave of everyone involved in the whole convoluted affair in which blood, arms, and money had all played a part.

I felt calmer, cleaner, purged. I was hoping Maya felt the same. Krishna gazed at us, put his cap and shades back on, and signaled to the pilot. The chopper rose.

There was only one thing left to do.

CHAPTER 43

DELHI

WE LANDED AT a military heliport in the heart of Delhi. I asked
Colonel Krishna if I could borrow his jeep.

I drove in silence with Maya beside me, both of us ignoring the
usual sights and sounds of the city, oblivious to the chaos around us.

Finally, Maya was unable to restrain herself any longer. "Where
are we going?" she asked.

I scrutinized her face and smiled. "Just after we arrived in Delhi,
I made you a promise."

It took her a minute to remember. "It had to do with some place.
But that feels like ages ago. There's no way I'll remember the name."

"Yes, India tends to make time lose all meaning."

I parked at the entrance to Humayun's Tomb, the garden-tomb
of the second Mughal emperor, son of Babur the Conqueror and
father of Akbar the Great. It was dusk, about an hour before sunset,
when believers turn to the divine and lovers seek to join together in
solitude. The most wonderful time of day in Delhi.

Stretching out in front of us was the magical garden of the mausoleum. Most visitors were already on their way out, leaving us
alone in the empty garden. We sat down on a white stone bench
and breathed in the clear air, gazing at the infinitely changing
play of shadows on the arches and marble inlays of red, black, and
white. Moved by the beauty of the mute architecture, we listened
to the chattering of the monkeys, the buzzing of the wasps, and the

chirping of the birds scouting out a perch for the night among the thick trees.

"There's one thing I left out on the flight from Kashmir to Delhi," I said.

Maya looked at me without speaking. She was waiting.

Our eyes met, the most intimate of looks.

"Nothing real can be threatened," I said, adding, "and the only thing that is real is love."

Tears welled up in her eyes. She touched my arm and moved closer. I put my arm around her and drew her to me.

There was a guileless smile on her face. Her smile eclipsed the rivers of blood, easing the aching sense of loss and pain.

Willy would have said a smile like that made everything worthwhile.